PROCESS OF ELIMINATION

ROBERT STRICKLIN

Outskirts Press, Inc.
Denver, Colorado

This is a work of fiction. The events and characters described herein are imaginary and are not intended to refer to specific places or living persons. The opinions expressed in this manuscript are solely the opinions of the author and do not represent the opinions or thoughts of the publisher. The author has represented and warranted full ownership and/or legal right to publish all the materials in this book.

Outskirts Press, Inc.
http://www.outskirtspress.com

ISBN: 978-1-4327-4101-3

Outskirts Press and the "OP" logo are trademarks belonging to Outskirts Press, Inc.

PRINTED IN THE UNITED STATES OF AMERICA

DEDICATION

For Carrie and Jaime,
my pride and joy

Chapter 1

To each his own.

That was Mitch Cooper's motto. But as far as he was concerned, *nothing* – absolutely nothing in the whole, wide world – beat fly-fishing all by himself on a Saturday morning in the mellow month of May.

The fact that it was a warm, clear day along the banks of the scenic Delaware River – that a light, refreshing breeze tempered the prickling sunlight on the back of his neck – and that the cooler in the rear of his flatbed truck was filled with long-neck Coronas on ice only made the experience that much more sublime. It didn't even matter that he'd been knee-deep in cold water – sans a pair of waders or rubber boots –for more than an hour and hadn't caught a single fluke. It just felt good to be alive, twenty-seven years old and miles away from the nearest care.

Only twenty-four hours earlier Cooper had been wedged in bumper-to-bumper gridlock, cussing and fidgeting behind the wheel, inching his way to a dead-end job that barely paid the rent. Then, once he had reached his dreary destination, trapped at the front counter of Tire Emporium, he spent the entire day enduring the usual verbal abuse from a menagerie of surly customers, a boss who reminded him of his boorish old man, and the occasional harassing phone call from a bitter, speed-dialing ex-wife to whom he owed two-month's alimony.

But all that day-to-day, in-your-face, dog-eat-dog crap that defined his life of late would have to wait till Monday. Today, he was his own man, free as an unfettered bird, beholden to no one if for only a few precious hours, and nobody could take it away from him.

Or so he thought. For no sooner had Cooper changed his fly pattern and recast his line into the shallow rapids than the stillness of his tranquil repose was suddenly disturbed by the puzzling and pestering drone of an approaching aircraft.

Odd, he thought, lowering his rod and lifting his squinting eyes to the bright sky. This area was not in the traffic lanes of commercial airliners. Rarely was it the domain of private aircraft, either. But that was definitely a jet he heard, growing louder by the second. Even stranger, it sounded like the plane was descending. No – he had heard that distinct sound before at a military air show. It sounded more like … like … a nosedive.

And then Cooper spotted it – a fairly large jet, a 757 by the looks of it, approaching from the west, plummeting from the sky just a quarter of a mile downstream. He reversed his Phillies baseball cap to get the brim out of his eyes and gazed in disbelieving wonder, realizing that at its steep, downward trajectory this bird was definitely going to crash. "Jesus Christ," he muttered apprehensively, hastily reeling in his line and backing out of the water.

By the time he reached the riverbank, the plane momentarily disappeared beyond a cluster of evergreens on a hill. Then Mitch flinched violently as the dreadful sound of a thunderous explosion shattered the perfect stillness and shook the earth beneath his feet. Seconds later, an orange ball of flame and black smoke mushroomed above the treetops like an awesome specter.

Too stunned to react immediately, Cooper stood frozen in his tracks. Then, starting to hyperventilate, his adrenaline kicking in, he dropped his rod and began to trudge in his soggy jeans and bare feet toward the scene of the disaster. His plodding soon became an anxious trot, propelling him over a rough terrain of dirt, rock and pine needles that felt like shards of broken glass on the tender soles of his feet until he doggedly plunged headlong into a dense thicket.

Zigzagging at a desperate gait, he swiped aside jutting branches that clawed at his face and impeded his progress. There was no time to think – he had to get closer.

Then a second jarring explosion and a hot blast of air from the flaming wreckage forced him to pause, his crisscrossing arms instinctively covering his face in its searing wake. But within seconds, the heat diminished and Cooper resumed his intrepid advance, fearful yet willful at the same time. He simply couldn't restrain himself. He had to do *something*.

Yet, when he emerged from the woods and beheld the scorched clearing strewn with fiery fuselage, scattered debris, and charred body parts, Cooper was so overwhelmed by the sight that he lurched and fell to his knees in awe and horror. Radiating waves of hot wind seemed to blow straight through his body and the stench of catastrophe engulfed his lungs and nearly made him gag.

"Oh, my God," he declared in breathless disbelief as a veil of black smoke dissipated and revealed its horrible aftermath.

So much for an idyllic Saturday morning …

Chapter 2

At 10:19 a.m. EDST, White House Chief of Staff Hunter Davidson placed an urgent call to Camp David, Maryland. "Mr. President," he declared, dispensing with the usual pleasantries, "I'm afraid I have some bad news."

Having just completed a set of tennis with his wife Irene, James J. Hartman was still toweling beads of perspiration from his brow as he cradled the phone receiver between his ear and shoulder. He knew by the uncharacteristically solemn tone of Davidson's voice that this was serious. Snatching the receiver in his fist and turning on the spot, he braced himself for what he assumed would be a grim update on the fate of several Americans workers believed kidnapped by terrorists in the Philippines. "What is it, Hunt?" he asked breathlessly.

Davidson hesitated, but then evenly responded, "Air Force Two has gone down."

There was a tense pause. Eventually, President Hartman replied, "What do you mean, *it's gone down?*"

"It crashed about 10 minutes ago in Pennsylvania. We're not sure how or why. All we know at this point is that Philadelphia International suddenly lost contact with the flight while it was on initial approach. It suddenly veered off course, and then disappeared from radar. Several minutes later, someone near the crash site called 911 on his cell phone."

"Any information on casualties?" asked the President.

"Not yet. But it doesn't look good."

"How many were on board?'

"Seventeen. That includes the crew, the Vice President's entourage and a few members of the press."

"Mrs. Talbot?"

"No," Davidson confirmed. "She decided to stay behind in St. Louis."

"Who's on it?"

"NTSB, FBI, DHS ... Secret Service."

"How long before the media gets wind of this?"

"Probably within a matter of minutes."

"Irene and I will need to return to the White House as soon as possible," said the President, thinking aloud.

"I'll arrange for the chopper, sir," said Davidson. "In the meantime, we'll follow protocol and get everything geared up on this end. Depending on what we learn within the next hour, we'll have to decide whether to hold a press conference or address the nation."

"Okay. In the meantime, call me on my cell as further details come in."

"Yes, Mr. President," Davidson affirmed and hung up.

Standing in the alcove of the presidential retreat, Hartman slowly lowered the receiver and stared at the floor in stunned silence. Then, sensing a presence, he turned abruptly and made eye contact with his wife, who was standing in the front doorway.

"What is it, Jim?" asked the First Lady anxiously, noticing her husband's pale complexion and sullen expression.

Glancing at her tennis outfit and his own T-shirt, shorts and sneakers, the President of the United States muttered, "We'll need to change."

At 10:34 a.m., CNN interrupted regular programming with breaking news. "This just in," the female weekend anchor announced gravely, "CNN has learned that a plane carrying Vice President Clayton

Talbot has reportedly crashed in southeastern Pennsylvania ... There are no other details at this time.

"Vice President Talbot was en route to Philadelphia from the Midwest, where he had been inspecting flood-ravaged disaster areas in Missouri and Illinois. As soon as we receive more information, we will pass it along to you. Repeating, a plane carrying Vice President Talbot has reportedly crashed in Pennsylvania. More news as it becomes available."

Presidential Press Secretary Pauline Cafferty looked away from the television monitor in her West Wing office and focused on her computer screen, where she was composing an official statement for the media. Initially traumatized, she was finding it difficult to write without making one typo after another. And yet she was also feeling a guilty exhilaration, a common phenomenon for a veteran journalist who had dealt with eventful circumstances before and was galvanized by the opportunity to manage such a momentous story. She had been a beat reporter for the *Boston Globe*, then a renowned Washington correspondent for the *New York Times* before being tapped by President-elect Hartman as his press secretary at the age of 34. This was not the first time she and the rest of this administration's staff had been in unexpected crisis mode, nor would it be the last, but experience never made it any easier to cope with.

"Hell of a way to spend a Saturday morning," said Davidson over her shoulder, startling Pauline in mid-sentence. Typically, he had noticed her open door and had crept up behind her. "Thanks for getting here so quickly. How's it coming?"

"Five minutes," she blurted without turning her eyes away from the screen or turning to face him, knowing that whenever Davidson asked for a progress report, he was merely asking when something would be ready.

"Good, good ..." Davidson muttered, bending over and scanning what Pauline had already written, practically breathing in her ear.

Uncomfortable, she leaned to her left and awaited his inevitable critique.

"I would just delete the second sentence in the third paragraph," he predictably suggested. "Otherwise, it's fine. We'll schedule the press briefing for 11:30 a.m."

"That works for me," said Pauline, peering over her reading glasses as she back-spaced and edited.

Davidson left to attend to other matters, but he was quickly replaced by Hannah Goodwin, Pauline's unassuming but diligent younger assistant. "Can I get you anything?" she asked her boss timorously.

"No, I'm good," Pauline replied in a tone that suggested all she needed was a few minutes without being interrupted. However, she reconsidered. "On second thought, a cup of coffee might help. *Black*."

As Hannah started to dash off, Pauline hastily added, "And tell the press corps there'll be a briefing at 11:30 sharp."

Secretary Wayne Kirkland arrived at his office at the Department of Homeland Security at approximately 10:55 a.m. and was immediately patched into agents on the ground at the Air Force Two crash site in Bushkill, Pennsylvania via a secured phone. Trenchant by nature, the former Marine and Philadelphia police commissioner kept interrupting one of his subordinates with impatient questions.

"So you've actually seen the wreckage?" he brusquely inquired. "No, that's not what I asked you. Have you ... *seen* ... the wreckage? Ah-huh. How bad is it? Yeah. Ah-huh. Was the plane intact before it hit the ground? Well, what do *you* think? You've seen crashes before. You can tell whether the aircraft came apart in flight or not. Is the debris contained to a certain area or scattered for miles? You see what I'm driving at here? We need to know what the hell happened and we need to know it as soon as possible. Ah-huh. Ah-huh," he grunted, habitually running a beefy hand over his sandy-colored buzz-cut. "Well, call me back as soon as you have more information ... especially if they find the black box. Right."

As soon as he hung up, Kirkland sighed deeply, lifted his stocky frame out of his chair and lumbered toward the door. It was bad enough that terrorist activity and chatter had been on the upswing in recent weeks, forcing him to post more overtime hours than usual. There was the attempted bombing of the U.S. embassy in Morocco, the kidnapping of several American defense contractors in Manila, and now this. Just when he had thought he was gaining an upper hand on the whole situation, finally getting the hang of the job he had reluctantly accepted several months earlier, Kirkland was back in the hot seat.

Bursting into the outer office, he scanned the room with his gray, wolf-like eyes and motioned to Bentley, one of his senior staff members in the bustling work area, who cut short his own phone call to rush over. "Sir?"

"We're raising the terror alert to orange," Kirkland ordered. "We haven't confirmed anything yet, but I'm not taking any chances. Instruct all personnel to follow crisis protocol until further notice."

"Yes, sir," Bentley acknowledged. "Anything else?"

"Yeah," Kirkland gruffly added. "Get me the White House. Redmond."

Eleven thirty a.m. came and went. The White House briefing room was filled with reporters and correspondents chomping at the bit for information, but Cafferty and Davidson were still ensconced in his office parsing the administration's official statement and formulating appropriate answers to likely questions. By then all the major television networks and cable news channels were promising live coverage of the press briefing after providing nearly an hour of sketchy reports on the Talbot tragedy. Finally, at 11:45, Press Secretary Cafferty was ready and headed for the briefing.

As she approached the podium emblazoned with the presidential seal, Cafferty could sense tension in the room. The White House press corps was barely restraining itself, anxiously waiting in silence for her remarks. Ordinarily, she would start by wishing the assembled journalist a good morning, but today required a terser demeanor. Poised, she calmly adjusted the microphone, took a deep breath, and began, "At approximately 10 a.m., Eastern Daylight Savings Time, a Boeing C-32 carrying Vice President Clayton Talbot and 16 other passengers en route from St. Louis to Philadelphia crashed in the Delaware Water Gap National Recreation Area in Bushkill, Pennsylvania. The cause of the accident has not yet been determined, but emergency personnel at the scene of the crash have confirmed that all 17 passengers on board the plane, including the Vice President, five members of the Vice President's staff, two Secret Service agents, several members of the press, and the pilot and copilot, perished in the crash. The names of the other victims are being withheld until their families have been notified.

"As you all know, the Vice President and his entourage had recently been dispatched to the Midwest to assess flood damage. He was on his way this morning to attend a housing and urban renewal conference in Philadelphia before returning to Washington.

"The President was made aware of this tragedy shortly after the White House was alerted, and he and Mrs. Hartman are on their way back to Washington from Camp David. It is expected that the President will address the nation later today. I will now try to answer any questions you may have."

Amid an initial flurry of frantic voices coming from every direction, Joe Halpern of the *Washington Post* was the first correspondent recognized. "Any indication that this may have been an act of terrorism?" he asked.

"As I said, we have no information on the cause of the tragedy and, therefore, will not speculate," Cafferty replied. "As soon as we learn more about the circumstances surrounding the crash, we will certainly share that information with the American people."

"Has the aircraft's flight recorder – or black box – been recovered?" Halpern followed up.

"Not yet – at least not to our knowledge," said Cafferty.

She then pointed to Gordon Ames of *Fox News*, who asked, "Has the Office of Homeland Security changed the nation's terror alert status?"

"As a matter of protocol, the terror alert has automatically been elevated from yellow to orange" Cafferty confirmed. "But I repeat, the cause of the crash has not been determined."

"Has Mrs. Talbot been notified?" Ames followed up.

"Yes, Mrs. Talbot was contacted immediately by Chief of Staff Davidson," Cafferty replied.

"How did she take the news?"

"I would rather not comment on that," Cafferty answered.

"How did the President react?" asked Stacey Moss of *U.S. News & World Report*.

"He was shocked and saddened … and, of course, concerned for the Talbot family, as were we all."

"Are any special precautions being taken to protect the President?" asked Tom Carswell of MSNBC.

"The appropriate security protocols are being followed," Cafferty vaguely assured.

Howard Casey of the *New York Times* raised his pen. "Will there be a formal investigation into the cause of the crash?"

"The National Transportation Safety Board and other federal organizations are already investigating," said Cafferty, "and pending their initial findings there is likely to be a concerted effort to pinpoint the precise cause of the crash."

"Will there be a state funeral for Vice President Talbot?" asked a representative from *Reuters*.

Cafferty brushed back a lock of brown hair that had fallen over her eyes. "No doubt there will be. However, it is premature to speculate on that. We're still trying to absorb what has happened and deal with it effectively. But also, we'll certainly want to respect the Talbot family's wishes concerning funeral arrangements."

It was then that Cafferty noticed an all-too familiar face in the crowd of reporters. They made eye contact and he took it as a sign of acknowledgement. "When does the President intend to name a successor to Vice President Talbot?" asked Gideon Burnett of the *American Observor*.

Cafferty was somewhat taken aback by the inappropriateness of the question and, judging by the appalled looks on other faces, she was not the only one. But she maintained her poise and, avoiding Burnett's inquisitive gaze, responded, "It is far too soon to deal with that. We're all just trying to absorb and cope with what has happened today. The nation will be in mourning for at least the next several days. At the proper time, the President will focus his attention on filling the vacancy. For now, however, our thoughts and prayers should be with the Talbot family and the families of all the victims of this untimely tragedy."

As dozens of hands shot up, Pauline discreetly cast a scolding glance at Burnett, who squinted back playfully.

Marine One landed on the White House lawn at approximately 12:17 p.m. As he disembarked from the helicopter, the Commander-in-Chief returned the salute of the Marine guard who had ceremoniously met the aircraft, then turned to offer his hand to the First Lady as she gingerly descended the steps. They were immediately greeted by Chief of Staff Davidson and National Security Advisor Sam Redmond, both of whom proceeded to fill the president in on the latest intel.

"You're sure this was not the result of a terrorist attack?" asked Hartman as the party made its way across the grounds toward the rear portico.

"There wasn't a bomb or a missile or a high-jacking involved?"

"No, sir," Redmond verified, striding with the clipped, graceful gait of a former Army sergeant, FBI agent and NSA administrator. "No evidence whatsoever."

"Then, what? Equipment failure? Pilot error? A mid-air collision?"

"We've got a team from NTSB sifting through the wreckage. As soon as they find the black box, we'll have a better idea of what happened."

"We'd better," warned the president. "The American people will expect answers – plausible answers. I want a very thorough investigation and full disclosure."

"Yes, sir," said Redmond. "I've also been in contact with Homeland Secretary Kirkland. He also has people on the ground and his office has raised the terror alert as a matter of procedure. However, he assures me there is no cause for alarm. Still, it would be advisable to contact our allies and other foreign leaders to allay any concerns they may have."

"I'll get on the phone right away."

"May I also suggest, sir, that you place a call to Grace Talbot?" Davidson interjected.

"Yes, of course."

"I'd like to speak with Grace, as well," the First Lady chimed in, although she wasn't sure anyone had heeded her soft-spoken request.

"We'll also coordinate the funeral arrangements with the Talbot family," Davidson added.

"A full state funeral," the President insisted.

"Yes, sir. Of course."

"I'll also need to address the American people."

"May I advise, sir, a primetime broadcast? That will give us sufficient time to get our facts straight and craft a fitting tribute to the Vice President."

"Fine," Hartman agreed. "What about the Cabinet? Everyone safe and accounted for?"

"Yes, sir," Redmond confirmed. "As you instructed, each member has been assigned temporary Secret Service protection – just as a precaution."

"Good. Perhaps we should schedule a meeting at our earliest

convenience," the president suggested. "Say, shortly after the funeral."

"I think that would be wise, sir," Davidson concurred.

As they reached the rear entrance to the White House, where an attendant was holding the door open, the three men paused to allow the First Lady to enter first. The president started to follow, but turned at the threshold for one last remark. "Thank you both," he gratefully acknowledged. "I know it's going to be a rough few days, but I'm sure we'll all bear up."

Glancing at Redmond, Davidson muttered, "What's the alternative?"

Over the next few hours, President Hartman worked the phones in the Oval Office, conferring with NATO allies, various dignitaries and prime ministers, members of the Joint Chiefs of Staff, key Cabinet officials and Congressional leaders. Periodically, he would receive updates from advisers that were in direct contact with the federal agencies involved in the investigation. Only tidbits of information were trickling in and none of it provided the specific cause of the crash, but at least it did rule out an act of terrorism which, despite the circumstances, was cause for relief.

Meanwhile, designated White House liaisons made funeral arrangements with members of the Talbot family. Overseeing their progress, Hunter Davidson also supervised the drafting of a planned presidential address penned by White House speechwriter Clancy Ackerman. Practically every member of the West Wing staff was now on premises, lending whatever support was necessary to handle the situation as efficiently as possible.

Elsewhere, the major networks and cable news channels were in all-Talbot, all-the-time mode, providing bits and pieces of fact and conjecture about the crash and recovery, airing retrospectives of his life and political career, and interviewing friends, associates and citizens throughout the nation. This included the sole witness to the crash, whose surname was initially misspelled as Mitch Copper. Relishing his 15 minutes of fame, Cooper repeatedly and excitedly related his first-hand knowledge of the disaster – his near brush with catastrophe and his heroic search for survivors until the authorities arrived at the crash scene and, of course, his shock, awe and sorrow in the midst of the devastation. It was a story he would tell – and embellish – to anyone who would listen for many years to come.

The usual pundits – more than eager to put in weekend duty – were also on hand to offer their analyses and assumptions of how the tragedy would affect the course of American history, already speculating on who the next vice president should be. The relentless marathon would last for days with no shortage of revisionist adoration for the heretofore disregarded and now departed occupant of Blair House.

At 4:15 p.m., Davidson entered the Oval Office and gave the President the thumbs up – code for a breaking development.

Seated at his desk, Hartman apologized and placed House Speaker Jeb McDonald on hold. "What is it, Hunt?" he asked.

"They found the black box, Mr. President."

"How long until we know what's on it?"

"They're not sure, sir. It seems to be in reasonably good shape, but we won't know if it's audible until it reaches FAA headquarters."

"How's the address coming?"

"Ackerman's applying the final touches now. You'll have it by five."

The President raised his hand as a thankful but dismissive gesture. Davidson obediently left and closed the door behind him. In the outer office, he gave Mrs. Garrett, the President's personal secretary, an earnest nod of encouragement, then strode off toward his own office.

Shortly before 5 p.m., Senate Majority Leader Henry "Hank" Howard received several impromptu guests at his Arlington, Virginia home. Attendees included Senate Whip Bill Bryce, Republican Party Chairman Ralph Patterson, House Speaker Pierce Allman and G.O.P. political strategist Dale Cardigan, all of whom were in a somber mood, but not necessarily for the obvious reason.

"Drinks?" Howard offered as his colleagues and friends settled into various seats in the Senator's spacious study.

"The usual," Bryce readily replied.

"I'll have what Bill's having," said Patterson.

Cardigan shook his head and Allman refrained with a wave of his hand.

"Hell of a day," Howard observed, pouring three bourbons, including one for himself.

"Now, that's an understatement," muttered Cardigan.

Patterson was blunter. "Certainly changes the political landscape, wouldn't you say?"

"You know what this means," said Howard, handing Ralph and Bill their drinks. "A sympathetic boost in the President's approval ratings heading into next year's primaries."

Allman tried to be philosophical. "Better now in the off-year than a few months before the election," he declared.

"It's hard enough unseating an incumbent president …" Howard complained, pausing to take a gulp. "Now I've got to run against a political widower."

"The election's a year and a half away," Bryce optimistically reminded everyone. "That's an eternity in politics."

"Depends on whom Hartman chooses to replace Talbot," Cardigan was quick to point out.

"My money's on Singleton," said Howard. "That would be the smart move. It would cut into our southern strategy and tip Texas in their favor."

"Then we should steer him away from Singleton," Patterson suggested.

"Or discredit anyone he does nominate," Patterson added.

"That could backfire," Allman warned. "A prolonged confirmation might hurt us more than the administration."

"I'm with Pierce on that," said Bryce. "The sooner we confirm the President's nominee, the sooner we can get back to the status quo."

"And the sooner the President's approval ratings return to the low 40's," Cardigan chimed.

"But will they?" wondered Howard with a note of anxiety.

"Come on, Hank," Cardigan scoffed. "His health care initiative was D.O.A., his energy bill and tax reform has Wall Street in a tizzy, the perception is that we're losing the war on terror, and both the economy and crime rate have seen better days. Another pretty face on the ticket isn't going to do him a lick of good."

Snickering, the others took heart in Dale's assessment. "At any rate," said Howard, "after the funeral, I think we should arrange a visit with the President. Offer our condolences and suggestions on a successor. Feel him out on whom he's considering. Then do some research on the major candidates and formulate campaign talking points."

"Sounds like a plan," said Patterson. Bryce and Allman nodded in agreement.

"If I may," Bryce gingerly suggested. "When we convene both houses of Congress this week, we should have a moment of silence for Vice President Talbot."

"Of course," everyone agreed in unison.

Goaded into the façade of sympathetic respect, Howard impulsively raised his glass to offer a toast. "Gentleman," he declared, "to Clayton Talbot ... friend and colleague ... may he rest in peace."

By 6:15 p.m., funeral arrangements had been finalized and released to the press. Vice President Talbot's remains were already identified and en route to Washington, D.C. His closed casket would lie in state in the Capitol rotunda for two days – Sunday and Monday – where the general public would have the opportunity to pay their respects. A service would be held on Tuesday morning at St. Matthew the Apostle Cathedral, the church the Vice President and his widow Virginia had attended on most Sundays over the last two and a half years. Following the ceremony, the Vice President's coffin would be flown, along with his family, to Talbot's hometown of Athens, Georgia where he would be honored and eulogized again before being accorded a military burial complete with a 21-gun salute in recognition of his service as a colonel in the Persian Gulf War. In lieu of flowers, mourners and well-wishers would be encouraged to contribute to numerous charities. In years to come, boulevards and high schools in Georgia and elsewhere would be renamed in Clayton Talbot's honor, but for now this hastily but meticulous planned tribute would have to do.

FAA Secretary Evelyn Morales placed a call to the White House at 7:10 p.m. that was promptly transferred to the Oval Office.

"Evelyn, I'm putting you on speaker phone," said the President. "Chief of Staff Davidson and National Security Adviser Redmond are with me. What have you learned?"

"Mr. President," Morales replied, "as you know, we retrieved the black box from the crash site a few hours ago. We've finally been able to listen to the flight recording in its entirety."

"And?"

"The final excerpt of that recording indicates that there was a sudden and irreversible loss of cabin pressure aboard the aircraft resulting in hypoxia, or lack of oxygen, just before the crash."

"What do you mean, 'irreversible?'" the President interjected.

"Apparently," Morales explained, "the pilot, co-pilot and everyone else on board slipped into unconsciousness before any evasive action could be taken."

"How is that possible?" the President challenged.

"Well, you might recall that a similar incident occurred in 1999, claiming the life of professional golfer Paine Stewart."

"So you're saying this was the result of a mechanical problem?" asked Redmond.

"Apparently."

"What about sabotage?" Davidson suggested.

"Doubtful," said Morales. "The plane underwent a thorough inspection before the flight and was cleared for takeoff."

"People make mistakes," the President muttered uneasily.

"Every precaution was taken. Still, I would recommend a full-scale investigation."

"Oh, you can be sure of that," Hartman promised. "But for now we can rule out pilot error or an act of terrorism?"

"We can, sir," Morales confirmed.

There was a momentary lull in the conversation in which Hartman looked off, pondering what he had just learned. "Thank you, Evelyn," he finally declared. "Let me know if and when you have any other details."

"Yes, Mr. President."

Disconnecting, Hartman looked up at Davidson and Redmond and cynically predicted, "The conspiracy theorists are going to have a field day with this."

At 8:01 p.m., EDST, the President of the United States appeared behind his desk in the Oval Office, flanked by the American flag in the background to his right and the presidential flag to his left with finely sculptured busts of Abraham Lincoln and John F. Kennedy visible on the corners of the file bureau behind him, and somberly began his televised address to the nation:

"My fellow Americans, today our nation suffered an untimely and tragic loss. Vice President Clayton Talbot was more than a public figure, more than a private friend and colleague. He was a man of unquestionable integrity whose devotion to his family, his constituents and his country was an example to all who knew him.

He – and 16 other people – died today while returning from a mission to the flood-ravaged regions of the Midwest, where he had offered hope, compassion and assistance to those who were left homeless and destitute. His life ended as he probably would have wanted it, in the service of others."

Watching from his sprawling mountain retreat in Provo, Utah, Malcolm Everett Tate couldn't help but gloat. On his wall-mounted, 63-inch high-definition screen, perched above an opulent cultured stone fireplace, the President's face was a portrait of earnest solemnity. Tragedy became him, thought Tate with a cynical smirk.

As Hartman paid tribute to Clayton Talbot and assured the nation that the goals of the administration would not waver, the 72-year-old billionaire squinted at the screen, his bushy silver eyebrows squeezed together in one long scrutinizing zigzag. His contempt for the man knew no limit; his delight in his sadness was uncontainable.

For it was popular knowledge that Malcolm Everett Tate was no friend of James J. Hartman and his "radical liberal agenda." In fact, as the founder and Chairman of the Board of the Tate Energy Consortium and the majority shareholder of Uniplex Industries, one of the nation's most prominent energy providers and defense contractors, he considered the Hartman administration's efforts to increase regulation of the oil and gas industries, cut "waste" in military expenditures and boost the taxes of wealthy Americans a threat to his interests and, therefore, a threat to the nation itself.

"I have declared Tuesday a day of national mourning," the President announced. "And for the next 30 days, flags at all federal agencies throughout the United States will be flown at half-mast in tribute to Clayton Talbot. It is my sincerest hope that his family, friends, colleagues and every American will find solace in the wake of his passing, and that his life will serve as an inspiration for all of us. Thank you and good night."

Aiming his remote control, Tate clicked off the television. Then, feeling a twinge of stiffness in his fingers, he flexed his hand and reached for his glass of gin. Savoring a mouthful, he gazed out the plate glass windows that provided a panoramic view of the majestic Sierra Nevada's with their snow-capped peaks. It was dark back east, but here the sun had yet to set, and in its brilliant illumination Tate's horizons were endless. He reflected on the day's events and their significance, and looked beyond to the task still at hand. Arthritis may have been setting in, the wrinkles on his furrowed brow may have been deepening, but his vision was clear and his mind was still as sharp and deadly as a steel bear trap.

Narrowing his eyes in malevolent glee, he muttered, "And so ... we begin."

Chapter 3

Over the next three days, more than a million and a half people paid their respects to Clayton Talbot by filing past his flag-draped casket as it lay in state in the Capitol rotunda, this despite inclement weather as rain and fog slowly made its way east, casting an appropriate pall over a sober Washington, D.C. For much of the viewing, members of the Talbot family – with the notable exception of the Vice President's widow – were in attendance, personally thanking each and every visitor for their condolences.

Reportedly, Virginia Talbot was devastated by her husband's sudden death and was heavily sedated. She did, however, attend the state funeral service on Tuesday, supported by her three adult children – two sons and a daughter. Also in attendance were several hundred foreign dignitaries, all but two members of the Cabinet, numerous Congressmen and Senators, administration officials, other family, friends and, of course, the President and Mrs. Hartman.

Televised on the major networks, the various news channels and C-Span, it was a somber and reflective ceremony that seemed more perfunctory than anything else. In his eloquent eulogy, the Reverend Thomas McGee called Clayton Talbot, "a champion of American ideals, a tireless defender of freedom and justice who inspired millions and stood for all that is noble about public service."

The President also rose to the occasion, delivering a stirring tribute only he and a few others knew had been written for him by

Clancy Ackerman. Recognizing a defining moment when he saw one, Hartman poignantly paid homage to the departed and offered solace to a grieving nation. By the time he concluded his acclamation, there wasn't a dry eye in the house.

However, it was Irene Hartman who made the most indelible impression on the national consciousness as the best supporting participant at this sobering event. All but dispelling the prevailing impression that pegged her as "The Reluctant First Lady," she not only carried herself with grace and dignity throughout the ordeal, but also took charge of many of the funeral arrangements and accommodations for visiting heads of state. It was she who dispensed with formality to cling consolingly to a weeping Virginia Talbot throughout the long and distressing ceremony. And it was she who was at her husband's side as he escorted Virginia out of the cathedral to her waiting limousine when it was done.

The world watched that day as America paused to do what it did best – honor its own and move forward with a renewed sense of hope and resiliency.

Later that evening, alone in the Oval Office, President Hartman behaved like a chronic workaholic, poring over paperwork best left for a more lucid opportunity, reluctant to call it a day. Unlike many of his predecessors, he preferred to burn the midnight oil, not because he was particularly diligent, but because it was the one time when he was unlikely to be disturbed. Tonight, however, he was too pensive to get anything meaningful done. Preoccupied in his wandering thoughts, he was startled by a knock on the door. "Yes?" he called, peering over his bifocals.

It was Davidson. "Mr. President," he murmured, standing in the doorway. "May I come in?"

"Of course, Hunt," Hartman replied, removing his reading glasses. "Pull up a chair."

Davidson did just that, seating himself beside the President's desk. He was close enough to notice the fresh lines under Hartman's usually bright eyes. Evidently, his insomnia, a telltale sign of increased anxiety, was back. Although he was still relatively youthful in appearance for his age, the presidency had added a few more gray hairs to his once dark brown temples and a few creases to his ruggedly handsome face, as well.

"Did you know, Hunt," the President asked out of the blue, "that this desk dates back to the Hayes administration, circa 1880?"

"No, sir. I didn't know that," Davidson replied.

"It's known as the Resolute Desk. That's because it was made from the timbers of an abandoned British ship named the H.M.S. Resolute. It was discovered by an American vessel and returned to Queen Victoria as a token of friendship. When the ship was retired, the queen returned the goodwill gesture and gave it to us."

"And we chopped it up for furniture?" Davidson quipped.

"Mmm," the President smiled. "American ingenuity."

But his smile quickly faded. "It's been a long day, Hunt," Hartman remarked with a deep sigh. Then, impulsively checking his wristwatch, he noted, "Shouldn't you be on your way home by now?"

"I thought I'd stay here tonight, sir," Davidson replied dutifully, smoothing out his rumpled suit and straightening his tie. "Tomorrow will be just as grueling and I think it would be best to get an early start. I also thought you might welcome the company."

"I would," said Hartman, "but I don't think we have a spare bedroom. They're all occupied by foreign ambassadors."

"The couch in my office will be fine, sir."

Davidson expected the President to discourage him, but he was obviously too distracted to even acknowledge the comment. He had a faraway look in his eyes and was silent for what seemed like an unusually long time. Then he suddenly blurted out, "I didn't even like the man when I chose him as my running mate."

Davidson stared at the President quizzically until he realized to whom he was referring.

"I didn't even want him on the ticket," the President confessed. "It was pure political expedience."

"I wouldn't dwell on it, sir," Davidson awkwardly responded, somewhat surprised by the President's candor.

"I needed a moderate Southern governor to balance things out," Hartman elaborated, "to give us a fighting chance at a few electoral votes in the Bible Belt. It worked. We won the election. And how did I reward him? By treating him like ..."

"Don't be so hard on yourself," Davidson interrupted, speaking as a compassionate friend and confidante. "Clayton knew why he was chosen. He knew what he was getting into. He knew the two of you had your differences, that you were never going to be the best of buddies, and that his role would be limited. He saw an opportunity to be a heartbeat away from the presidency ... and he took it. Neither of you could have known it would come to this."

"I sent him to Illinois and Missouri," the President persisted. "I had him tour the flood zones because I was too 'busy.'"

Davidson leaned forward. "Sir, you're not suggesting that you were to blame for his death?"

"Had I gone instead on Air Force One, he'd be alive today."

"Yes, and if Kennedy hadn't gone to Dallas ..." Davidson muttered. "That kind of second guessing is pointless ... and it won't bring him back."

Several long seconds of silence followed. Then the President wondered aloud, "Now what do we do?"

"Well," sighed Davidson, "first we postpone your European trip. Our allies will certainly understand. Then we move up our next scheduled cabinet meeting from next Monday to later this week ... say Thursday or Friday. And then ... we choose a nominee to replace Clayton."

"But not so soon," Hartman advised. "That would appear cold and insensitive. There must be a respectful period of mourning before we deal with that issue."

Davidson disagreed. "Frankly, Mr. President, I think it's in the country's best interest to dispense with the prolonged grieving and begin the selection process as soon as possible, if only behind the scenes. It will take time to interview candidates and conduct background checks and ... "

"It can wait," the President insisted. "The line of succession as stated in the 25th Amendment provides for this situation. It's not a national emergency."

But Davidson begged to differ. "The line of succession places the Speaker of the House and the President Pro Tem of the Senate – both members of the loyal opposition – one and two heartbeats away from the presidency, respectively."

That didn't seem to concern the President. "I assure you, Hunt, I have no intention of kicking the bucket any time soon."

Davidson bit his tongue for a moment, but then couldn't resist replying, "Neither did Clayton."

Hartman pursed his lips and turned his head to gaze out the window at the darkened Rose Garden. "We'll get on with it, soon," he promised. "Just not right away. I need a little time to catch my breath."

"Of course, Mr. President," said Davidson, studying his brooding profile. Eventually, Hartman swiveled in his chair and faced him again. "Will there be anything else this evening, sir?" asked the Chief of Staff.

"No," the President replied. "It's late. And you should go home instead of staying here."

"Honestly, sir, I don't mind ..."

"But I do," said Hartman firmly. Leaning forward, he reminded his colleague, "It's just a job, Hunt."

Davidson shrugged, but the President was having none of it. "You need to spend as much time with your family as possible," he declared with a feeble smile, adding, "We never know how much time we have, do we?"

"Alright, sir," Davidson conceded, rising from his chair. "Then I'll see you in the morning."

"Give my regards to Melissa and kisses to young Tina and Jane," said the President.

"I will, sir," Davidson nodded. "Good night."

As the door to the Oval Office closed, President Hartman donned his reading glasses again and half-heartedly reviewed some of the lingering documents sprawled across the Resolute Desk. After a few moments of scanning the same sentences more than once though, he wearily decided to pack it in for the night. Try as he might, he could not put off tomorrow. Perhaps it would be a better day. Lately, however, each day was becoming harder than the one that preceded it.

As he strolled through the late evening ground floor corridors, the President glanced at various portraits of his predecessors. Some were true statesmen, others merely glorified custodians, but all had an aura of distinction, a sense that fate had led them to a position of power that suited their abilities. Hartman couldn't help but wonder if some future president would have the same impression of his portrait.

He skipped the elevator and instead took the stairs to the first and second floors, acknowledging the skeleton crew of White House staff and Secret Service agents posted along the way from the Center Hall to the West Sitting Room and finally the President's Bedroom. Once inside his private chamber, he leaned against the closed door and stared wistfully at the impeccably fitted, king-sized bed that awaited him. The First Lady had long since retired to the Lincoln Bedroom at the other end of the mansion, and he wondered if she would ever sleep in this room with him again.

Whoever said that the presidency was the loneliest job in the world didn't know how right he was.

Chapter 4

Washington, D.C. had had a relatively mild winter and early spring that year. Most of the cherry blossoms that had bloomed in mid-March in West Potomac Park along the shore of the river's Tidal Basin were all but gone by May. Nevertheless, a few hearty remnants remained near the Thomas Jefferson Memorial, much to the enchantment of the lunchtime strollers, groups of high school students and tourists who congregated there on the day after Clayton Talbot's state funeral.

One anonymous member of the crowd, a tall, bespectacled man in a beige raincoat, was there killing time before a scheduled rendezvous at 12:30. Quite early for the meeting, he leisurely sauntered through the building, admiring its circular colonnade of Ionic columns, its lofty dome and circular marble steps, and pausing to read and reflect on the engraved quotations of its prolific namesake.

Something of a history buff, it was not the first time he had visited the Memorial, nor was it the only landmark he had perused on his many trips to Washington. He had covered most of the tour bus stops – the Great Mall and the Washington Monument, the Capitol, the Ford Theater, even the White House itself when he had been a younger man and well before 9/11. He had enjoyed these brief but enlightening sidetracks, particularly in light of the nature of his work. But he had a particular affinity for the Jefferson Memorial, perhaps because he viewed it as a shrine to a more idealistic time and a nobler school of thought.

In the present, however, the work was his overriding priority. So, punctual to a fault, he left the Memorial and took his predetermined seat on a vacant park bench by the riverside ten minutes earlier than necessary and waited patiently for his new contact to arrive. He bided his time gazing at the Potomac, mesmerized by the glistening sunlight on the water, tuning out the sounds of the surrounding city, the occasional patter of a passing jogger and birds chirping in nearby trees. These moments of solace were rare; one had to savor them whenever one could.

Eventually, a man in a dark tweed jacket and collarless T-shirt arrived and casually sat down a few feet beside the man in the raincoat. He looked like a college student or some radical junior college professor, more than a bit younger and certainly scruffier than the clean-shaven man in the raincoat had expected, sporting days-old stubble and fashionably unkempt brown hair. The man in the raincoat knew he was the one he had been waiting for because the young man kept giving him nervous sideways glances without speaking. Nevertheless, the man in the raincoat followed protocol. "Good day for a stroll in the park," he remarked, looking straight ahead at the river.

Sure enough, the man in the tweed jacket flatly replied, "But a bit chilly for this time of year."

Satisfied, the man in the raincoat reached into his pocket and removed a pack of cigarettes and a gold-plated lighter. He lit up without offering one to his contact who, as it turned out, was obviously not a smoker because he disapprovingly slid to the far end of the bench.

After a long, awkward silence, the man in the tweed jacket felt compelled to speak. "Well, now that that's out of the way ..." he said. "My name is ..."

"Uh-uh-uh-uh-uh," the man in the raincoat cautioned, taking a puff of his cigarette and keeping his eyes on the river. "No names."

"Don't you want to know who you're talking with?" asked the man in the tweed jacket.

"No," the man in the raincoat replied, "and neither should you. The less you know, the better."

"For whom?" asked the man in the tweed jacket.

The man in the raincoat exhaled smoke from his nostrils and replied, "For everyone concerned."

The man in the tweed jacket huffed and smirked.

"You're new to this, aren't you?" the man in the raincoat inquired. His suspicion was confirmed when the man in the tweed jacket hesitated to respond. "Well, then," he said, leaping at the opportunity to educate this novice. "Allow me to explain it to you … as simply as possible."

But before he did, he paused for another drag on his cigarette as the man in the tweed jacket regarding him with a mixture of amusement and incredulity.

"You and I," said the man in the raincoat, "are part of a long chain of messengers. The chain begins with Mr. A and extends to Mr. Z. I am … oh, let's say … Mr. L. Since you're my immediate contact, that makes you Mr. M. I receive messages from Mr. K, pass them on to you, and then you pass them on to Mr. N. I don't know who Mr. A through Mr. J. are, or Mr. N through Mr. Z. By the same token, you have no idea who Mr. A through Mr. K are, nor Mr. O through Mr. Z. No one along the chain deals directly with anyone except their immediate contacts. And no one between Mr. B and Mr. Y knows anyone by name. That way, no one is accountable – especially Mr. A and Mr. Z."

"Accountable for what?" asked Mr. M.

"That doesn't concern us," Mr. L replied, taking another puff of his cigarette. "All we need to do is pass along messages."

"That's all?"

"That's all."

Mr. M took a moment to digest this convoluted explanation. "Whatever," he finally shrugged indifferently. "As long as I get paid."

"Exactly," Mr. L muttered, tapping ashes.

"So how do we do this?" asked Mr. M.

"We'll meet here every three days," Mr. L replied. "Same time.

That'll allow the messages to flow at a steady pace without delay or any overlapping along the chain."

"Why here?"

"Because it's public, yet private," Mr. L maintained. "We're in broad daylight, yet unnoticed. Less likely to be observed or overheard. Less apt to arouse any suspicion."

"Why do we have to meet at the same time?"

"Easy to remember. Orderly."

"Sounds anal, if you ask me," Mr. M snickered, waving his hand to ward off Mr. L's drifting second-hand smoke.

"Since this is a two-way system, we'll alternate our messages," Mr. L continued. "I'll have one for you, then the next time we meet you'll have one for me. And each of us passes the message along to the next link in the chain."

"And that's it?"

"That's it. Think you can handle that?"

Mr. M ignored the sarcasm. "So what's today's message?"

Mr. L took another drag and declared, "White knight to bishop four."

Mr. M did a double take. "*Huh?*"

Mr. L sighed in feigned frustration. "White knight ..."

"I heard you," Mr. M cut him off. "I just didn't think you were serious."

For once, Mr. L turned his head slowly to face Mr. M and dryly retorted, "Do I look like I'm being facetious?"

Mr. M raised his eyebrows and looked away. "I guess not. It's just ..."

"What?"

"It's like we're playing a scene in some old, hackneyed spy movie."

Mr. L rolled his tongue in his cheek, but kept his simmering annoyance in check. "Do me one small favor," he said, looking down at his brown, spit polish patent leather shoes. "Keep your caustic remarks to yourself and just make sure you get the message straight. You are capable of getting the message straight, aren't you?"

"Yeah," Mr. M replied with a cocky smirk. "I'm capable all right."

"Then repeat it."

"What?"

"Repeat … the message," Mr. L demanded.

Mr. M rolled his eyes and shifted restlessly on his half of the bench. He took his sweet time, but nonetheless reiterated slowly and ever so distinctly, "White … knight … to … Bishop … Four. Okay? Are we done here?"

"Yes. We'll meet again on Saturday," Mr. L instructed. "Same time, same place."

"I can't wait," Mr. M muttered sarcastically, springing to his feet. "Oh, and by the way," he added, referring to the cigarette, "you should try a nicotine patch. Those things will kill you." Then, without further adieu, he turned and walked swiftly away.

As he left, Mr. L glanced in his direction, albeit disapprovingly, then back at the river and the Memorial. Some people just don't take any pride in their work, he thought, dropping the cigarette to the ground and crushing it beneath his heel.

Chapter 5

A s First Lady, Irene Emerson Hartman had yet to find her niche. Whereas Jackie Kennedy had refurnished the White House, Nancy Reagan had served as an anti-drug spokesperson, and Hillary Clinton had advocated for universal health care, Irene Hartman was simply known as the wife of a U.S. president. She was neither a fashion trendsetter nor the driving force behind any social initiative. She was an adequate hostess, but hardly the belle of the Beltway or the grand dame of D.C. With the aid of her resourceful staff, she did what was required of her, but little else. In fact, her reluctance to engage enthusiastically in campaign events and her aversion to the public spotlight was almost palpable. While some considered her tenure a throwback to another era and a refreshing change from the age of well-meaning but exasperatingly proactive first ladies, others quietly questioned whether her heart was really in it. Still others cynically referred to her as "The Prisoner of Pennsylvania Avenue."

Born 49 years earlier in Andover, Massachusetts, she was an only child whose father was the founder of a lucrative used car franchise. The business' success enabled Albert and Alma Emerson to live in a Victorian mansion in a posh section of town and send their daughter to one of the best private schools in the area. In time, the Emersons moved to Boston, where Albert's enterprise thrived and Alma became a fixture of Beacon Hill society.

As for Irene, life was a relatively dull but blissfully uneventful stream of prep school adventures, long summers on Cape Cod, surreal debutante balls and but a few youthful indiscretions – until she left home for college. For it was there, in her freshman year at Dartmouth, that she met James J. Hartman, although the encounter would hardly qualify as love at first sight.

A serious student majoring in Sociology, Irene ironically refrained from extracurricular socializing, preferring the company of her roommate Mitzie Callahan and a small circle of bookish girlfriends. They'd spend much of their free time in the student lounge, discussing Margaret Mead, mocking the activities of various campus sororities and fraternities, and, on rare occasions, gossiping about particular members of the male student body.

One of them was a certain tall, dark and cocky junior who was both a running back for the university football team and captain of the debate club. "Brains and brawn," noted Mitzi as she and Irene sat in the stadium stands one autumn afternoon, watching a practice scrimmage as number 17 took the handoff and zigzagged his way through a maze of would-be tacklers.

"Broad shoulders and a big head," Irene dismissively replied.

"You neglected to mention his cute butt," Mitzi quipped.

"Please ..." Irene scoffed in exaggerated disgust.

"Right ... like you wouldn't date him if he asked."

"I wouldn't," Irene adamantly vowed. "And he wouldn't."

"I don't know, Emerson," Mitzi teased. "I've seen him scoping you out on numerous occasions."

"I imagine he's been scoping out everyone on campus who's wearing a skirt," Irene scoffed.

"Me thinks thou doth protest too much," Mitzi nudged with a sly grin.

"That's because you're a Psych major. You think everyone has subconscious desires."

"Well, don't they?"

"I know what I want," Irene assured her friend, "and it is definitely not him."

Mitzi dropped the subject, although she did notice that for someone who wasn't the least bit interested in Jim Hartman, Irene seemed to be looking in his direction an awful lot.

It wasn't until the following spring semester, while Irene was attending a screening of Ingmar Bergman's *Scenes From A Marriage* in a campus auditorium, that she actually *talked* to Jim Hartman. She was seated alone in the front row, one of only a handful of attendees scattered throughout the darkened, makeshift theatre, engrossed in the domestic drama unfolding on the screen. During one lull in the pathos, however, her attention wandered and she glanced to her left and right, noticing no one else in her row. She then turned in her seat to check the audience behind her and was dismayed by the scant turnout. It was a sad commentary on American culture, she indignantly surmised, that more people, even the student body of Dartmouth, preferred the likes of *Star Wars* to a Bergman festival.

It was while she was surveying the auditorium that she suddenly spotted a familiar face several rows back. Inadvertently, she had caught the eye of none other than Number 17, who jokingly returned her quizzical stare with a goofy grin and a fluttery wave. Embarrassed, Irene quickly turned back around in her seat and kept her eyes glued to the screen. Yet, as hard as she tried, she suddenly found it difficult to follow the film. It was as if the English subtitles were in an unfamiliar language and her concentration had been shattered.

"Is this seat taken?" a startling voice inquired shortly thereafter.

Irene looked up at a looming Jim Hartman standing beside her in the aisle. Befuddled, she glanced to her left and right at all the empty seats, then back at Hartman.

"I guess not," he shrugged and plopped himself down in the seat to her right.

At a loss for words, Irene turned her eyes back to the screen, determined to ignore him. But a minute later, he shoved a box of popcorn under her chin and whispered, "Want some?"

She shook her head without so much as a sideways glance.

Hartman didn't press the issue. Nor did he bother her for the rest of the film. In fact, aside from chomping on his popcorn, he sat quietly and watched the movie while Irene was preoccupied with her thoughts. Why, she wondered, would a jock sit through a Swedish film devoid of car chases, gun battles and pyrotechnical explosions? Was there more to James J. Hartman than met the eye, or was he simply playing her? And why would an admittedly handsome guy like him be interested in an antisocial, passably attractive wallflower like her? Something didn't jibe. Could she be the intended victim of a fraternity prank? Was a bucket of pig's blood about to splatter her head?

By the time Irene had considered all the possibilities, the film ended and the houselights came up. Rather than glance toward Hartman, she sat frozen, staring at the blank screen.

"So?" he asked, depositing his empty popcorn box under his seat. "What did you think?"

"About what?" Irene awkwardly replied, gawking at him.

"About the film."

"I thought it was … poignant."

It was Hartman's turn to gawk. *"Poignant?"*

Irene cast a stern, defensive look. "I suppose you thought it was stupid."

"Stupid? Why would I think that? On the contrary, I think Bergman is a brilliant filmmaker."

Irene smirked skeptically. "Oh, like you've seen a lot of his films."

"As a matter of fact, I have," Hartman informed her.

"Name one," she challenged. "Besides *Scene From A Marriage*."

"I'll name several off the top of my head – *Wild Strawberries, The Virgin Spring, Persona, The Seventh Seal* … that happens to be my favorite."

"You've seen all of them?" she replied doubtfully.

"Sure … not that I have the ticket stubs to prove it. Why? You find that hard to believe?"

"You don't seem to be the type."

"What type is that?"

"The art-house, foreign cinema type."

"Well, I guess you can't judge a book by its cover," Hartman shrugged with a sly, playful smile. He glanced over his shoulder, noticed that they were the only two people left in the auditorium and rose from his seat. "Shall we?" he suggested.

"Huh?" said Irene, looking up at him quizzically. "Oh," she added, realizing it was time to leave. She self-consciously sprang from her seat and started heading quickly for the exit with Hartman in striding pursuit.

"Hey, I'm kinda' thirsty after all the popcorn and Scandinavian angst," he muttered, walking alongside Irene. "Care to join me for a beverage at the student union?"

Irene could scarcely believe this whole conversation, let alone the idea that J.J. Hartman wanted to spend time with her. "I've got to get back to the dorm," she impulsively declined. "I've got a lot of studying to do."

Of course, he wasn't buying it. "Come on," Hartman cajoled. "One can of Dr. Pepper. We can rap a little, get acquainted, share each other's misconceptions about the other …"

Looking down at her feet as her pace slackened, Irene couldn't help but smile. She wasn't used to being an elusive object of interest. To her surprise, it felt good.

"Did I hear a 'yes?'" Hartman persisted, leaning her way and cupping a hand behind his ear.

Irene stopped walking and shyly lifted her head to look at him. His dark blue eyes had a definite twinkle, but they seemed to convey sincerity. "By the way," he said. "My name is Jim, Jim Hartman."

"I know who you are," she replied. "My name is …"

"I know who you are, too," he interrupted, studying the features of her face with meaningful fascination.

Seeing him in a new light, Irene tentatively returned his smile and said nothing else all the way to the student union.

In the days, weeks and months that followed, Jim and Irene became what Mitzi Callahan referred to as "an item." Occasional run-ins evolved into casual on-campus dates, then Friday and Saturday nights out on the town and, eventually, whole days spent together. Often, they'd simply stroll the grounds of the campus or lounge beneath a shady tree on the commons and talk about their respective families, friends, classes, beliefs and ambitions. Other times they'd go for long rides in Jim's late model Chevy Impala, exploring the back roads of Plymouth County, picnicking in Wompatuck State Park, or driving all the way to Boston to go dancing or catch a show.

During the winter, Jim convinced Irene to join him at Blue Hills Ski Area in Saint Canton. He taught her to ski, although she preferred ice skating and long, cross-country rides on a snowmobile, where she would sit behind Jim, her arms strapped around his waist and her chin resting on his shoulder as he drove fearlessly through the powdery drifts and across frozen lakes against the frigid wind. Clinging to him, she felt safe, adventurous and alive.

During spring break, Jim accompanied Irene to Boston to meet her parents, both of whom were immediately taken with the self-assured junior. Of course, it didn't hurt that Jim was a motivated pre-law student and gifted athlete from a prominent political family. In fact, given Irene's shy, aloof disposition, her parents were secretly surprised that she had landed such a promising beau. Nevertheless, priority ruled the Emerson household and although they had consummated their relationship back on Valentine's Day, Jim and Irene dispensed with overt displays of affection while visiting and did not press the issue of Jim sleeping in a separate bedroom during their stay. There would be plenty of opportunities to make up for lost time when they returned to Dartmouth.

In a way, abstinence in the midst of a family environment put their courtship in a whole new perspective, especially for Jim. It made him think of Irene as more than a girlfriend, more than a college fling. He could see himself spending the rest of his life with her, fathering her children, conquering the world with her at his side.

What he didn't anticipate was her answer when, while sitting together alone on her parents' backyard deck one night, Jim proposed to Irene. He had expected her to look shocked at first, then excitedly throw her arms around his neck and profusely accept. Instead, she cocked her head and stared at him quizzically.

"You heard me," he said. "I love you and I want to spend the rest of my life with you. Will you marry me?"

Irene glanced up at the stars and sighed. "Jim," she replied, "I'm only 19 years old. You just turned 21. We've only known each other for a few months."

"Six," he corrected her. "Six months."

"Still ... we've got years of school ahead of us. I have another three. You're going for your Masters, then law school ... We're too young."

"Is that a 'no?'" he asked, looking disappointed to say the least.

Irene placed her hand on his cheek and tenderly replied. "It's a 'not yet.'"

"But you do love me, don't you?"

"Of course I do," Irene scoffed. "You wouldn't be here if I didn't."

"Well, then," Jim argued, "that's all that matters."

"No. That's not all there is to it. We hardly know each other."

"How could you say that?" Jim replied indignantly. "After everything we've done, everything we've been through."

"That's the point," Irene insisted. "We *haven't* been through everything yet. We've been dating, having good times together. But we haven't been together long enough to deal with the kind of problems every couple goes through."

She was right, and Jim knew it. His bruised male ego wanted him to throw a tantrum or at least punish her with wounded silence. But his rational mind prevailed. In fact, he admired her all the more for her grace and maturity. Yes, this was the girl he wanted. But there was time. First, he needed to grow up. They both did.

And so, Jim and Irene continued their courtship while fulfilling their academic commitments. He went on to complete his bachelor's degree and Master's in political science. Then it was off to Harvard Law. She completed her four years at Dartmouth, but instead of pursuing her Master's, Irene became a social worker in Boston, so she could live off-campus with Jim.

The day after he graduated from Harvard, Jim revealed to Irene that he had landed a job at a prestigious New York law firm. He also took the opportunity to offer her a 24-karat diamond engagement ring. This time, she accepted.

The wedding took place the following year. By then, Jim and Irene were settled into a cozy single-family house in Great Neck, Long Island, a wedding present from Irene's Dad. Both would commute each morning to Manhattan, via the Long Island Railroad, where they held their respective jobs – Jim at Hazelton, Collins & Dern, Irene at the Department of Social Services. Six months later, however, Irene learned she was pregnant. By then, Jim's career was in full swing and he was earning top dollar for his services. At his insistence, Irene quit her job and became a homemaker and expectant mother.

It didn't take long for Irene to realize that she had made a mistake. Despite her "delicate condition," as Jim had put it, she was bored by her new role as house frau and missed the interaction of her job. Her only refuge from a mundane existence was shopping for maternity clothes and planning the conversion of their guest room into a nursery.

And then, six weeks into her pregnancy, it happened. While having lunch at the mall with her visiting mother, Irene suddenly felt ill and was rushed to a local hospital. An hour later, she was no longer an expectant mother. The loss generated awkward sympathy from everyone she knew, including Jim, who took it worst of all. Yet even amid his comforting words and assurances that they could "try again" when she was ready, Irene was at the mercy of conflicting emotions. Certainly, there was sadness and a nagging sense of failure. But much to her dismay, there was also a strange, unsettling sense of relief.

Not long thereafter, Jim announced his plans to run for Congress. It was always assumed that he would follow in his family's political footsteps, but his rationale also included a change of scenery and a means for Irene to become involved in something.

Despite her reluctance to relocate to D.C., Irene gamely supported the candidacy. She was not about to deprive her husband of his inherent aspirations and, faced with the alternative of remaining alone in Great Neck while Jim worked and resided more than 200 miles away, she resolved to make the best of the move. So, with the help of the Hartman clan and the Nassau Democratic Party, Jim eked out a narrow victory, thus beginning what promised to be an illustrious career in government – even at the risk of straining his marriage.

On the heels of the victory, Jim and Irene rented a townhouse in Georgetown, which Irene perpetually refurnished to keep herself occupied while Jim established a voting record in the House of Representatives. They attended their share of cocktail parties, charitable benefits and fund-raising events, and hobnobbed with a whole new class of people from every corner of the nation. But although she hardly had a dull moment, Irene felt distinctly out of place, often yearning for a simpler, quieter life.

As it turned out, she was not the only one who had misgivings about their D.C. lifestyle. Jim had come to Washington with all sorts of idealistic ambitions, only to discover that as a lone voice of progressive reform in a complacent, capitulating 435-member legislative body, he was hardly in any position to advance real change. It didn't take long for frustration to set in, and no sooner had he arrived in Congress for his two-year term and acclimated himself than he had to gear up for reelection. Fortunately, during his second term, opportunity knocked and he was offered a place on the ticket as a candidate for New York State Attorney General, a position better suited to Jim's hands-on, public service mindset. He didn't have to be asked twice.

PROCESS OF ELIMINATION

Seven weeks after Jim won the election and relinquished his Congressional seat, Irene found herself back in Great Neck. They had kept their split-level brick house there as a permanent residence while renting in D.C., and now it was back to their previous routine with Irene playing homemaker while Jim commuted to the Attorney General's office in Manhattan.

However, there was one significant difference – Jim's duties were such that he spent far more time in the city than he did at home. In addition to 12-hour work days, there were frequent trips to the state capital in Albany, political affairs, television appearances and other events that required his attention. Although Irene did not complain about their lack of quality time together, it was something she had not counted on when they had returned to New York. She had long since resigned herself to the reality that a career in public service required a certain amount of time away from home, but these absences were worse than those when Congress was in session.

It was then that the idea of a family began to appeal to Irene once again. Having overcome the painful experience of her miscarriage, she broached the subject with Jim, who agreed it was time to try again and promptly whisked his wife to a hastily arranged vacation in the U.S. Virgin Islands. Several weeks later, Irene learned that she was pregnant again and this time, she was determined to carry to term.

But less than a month later, in the middle of the night, Irene was awakened by a piercing throb. Panicking, she awoke Jim, who hastily drove her to the nearest emergency room. By the time she was wheeled into the hospital, she was no longer with child.

If the first miscarriage had been a shock, the second was a devastating blow that plunged Irene into a state of depression. To make matters worse, she learned that she was unlikely to carry a child, any child, to full term. Despite Jim's comfort and the support of countless family members and friends, Irene harbored a deep-seeded sense of failure and unfulfilled longing. Mitzi suggested therapy, but as the wife of a high-profile politician, Irene knew this wasn't a viable option.

When Irene was well enough to deal with it, she and Jim reassessed their familial plans. There were discussions about adopting a child, but neither Irene nor Jim were enthusiastic about the idea. For Jim, coming from a large family, simply adding a child to the equation for the sake of having a "typical American family" seemed politically expedient. For Irene, raising a child that she hadn't born would be a subconscious reminder of her shortcomings as a woman – such were her insecurities. For both, it felt like an act of desperation and put a strain on their relationship. Besides, with Jim's hectic schedule and Irene's restlessness at home, how attentive would they be as parents? For all of these rationales, they decided to forego parenting.

The decision seemed to be a wise one when Jim was presented with the opportunity to run for Governor. Although the prospect of being New York's First Lady hadn't been one of Irene's lifelong ambitions, especially if it involved moving to the state capital at Albany, it was an intriguing option. She certainly didn't want to deny Jim what she believed would be his ultimate political achievement. And so, she put her natural reticence to campaigning aside and whole-heartedly helped her husband get elected.

But Irene's support extended only as far as Jim's professional ambitions. In their evolving personal relationship, there had been a subtle but seminal shift. Now in their forties, they had entered a new and significant phase. After two miscarriages, Irene's libido had diminished considerably. Absent the desire, neither was the opportunity to indulge what now seemed like an ancient ritual often presented, and whenever Jim initiated a sexual overture, Irene's utter lack of enthusiasm for his advances quickly doused the flames of passion.

At first, Jim was in denial about his wife's diminishing capacity for affection. He treated it like a transitory ailment rather than a symptom of a deeper, more complicated problem, joking at times about the honeymoon being over. In time, however, it would become an issue. Never did either of them suggest couple's therapy – such a move, however beneficial, wouldn't play well politically. So their lack of intimacy became the norm – and something of a moot point, considering Jim's grueling schedule as Governor.

Later, when Jim was coaxed into running for the Democratic presidential nomination, the fact that he and Irene were childless was seen as both a political liability and an asset. There were no cute and cuddly offspring to trot before the media at campaign rallies, no First Family to pose for a group portrait. But there was also no one besides Irene to dissuade Jim from seeking what she felt was a grueling, thankless and potentially dangerous job. Neither was she eager to become the most scrutinized female role model in the country.

Yet, in the end, Irene did what she had always done, and that was to support her husband's ambitions, no matter where they led and how they affected her emotional wellbeing. Always the self-sacrificing team player, she put on her brave face and gamely campaigned on his behalf, sometimes to the point of exhaustion and always in a thinly disguised state of anxiety. Fortunately, Jim swept the early primaries and by Super Tuesday was the party's presumptive nominee.

But it wasn't the years of exhaustive campaigning, conflicting emotions and unrealized parenthood that all but destroyed Jim and Irene's marriage. It was something else. Or, to be more specific, someone else. And her name was Shannon Cole.

Nearly three years later, Irene Emerson Hartman found herself sitting alone one evening on the balcony of the White House, overlooking the Great Mall and Washington Monument in the distance and thinking about what was and what might have been. Despite her wistful mood, it was a relatively peaceful respite from the rigors of her demanding schedule and a rare moment for reflection. But no sooner had she succumbed to a sense of calm and equilibrium than her privacy was disturbed by a less than welcome visitor.

"I thought I might find you here," said the President, moving closer but respecting a certain space.

"It's a lovely evening," she replied nonchalantly, scanning the D.C.

skyline. "Although you can scarcely see the stars for the city lights."

"You aren't cold, are you?" he diffidently asked, noting a slight chill in the air.

Irene regarded him skeptically. "What is it?" she replied. "What do you want?"

Her abruptness pained him. In public she was his wife, his companion, his tennis partner, little more than a glorified escort. In private, however, she was a perpetual fount of dismissive scorn.

"I just wanted to thank you," said Jim innocently.

"Thank me for what?"

"For the way you've helped the last few days."

The corner of Irene's mouth curled into a sarcastic smile. "You mean the way I've performed my role as First Lady?"

"The way you helped console Virginia Talbot and her family," Jim gently amended. "The way you helped comfort the entire nation."

Irene suppressed a mocking laugh and looked away.

"Anyway," said the President, "it meant a lot to them ... and to me. And I know it couldn't have been easy for you."

"On the contrary ... it was very easy," Irene claimed. "If there's anything I've learned over the years, it's how to pretend."

Her remark was followed by an awkward silence. Jim simply didn't know what to say.

"How is your search for a new vice president coming along?" Irene finally asked, changing the subject.

"We've yet to consider a replacement," the President replied.

"What are you waiting for?"

Her prodding tone made Jim bristle. "We'll deal with it soon enough," he insisted. Then, as an afterthought, he added, "I don't suppose you have any suggestions?"

Irene turned her frosty green eyes on his. "Since when does my opinion matter?"

"That's a bit harsh, don't you think? You had considerable input when I chose Clayton as my running mate."

"That was some time ago. Back when you used to confide in me. Before you had someone else to confide in."

Jim sighed. "Are we ever going to get beyond that?"

"I don't know," said Irene. "How does one get beyond that?"

"Well," Jim answered as gingerly as possible, "if you tried ..."

"To forgive and forget?"

"Yes. That's what I'm asking. That's what I've been asking for nearly two years."

Irene said nothing, refusing to face him.

"Look, I've apologized a thousand times."

Still no response.

"It didn't mean anything," Jim insisted.

"Not to you," she muttered.

"It was a mistake. I'm sorry. It's over. It will never happen again. I ..."

"You, what?" Irene demanded, finally confronting her husband. "You love me?"

"Yes. And you love me. If you didn't, you wouldn't have taken it so hard."

But Irene's icy glare did not thaw. "It's not a question of love."

"Then, what?" asked Jim, barely able to contain his exasperation.

"It's a matter of trust ... and respect."

"I do respect you."

"But not my wishes," Irene declared. She took a deep breath and sighed, "I never wanted *this*. But you went for it, anyway. It didn't matter what I wanted. It was what you wanted. Always what *you* wanted. And I, the dutiful wife, went along with it. I didn't want to be selfish, didn't want to deprive you of your moment of glory." She paused and stared deep into her husband's eyes. "Well, you got what you wanted, Jim. Are you satisfied?"

"What would you have me do, Irene? Resign?"

"Don't be ridiculous," she scoffed. "You couldn't do that. And even if you could, you wouldn't. You're already planning your campaign for a second term. Aren't you?"

"I don't have to run again."

"Of course you do. It's in your blood, it's who you are."

"I'd give it up for you."

"Oh, *please.* "

"I would," Jim insisted with conviction.

"Well … at this point that would be very foolish," Irene surmised, placing her hands on the balcony railing and looking off into the void. "After all, this job is all you have."

The last remark cut the deepest because it happened to be true. Still, Jim bit his tongue and maintained a stoic silence. It was better for Irene to vent than keep all this bitterness locked inside.

"As for my 'suggestions' about replacing Clayton," she said, "my advice is not to waste the opportunity by playing it safe."

Jim regarded her with a puzzled expression.

"Go with someone fresh and dynamic, slightly younger than yourself. It'll make you look more like a father figure. Clayton was your elder," she explained. "He was perceived as the true statesman of the administration, your mentor. Now *you* need to assume that role. For once, think about the future of the party and the country, instead of what's convenient for you. That's my advice – for what it's worth."

The President bowed his head and nodded thoughtfully. "Thank you," he said with more politeness than sincerity.

Irene looked away, concealing an ironic smirk. If there was anything she was familiar with, it was advice that fell on deaf ears.

Rather than endure her silence any longer, Jim muttered, "Well, good night," and wandered away.

Ignoring his departure, Irene lingered on the balcony, surveying the glittering view and wondering how she had gotten to this bleak and lonely place. All too content with her sullenness, she closed her eyes as a cool breeze caressed her uplifted face.

Chapter 6

Gideon Burnett awoke to the dulcet tones of an instrumental he recognized as Henry Mancini's theme to *Two For The Road* on a clock radio on his side of the queen-size bed. As the time – 7:14 a.m. – came into focus, he groggily reached out and tapped the snooze button and the impromptu musical interlude came to an abrupt pause.

Only one person he knew would set her alarm clock to easy listening music and he rolled over to confirm that it was indeed Pauline with whom he had spent the night. There she laid beside him, flat on her back in the morning daylight, her shoulder-length auburn hair sprawled across her pillow. Were it not for her gaping lips and gentle snoring, she would be a waking man's vision. And yet, there was a childlike, endearing quality about her in slumber that even a self-centered cad like Burnett could appreciate.

Taking great pains not to rouse her, he lifted the covers and slid stealthily out of bed, then trudged wearily into the adjoining bathroom and quietly closed the door. Still disoriented, he nevertheless had the presence of mind to put down the toilet seat and flush after relieving himself. Then, slouching over the sink, he glanced at his murky reflection in the mirror, turned on the tap and doused his face with bracingly cold water. Refreshed, he closed the tap, reached for a nearby towel and dabbed himself dry. A clearer view in the mirror revealed a few crow's feet in the corners of his dark blue eyes and a gray hair or two in each of his jet black temples, but otherwise he looked remarkably youthful for a bachelor pushing 40.

Satisfied with the visual reality check, Burnett decided to take a quick shower while he had the bathroom to himself. But no sooner had he stepped into the tub, drawn the curtain and turned the valves than he heard the door open and Pauline coughing over the sink.

"Hey!" he shouted as she turned on the hot water, sending the temperature of his warm shower plummeting.

"My bad," she apologized, lowering the tap. Pressed for time, she plopped herself down on the toilet seat and relieved herself while brushing her teeth.

"Multitasking?" quipped Burnett, peeking through the shower curtain as he lathered his chest.

Without thinking, Pauline flushed. "Ahhh!" cried Burnett, momentarily scorched.

"Come on," sighed Pauline, climbing into the shower and slapping his bottom. "Stop being such a baby."

"You're in a chipper mood," Burnett noted in a self-congratulatory manner.

"Don't flatter yourself," said Pauline, stealing the soap and lathering her armpits. "I feel like crap. I should know better than to have a couple of mohitoes on a school night."

"Mmm," Burnett agreed, wrapping his arms around her slender waist from behind and planting a wet kiss on the nape of her neck. "But it was the only way to get you in bed."

"Shut up and do my back," she shrugged, handing him the soap. "I'm running late and I've got to get to work."

"That makes two of us," Burnett grumbled, nonetheless catering to Pauline's request. "It must be pretty hectic on your side of the building this week."

"We're coping," she replied, rolling her head and flexing her shoulders. "Things will calm down soon enough."

"Especially when the President chooses another Veep," Burnett remarked. He waited a few seconds, expecting a reply. When he realized none was forthcoming, he asked, "How's the search coming along?"

Pauline turned around to face him with a suspicious glare.

He glanced at her wet breasts, then feigned innocence. "Just making shower chit-chat. So? Any idea who has the pole position?"

"Now, now," Pauline cautioned, wagging her finger. "You know the rules. No pillow talk."

"You won't throw me a bone?"

"I'm your girlfriend," she reminded him, "not Deep Throat."

"You're my significant other," Burnett corrected.

"Oh, really?" Pauline replied, sounding amused. "How significant?"

"Enough to give me a hint or two."

"Here's a hint …" she said, hastily stepping out of the shower and wrapping herself in a towel. " … Find yourself another source."

"That's cold," Burnett replied, shutting off the shower faucets. "If I was in your position, and you were in mine, I'd share information with you."

"Would you?"

"Absolutely," Burnett maintained, grabbing a towel and buffing himself.

"Well, that would be foolish."

"Why?"

"Because if I were in your position, I would probably use that information to scoop the competition."

"What's wrong with that?"

"Nothing. But you would be in a world of trouble."

"How do *you* figure?"

"You'd be leaking confidential information."

"But I'd be an unnamed source."

"An unnamed source *within the White House*," Pauline corrected, combing out her wet hair. "Considering that only a handful of people would be privy to that information, that would narrow it down quite a bit, don't you think?"

"But no one knows that you and I …"

"Oh, come on, Gid. This is Washington, for Christ's sake. Nothing goes by unnoticed."

"Alright," Burnett relented. "Keep it to yourself. It's not like I don't have a pretty good idea which way the President's leaning." He paused and waited for a response. But when Pauline failed to take the bait, Burnett blurted out, "It's Singleton, isn't it? He's definitely on the short list. You don't have to confirm or deny, just blink twice if I'm right."

Pauline sighed, placing her comb aside. "As far as I know, the President hasn't even begun to consider nominees. Okay?"

"I don't believe you," said Burnett with a sly, crooked smile.

Pauline rolled her eyes and headed for the kitchen. "Coffee?" she called over her shoulder.

"Black," Burnett replied, scrutinizing himself once again in the foggy bathroom mirror.

When Pauline arrived at the West Wing later that morning, she ran into her Hannah Goodwin in the hallway. "He's looking for you," her assistant warned with arched eyebrows.

"Thanks," Pauline replied, then headed straight for her office to check her e-mail. Sure enough, there was a message from Chief of Staff Davidson: "P.C. – Drop by when you get the chance."

Pauline sighed as she erased the directive. Meeting with Davidson wasn't how she preferred to start her day and she hated being referred to as "P.C." Nevertheless, like the faithful team player she considered herself, she wasted no time answering the summons.

Davidson's office door was wide open and he was seated behind his hopelessly cluttered desk. "You wanted to see me?" said Pauline, drawing his attention from a stack of paper work.

"Ah, yeah," he replied. "Close the door and have a seat."

Wondering what this was all about, Pauline shut the door and traipsed across the room to a cushy leather chair facing the Chief of Staff. As she sat down, she made sure her hemline was as low as possible, refraining from crossing her legs having more than once caught Davidson glancing at her thighs. Today, thankfully, his eyes remained north of her torso.

"As you know," he said, "the President will need to choose a successor for Vice President Talbot. He's put it off temporarily, but he'll have to deal with it soon enough. When he does, he'll confer with a small group of close advisors, including me. I want you to be a part of those discussions."

Surprised, Pauline was momentarily speechless. Then she modestly replied, "I'm not an advisor. I don't have that kind of clearance."

"No," Davidson acknowledged. "Not for daily security briefings. But on a matter like this, I can grant you special privileges."

"And why would you do that?" Pauline wondered. "I'm the Press Secretary. Why would my input matter?"

"It's not so much your input that's vital," Davidson conceded in his usual, less-than-subtle way. "You're the administration's media liaison. There will be a lot of speculation and disinformation regarding this decision. We'll want to keep a tight lid on our deliberations, hold the press reasonably at bay and avoid any leaks until we've made a sound and acceptable choice. We can't do that unless you're in the loop."

"Well, then," said Pauline, flattered. "I'll do my best."

"You do understand," Davidson added, "this means maintaining the strictest confidence about the selection process?"

"Of course."

"That includes significant others," he stressed.

Pauline blinked, surprised by his choice of euphemisms. "What are you getting at, Hunter?"

"Well, I know you've been … seeing a certain member of the White House press corps …"

"And how do you know that?"

"You've been seen together in public … at restaurants and such. Word gets around."

"Does it?"

"Which is fine," Davidson hastened to add. "What you do in your private life is no concern of mine … within certain limits, of course. All I'm saying is …"

"I know what you're saying," Pauline interrupted, "and you have nothing to worry about."

"Good," nodded Davidson. "Well, I'll let you know when the President's ready to deal with the matter. Do you have any questions?"

"None."

"Well, then … Have a good day."

And with that gracious dismissal, Pauline returned to her own office where she sat for a moment considering the task she had just agreed to undertake.

Initial uncertainty quickly gave way to exhilaration. She impulsively reached for the phone to give Burnett a call but hesitated, then refrained. Discretion, she realized, was advisable. After all, they had been *seen together in public*.

For the first time ever, Pauline fleetingly entertained the possibility that her phone might be tapped. Then, dismissing the idea as utterly paranoid, she cleared her mind and finally got down to work.

Chapter 7

James Joseph Hartman was born into a family of perennial public servants, but not one that historians could label as a political dynasty. The youngest of four children, he would far surpass his siblings and forebears in terms of career achievement, but their individual accomplishments were nonetheless a source of pride worth noting. His grandfather, Jacob Andrew Hartman, served two terms as Mayor of Elmira, New York. His father, James Jacob Hartman, was a town alderman in Elmira and later a State Senator. His oldest brother, Lawrence Hartman, was the current Dutchess County Executive. His other brother, Edward Hartman, was a sheriff in Columbia County, and his sister, Rachel Hartman Porter, was School Board President of Putnam County.

The Hartman family's political and social connections not only paved the way for Jim's entrance into Dartmouth and Harvard, but also served him well in his later endeavors. When he decided to take the leap and run for Congress, he had the full support of numerous local and national Democratic leaders, as well as the backing of various labor unions and political action groups. That alone, however, did not ensure his election in a predominantly Republican district. So, combining the campaign savvy he had acquired "genetically" and taking a page from the old Kennedy playbook, he took to the streets, neighborhoods, factories, union halls, even bars to appeal face-to-face to his would-be constituents. Armed with as many fliers and literature as he could afford and reinforced with a rag-tag group of volunteers, he went door-to-door to introduce himself and engage voters in often lively dialogue, getting an earful at times but at every opportunity making his presence in the community well established.

The hard work paid off with a narrow but impressive victory in a heretofore Republican district and led to another term before Democratic Party officials in New York urged Hartman to run for state Attorney General. Somewhat disillusioned by his experience in Congress, particularly seeing his efforts for significant legislation thwarted at virtually every turn by lobbyists and special interests, Hartman saw this opportunity as a better fit, one that would allow him to deal more effectively with the issues he cared about and do so closer to home.

As Attorney General, Hartman focused on white-collar and corporate crime, prosecuting numerous CEOs, stock exchange officials and hedge fund managers for everything from insider trading to outright fraud. He also targeted several high-profile companies that were engaged in questionable retirement fund practices and influence peddling.

One of those targets included JTN Chemical, a subsidiary of Uniplex Industries, a multinational energy services corporation based in Texas with offices throughout the country and in several foreign cities. Evidence surfaced that JTN's plants in upstate New York were engaging in illegal dumping of waste which polluted lakes and tributaries of the Hudson River, prompting hefty EPA clean-up costs. However, the Attorney General's office also uncovered a paper trail of corporate payoffs to state and local officials dating back at least a decade and not only relentlessly prosecuted several of JTN's upper level managers, but also indicted a number of government administrators. The scandal nearly bankrupted the company and Uniplex stock took a hit. Eventually, the parent corporation severed ties with JTN, but not until considerable financial and public relations damage had been done. In the process, Jim Hartman enhanced his credentials as a citizens' watchdog, but also initiated a longstanding feud with one Malcolm Everett Tate, the iconoclastic founder and chairman of Uniplex.

With a solid reputation as an effective prosecutor and consumer advocate, not to mention his familial roots in the Democratic Party machine, Hartman's ascent to the governorship was a given. Although his campaign met with some opposition from certain sectors of Wall Street and corporate lobbyists, a majority of New York voters decided otherwise.

As the governor of a major state, it was only a matter of time before Hartman was routinely mentioned as a possible presidential contender. After several troublesome years of a Republican administration, Democrats were motivated to find a formidable standard bearer in the next general election. Although the field of possible candidates was vast and diverse, only two aspirants seemed to have a clear shot at the nomination – one of them was Georgia Senator Clayton Talbot, the other the Governor of New York.

But Hartman's decision to run was not a slam-dunk. Although the prospect was enticing and there were plenty of supporters urging him to throw his hat into the ring, his wife Irene was not one of them.

"It's a thankless job," she argued. "No matter what you stand for, your hands are tied by Congress, the media, the whole system. And no matter what you do, half of the country will hate you. Besides, can you see me as First Lady?"

"I think you would make a wonderful First Lady," her husband naturally replied.

"I hardly have the wherewithal to be the First Lady of one state. Never mind 50 of them ..."

"Is that your only reservation?" he asked.

"That and your personal safety," she admitted.

Hartman looked deeply into his wife's eyes. "We can win, you know."

"Is that what it's all about?" she countered. "Winning?"

"It's about making a difference," he maintained. "It's about changing the direction of this country. Changing things for the better."

"Well," she sighed. "If it means that much to you …"

"It does," he insisted. "If I don't at least try … I'll always regret it."

Several days later, with Irene at his side as usual, Hartman announced his candidacy. With Hunter Davidson as his campaign manager, he embarked on an exhausting tour of the early primary states. He shook every hand within reach, kissed more babies than he imagined existed, participated in countless debates and town hall meetings and made his case with all the passion and stamina he possessed.

He was a close second to Talbot in the Iowa caucuses, but solidly won the New Hampshire primary. A week later, however, Talbot easily won South Carolina, setting up a do-or-die matchup on Super Tuesday. In a televised debate prior to the main event, Hartman scored points with viewers by outperforming Talbot on two key issues – energy and health care. As a result – and combined with a massive positive ad campaign – Hartman won a majority of states on primary day. Talbot took the South as expected, but Hartman prevailed in the Northeast, most of the Midwest and did surprisingly well in the West, including California. Suddenly, the governor from New York had a two-to-one delegate lead over his only viable opponent. Rather than prolong the race, Talbot suspended his campaign and endorsed Hartman.

Overnight, Hartman had become the presumptive nominee. His first *Time* and *Newsweek* magazine covers hit the newsstands, he became the darling of the Hollywood elite, and polls showed him with a slim lead against the Republican presidential front runner. The usual amount of scrutiny followed – investigative reports on Hartman's record as a congressman, state attorney general and governor through the prism of certain conservative media, questions of whether Hartman was up to snuff on natural security and whether challenging economic times called for his populist approach. His association – however indirect – with various think tanks, former radicals and special interests was also trotted out by a handful of media sources affiliated with Malcolm Everett Tate, but nothing resonated.

As the Democratic National Convention approached in late July, Hartman and his closest advisors huddled to choose a running mate. Internal polls indicated weakness among voters throughout the South, a factor that could tip the election to the GOP. J.J. Hartman, as he was dubbed by the mainstream media, was perceived as a Yankee liberal, out of touch with the views of the common man south of the Mason-Dixie line. To counter this liability, Team Hartman vetted a number of Southern moderates, including former Texas Governor and Senator Harley Singleton. In the end, however, the consensus was that Clayton Talbot would not only be a highly qualified choice for Vice President, but also one that could actually deliver his home state of Georgia and possibly Virginia and North Carolina. It proved to be a sound choice, unifying the Party and catapulting the Hartman/ Talbot ticket to a 10-point post convention lead in national polls.

And then, just when it looked as if the election were in the bag – it happened. *The National Enquirer* broke the story that the Democratic nominee for President of the United States, recently had been involved in an extramarital affair with a blonde, attractive, 24-year old campaign worker named Shannon Cole.

Led by Hunter Davidson, the Hartman camp went into immediate damage control mode, issuing a vehement denial and accusing the opposition of engaging in a desperate, groundless smear campaign. Of course, that didn't prevent a media feeding frenzy that distracted voters throughout September and drove the Hartman/Talbot ticket's poll numbers down to neck-and-neck territory. Shannon Cole's sudden reclusiveness and refusal to comment on the matter didn't help matters. Allegations that she had been paid off to lay low also plagued the campaign, putting the outcome of the election in doubt.

The turning point came when Irene Hartman appeared on *60 Minutes* and expressed her complete faith and confidence that her husband was not a philanderer. "I've known Jim for the better part of my life," she told correspondent Lesley Stahl. "He is the same honest, forthright and loyal husband today as he was when we married. He has never lied to me and he has always treated me with love and respect. I know he was not unfaithful to me. Unfortunately, we live in a time when many people choose to believe the worst about others, when some people will say anything to win an election and, in the process, discredit a good man and prevent him from implementing the positive changes this country so desperately needs. I trust my husband and I believe he – not the tabloids, not the media, not his detractors – deserves the trust of the American people."

Irene's appearance was the show's most watched segment in years and set off a backlash of sympathetic commentary. Suddenly, the talking heads were admonishing their own industry and disavowing the politics of personal destruction. The precipitous slide in the poll numbers gradually reversed itself, and on the first Tuesday of November, James Joseph Hartman was elected President of the United States with a respectable four-point plurality and more than 300 electoral votes.

Shortly after the election, James and Irene Hartman took a brief but much needed vacation to Bermuda to recuperate from the long campaign. Cloistered in their ocean view villa at an exclusive, private resort, insulated from the media, they spent several days attempting to relax before having to face the rigors of a new administration.

But James was anything but relaxed, unusually pensive and preoccupied. Irene presumed the initial euphoria of victory had given way to consternation, a realization of the awesome responsibilities he was about to assume. If only it had been that simple.

"I have something I need to tell you," he suddenly announced one evening as they sat on their patio overlooking the dark Atlantic under a vast canopy of stars.

Holding her breath, Irene stared at her husband's shadowy profile, sensing the worst, keenly attuned to the rhythm of the surf as turbulent waves tumbled against the shore and then quietly ebbed.

"What I told you …in September … wasn't entirely true …"

Irene began to feel an unsettling weightlessness. "What … what are you talking about?" she asked with a mounting sense of dread.

James shifted uneasily in his chair, unable to look at this wife. He took a deep breath and replied, "Shannon Cole."

"Oh, God …" Irene whimpered.

"I told you I didn't have an affair with her. The truth is … we were together …"

"Oh, God …" Irene wailed, covering her face with her hands.

"It only happened once," James insisted.

"*Once? Once?!*" Irene angrily repeated. She then leapt to her feet and headed toward the far side of the patio, anything to get away from him.

James hastily followed. "Please," he begged, reaching out for his wife's arm.

"Don't!" Irene cried, recoiling. She clutched her sides, as if in physical pain, and looked to the dark sky as if searching for a means of escape.

"I'm sorry I lied to you," James feebly offered.

""Lied to me?" mocked Irene. "You lied to *everyone!*"

"I know, I know …"

"You idiot! You stupid son of a bitch!"

"Irene, please. I didn't mean to hurt you."

"You made me vouch for you! On national television! You used me to save your political career! You made a fool out of me!"

"I made a fool of myself …"

"No!" Irene shouted. "No! No! You did more than that. You put your ambition ahead of everything. Ahead of your integrity. Ahead of the trust people had in you. Ahead of our marriage."

Ashamed, James was at a loss for words. Only now did the reality of what he had done become excruciatingly clear. He let the full force of her wrath wash over him, hoping it would purge him of his guilt.

"Why, Jim," Irene demanded to know. "Why did you do it?"

"Please …"

"No, I want to know. Why did you cheat? Was it so necessary at your age to have sex with another woman? Was it worth the risk? Was that what made it so … titillating?"

"It wasn't like that …"

"Oh, really? Then why did you do it? Tell me. Why?"

"Irene …" James groped for an explanation. "It's been so long since we've … since we've been a couple."

Irene quivered. "Ah, yes. It's my fault."

"I'm not saying that."

"Of course you are. Now I understand. Was that the only reason? Because I haven't been … putting out for you? Is that your excuse? Isn't it enough that I've been at your side for thirty years, supporting you every step of the way? Haven't I been the good little political wife, putting my own needs aside and indulging your selfish aspirations, enabling you? And this … *this* is how you reward me?"

"I'm only human!" James blurted out. And no sooner had he said this than he realized how hollow it sounded. Still, he sought some form of redemption. "Give me *some* credit for owning up to what I've done."

But Irene would have none of his newfound contrition. "Why are you telling me this now?" she demanded to know.

"Because I didn't want to lie to you anymore," James replied. "Because you had a right to know."

"How considerate of you," she cynically responded. "And how convenient. Now that you've won the election, now that it's a done deal, now … now, James … you can afford to tell the truth."

"Irene …" he persisted, mustering all the sincerity he could, "I made the biggest mistake of my life and I regret it. Please … please forgive me."

"You're right," Irene coldly replied. "It was the biggest mistake of your life."

After that night, Irene did not speak to her husband for two weeks. And when she finally did, it was with the bitter distance of a woman emotionally estranged from her companion. For a time, James feared she would leave him. But she did not. Apparently, she was resigned to her new role as First Lady, using the position as a distraction from her deep-seeded yet silent misery, perhaps perpetuating the joyless union simply to spite him.

So they continued the charade of a public marriage, dancing at the Inaugural Ball, touring veterans' hospitals and child care facilities together, posing for White House Christmas portraits, even vacationing together in the summer on Martha's Vineyard. But behind closed doors it was a different story. They slept in separate bedrooms and ate alone unless entertaining guests.

James came to depend on his presidency as an escape of his own. Immersed in the day-to-day minutiae of governing, he found a form of refuge from the guilt of this betrayal and the emptiness of his failing marriage. There was still hope in his heart that one day Irene would forgive him but until then, all he had was his work. And even that was tenuous. Saddled with a Republican Congress that had gained strength in the mid-term elections, the Hartman administration had yet to succeed in getting a major piece of legislation passed. Its health care reform initiative was a non-starter. Its attempts to lower the federal deficit by slashing defense spending were met with derision even among moderate Democrats. And an ambitious energy bill languished amid partisan bickering. With another election just 18 months away, James J. Hartman needed to get his act together, and to get it together fast.

Three days after Clayton Talbot's funeral, the President held a meeting with the senior members of his administration in the Cabinet Room of the White House. All but one seat was taken at the long, oval-shaped table – the one directly across from the President in the center, where the Vice President always sat.

Flanked by Secretary of State Harold Stanton to his right and Secretary of Defense William Chesney to his left, the President barely managed to smile for the preliminary photo op. Others in the room, including the Attorney General and the Treasury Secretary, who sat on either side of the empty chair, were also more subdued than usual – such was the somber mood of the gathering.

As soon as the press photographers and television video crews left the room, the President called the Cabinet meeting to order. "Thank you all for being here this morning," he began. "The last 10 days have been a trying time for the country and this administration," he acknowledged. "Yet despite the fact that we have sustained a significant loss and are currently in a period of national mourning, it is incumbent upon us to move forward with the people's business. Before we begin, however, I request a moment of silence for our distinguished and departed colleague – Vice President Clayton Talbot."

Respectfully, all in attendance bowed their heads and held their collective breath for one long minute. Finally, the President lifted his chin and cleared his throat. "Now then," he intoned. "Regarding the first item on our agenda …"

"If I may, Mr. President," Secretary of State Stanton interrupted.

"Harold," the President acknowledged.

"Sir, with all due respect to the Vice President's memory, I think it is important that we take this opportunity to address the important matter of who will replace him and when that will occur."

Somewhat surprised, the President hesitated a moment before responding, "Well, frankly, I haven't given that a great deal of thought just yet."

"Perhaps you should, sir," Stanton persisted with his usual flair for forcing an awkward issue. "I realize it has been a short time since the Vice President's untimely death … we all do … but the process of choosing a successor and having the nomination confirmed by the Senate will take time and there is the priority of ensuring continuity of government."

"I can appreciate that, Harold," the President asserted. "I just don't feel the same sense of urgency that you do."

"All I'm saying, sir," Stanton persisted, "is that it might be a good idea to discuss your intentions with the Cabinet. Or at least share your initial ideas on the subject."

The President glanced at Davidson, who was seated across at the far end of the table with a knowing, "I told you so" smirk on his face, then returned his attention to the matter at hand. "Very well, then," he replied, resting his elbows on the arms of his chair and folding his hands on his lap. "First, let me say how much I value the hard work and dedication each of you contributes to this administration," he said, addressing the entire group. "In fact, I believe your collective talents are so vital that I have decided that no current member of the Cabinet will be considered for the position."

Not much of a poker player, Stanton did a poor job of concealing his disappointment.

The President continued. "Over the next several days – and possibly the next few weeks – I will be giving careful consideration to the matter. And while I welcome any suggestions any of you may have … the ultimate decision will *solely* be my own."

A momentary silence followed the President's definitive statement that even Stanton did not dare challenge. "Now, if we could move on to a related issue …" said Hartman, turning to Transportation Secretary Morales. "Evelyn, have we pinpointed a conclusive cause of the crash of Air Force Two?"

"No, Mr. President," she replied. "We *do* know the reason why the aircraft went down. As I explained to you, there was a sudden loss of cabin pressure that incapacitated the crew and its passengers, and subsequently led to a fatal loss of altitude. What we haven't ascertained as of yet is why the equipment failed. We have recovered most of the wreckage and – with assistance from the FBI – are continuing our investigation. In particular, we are focusing on the procedures taken by the maintenance crew that worked on the aircraft prior to its departure from St. Louis."

"Please keep me advised of any developments," the President instructed. "If necessary, I will appoint a presidential commission to investigate the accident. I will hold off on that, however, until I receive your full and conclusive report."

"Of course, sir."

The President then addressed the Secretary of State. "Harold … "

"Mr. President."

"I understand you have an update on the hostage situation in the Philippines?"

"Yes, sir," said Stanton, clearing his throat. "As you know, several American advisors to a non-profit organization in the Philippines were abducted at gunpoint from a restaurant in Manila on April 27th and have been held hostage since then by terrorists claiming to represent a splinter group of Al Qaeda. However, we have been unable to verify this through our various diplomatic channels."

"Well, who else could be responsible?"

"We doubt any other known terrorist organization would undertake such an operation."

The President sought the advice of Homeland Security. "Secretary Kirkland, you've dealt with Al Qaeda before. Are you convinced they're behind this?"

Kirkland hardly flinched a muscle. "Convinced, sir? No," he responded, steely-eyed. "They're certainly capable, but it doesn't fit their modus operandi."

"Who's to say they haven't changed their tactics?" suggested Stanton.

"Since the crackdown on Abu Sayyaf, a splinter terrorist group, their presence and influence in the Philippines has been virtually non-existent," Kirkland maintained.

"Until now it would seem," the President muttered.

"Yes, sir," Kirkland conceded. "But there's another curious detail – we haven't received any demands."

"Not yet at least," the President sighed, obviously frustrated. "So where does this leave us? We don't want another interminable Iranian hostage situation on our hands."

"Well, as you know, Mr. President," Stanton interjected, "we don't negotiate with terrorists …"

"Yes, yes, we *all* know that, Mr. Secretary," the President replied testily.

"However," Stanton continued, "we are working diligently with our allies in the Islamic community to obtain as much information as possible so we can apply pressure where it needs to be applied."

"How involved is the Philippine government in the investigation?" asked the President.

"Sufficiently cooperative."

"That's what I thought," the President muttered. "Get the Philippine ambassador over here as soon as possible," he instructed. "We need to nip this situation in the bud sooner rather than later."

Next on the agenda was another bone of contention. "Where do we stand on the energy bill?" the President asked, directing his question to Energy Secretary Sam Brogan.

"Stuck in committee," Brogan replied.

"And what are we doing about that?"

"There's not a lot we can do, Mr. President – not as long as we're in the minority in both houses of Congress."

"That's no excuse," the President maintained. "We have some support on the other side of the aisle."

"But apparently not enough. If we want to undo the log jam, you'll need to take to the bully pulpit. But even then …"

"It's now or never," the President realized aloud. "Next year is a national election year – nothing will get done. And if the GOP gains an even greater majority in Congress … well, we can kiss the whole deal goodbye. It'll mean another generation of foreign dependency on oil. We need to take a more aggressive approach to this initiative."

"Frankly, Mr. President," said Brogan, "what we need is a pit bull.

I've been up to the Hill several times testifying before Congress and advocating our bill until I was blue in the face. We need someone with deep Congressional roots, a silver tongue and a big stick."

The President glanced again at Davidson. Both of them knew who Brogan was referring to, but rather than entertaining the notion, Hartman merely nodded and replied, "I'll see what I can do."

Chapter 8

Wayne Kirkland hated Washington, D.C. How anything meaningful ever got done in this town was a complete mystery to the man, what with all the red tape, political posturing, unethical chicanery and outright incompetence he regularly encountered. And don't get him started about the sheer stupidity, duplicity and insincerity of most of the government big-wigs he had to contend with on a daily basis.

Kirkland's appointment as Homeland Security Secretary had been a no-brainer. Yet this was not the job he had signed up for. For one thing, he was a hands-on kind of guy, toughened by a tour of duty in the Marine Corps in the early 80's fresh out of high school and 15 years on the Philadelphia police force, rising swiftly in rank from a rookie to sergeant to lieutenant to captain and, finally, commissioner. He knew first-hand what it was like to be in the field, to go undercover and to deal eye-to-eye with hardened criminals and both homegrown and foreign terrorists.

He was there in Beirut on October 23, 1983 when a massive car bomb decimated the Marine barracks, killing 241 of his brothers-in-arms and wounding countless others, including himself. He knew what it was like to wake up suddenly in the night amid utter chaos, devastation and carnage. He knew what it was like to patrol the mean streets of an American city riddled with crack addicts, gang-bangers and other assorted sociopaths, putting his life on the line day in and day out. He even knew what it was like to sift through the rubble of the World Trade Center, having volunteered when on the Philly force to join responders from all over the country and lend a hand during those bleak days in September of 2001.

But now he was warming an armchair behind a metal desk, responsible by title for the security of the entire nation yet hamstrung by other desk jockeys at other agencies who were far more powerful but much less cooperative than necessary. If it wasn't the NSA interfering in his operations, it was the tag team of the FBI and CIA not only blurring the boundaries of his authority but also failing to provide him with crucial intelligence in a timely manner. As a result, DHS was little more than the impotent appendage of a vast and counterproductive intelligence network with Kirkland as its hapless figurehead.

Of course, not everyone in the public sector rubbed Kirkland the wrong way. The President was more or less a stand-up guy who had his heart – if not his balls – in the right place. He treated Kirkland with deference and at least made an effort to encourage interdepartmental cooperation. But even the Commander-in-Chief couldn't significantly overcome the stubborn status quo and empower DHS. Much of the struggle to reinvent government effectively had fallen to Vice President Talbot. But now he was gone and Kirkland had no reason to believe the next Veep would be nearly as proactive, much less successful.

Yet, despite his misgivings, Kirkland made the best of his situation out of duty to God and country. What choice did he have? Either it was this or getting put out to pasture, a fate his wife of 32 years and his personal physician would have preferred, but one he dreaded more than death itself. Still, Kirkland's dedication was always a sore point with Dr. Reece, who felt it necessary to visit him in his office twice a month. Today's appointment was no different than the ones before.

"150 over 100," Dr. Reece declared, unwrapping the blood pressure band from Kirkland's outstretched arm. "Not where you need to be."

"Well," Kirkland sighed, rolling down and buttoning his shirt sleeve. "What can I tell you, Doc? I'm taking the pills you prescribed, I'm watching my diet ... sort of. I haven't smoked in three years ..."

"Under more stress than usual?" asked Reece.

Kirkland shrugged. "I wouldn't call it stress."

"What *would* you call it?"

Kirkland looked out his office window. "Uncertainty," he muttered. "Frustration."

"Job-related?"

"What else?"

"Home life okay?"

"Yeah," Kirkland scoffed, smiling. "Angie, the kids. If it wasn't for them ..."

"Any chest pains? Shortness of breath?"

"Nah. Heartburn, but that's it."

"Frequent?"

"I guess."

"We'll test you for acid reflux."

"I don't have time for that. It's nothing, I know it."

"Do you now?" Dr. Reece peered over his spectacles, regarding him skeptically. "And where did you get your medical degree?"

"At the school of hard knocks," Kirkland grumbled. "Are we done here? I have evildoers to keep at bay."

"In that case, I'll leave you to your work," said the good doctor, packing his black bag. "But you'd better stick to the plan," he warned, shaking his finger. "The next time I see you, your blood pressure had better be normal. Oh, and you're due for more lab work next month."

"Yeah, yeah. Thanks, Doc," said Kirkland, ushering him to the door. "I appreciated the house call."

"That makes one of us," Dr. Reece quipped.

No sooner had Dr. Reece left Kirkland's office than Bentley was standing in the doorway clutching his daily report. "Am I going to be pleased?" asked Kirkland doubtfully.

"Are you ever?' his assistant replied, depositing the brief on Kirkland's desk.

"Stick around," said the boss, motioning toward a nearby chair.

As Bentley settled in, Kirkland scanned a few of the pages with a characteristically dour expression. "What do you make of the latest chatter?" he suddenly asked.

Taken off guard, Bentley cleared his throat and adjusted his tie. "Well, sir … Frankly, I don't know what to make of it." No sooner had he made this admission than he regretted it.

Surprisingly, however, Kirkland concurred. "I don't know what to make of it, either. It's too generic, too frequent and too consistent. 'God willing, we will drive a Silver Dagger into the heart of the infidel,'" Kirkland quoted in a dubious tone. "Rather melodramatic, don't you think? Even by Al Qaeda's standards. It's not their style. Nor any of the usual suspects."

"But who else has the channels to put it out there?" Bentley wondered aloud.

"Only a foreign power," Kirkland maintained. "And that wouldn't make sense. Whoever is doing this isn't being very discreet. These messages were in Arabic?"

"Fluent."

"What about the repeated reference to 'Silver Dagger' in upper case?"

"Sounds like a mission," Bentley ventured a guess.

"Smells like misdirection to me," Kirkland contradicted. "Still … we can't afford to ignore it. Run this by Wilkins at the State Department – we'll see what he thinks. In the meantime, we'll keep the terror alert at yellow."

As Kirkland spoke, Bentley noticed him periodically rubbing the left side of his chest through his starched white shirt. "Are you alright, sir?" Bentley casually inquired.

"Hm?" Kirkland responded. Then, realizing what he was doing, he abruptly lowered his hand. "Yeah. I'm fine. Anything new on Manila?"

"No, sir."

Kirkland sighed deeply. "None of it makes sense," he muttered.

"Sir?"

"Nothing. That'll be all for now."

"Yes, sir," said Bentley, taking his cue to leave.

Left alone in his office, Kirkland took a closer look at the daily report and once again, feeling a twinge of discomfort, placed a hand on his chest. *Heartburn*, he told himself.

Peter Ames was dying for a cigarette. But not only was he cooling his heels in a smoke-free facility, he also couldn't step outside – not for a minute. He felt trapped, like a rat in a cage. Only in this case, the cage was a waiting room in the annex of a remote hangar at Lambert-St. Louis International Airport and he was the only one waiting.

He surveyed his surroundings -- four walls, two doors, a table, a few chairs and a clock on the wall that seemed to tick away the seconds as if they were hours. No magazines, no TV, no muzak, nothing. If this wasn't purgatory, it was the next worst thing.

Of course, the reason he was there had a lot to do with his impatience and anxiety. He had already been questioned by a small army of Feds. Apparently they weren't satisfied with what he had told them initially or wary of his body language – and who could blame them? As supervisor of the maintenance team that had prepped Air Force Two, he was more accountable than any of his crew for the systems failure that resulted in the death of the Vice President of the United States and 16 other people less than a week ago.

Suspiciously, his eyes scanned the room for any surveillance cameras. There were none in plain sight. But then he noticed the tinted mirror on the wall – two-way, no doubt. This was not good.

The door abruptly opened and in strode a tall, imposing African-American man. He looked like a clean-shaven linebacker in a spiffy suit and tie – a Fed, no doubt. "Good morning, Mr. Ames," he declared in a deep, no-nonsense voice.

Pete merely nodded solemnly.

"My name is Travis Clark," he said, flashing identification. "I'm a special agent with the FBI."

The acronym sent a chill down Pete's spine. The last group of inquisitors were all from the NTSB – routine questioning. Now it was a single agent from the Federal Bureau of Investigation – and a *special* agent at that.

Clark took a seat across the table. "And how are you, today?" he asked cryptically, folding his hands.

Pete didn't know how to respond. He felt as if a thousand eyes were watching him, weighing his demeanor and judging his reply. "Fine, I suppose," he finally answered.

"You must be wondering why you're being questioned again," said Special Agent Clark.

Ames shrugged. "No," he muttered unconvincingly. "Not really."

"You supervised the inspection of flight H478."

"That's right."

"You've had some time to think about it since you last spoke with officials from the NTSB. Anything to add to your previous statement?"

"No. I think my previous statement was pretty thorough."

Apparently, Special Agent Clark disagreed. "You claimed the aircraft passed inspection."

"That's right, it did."

"And yet there was a mechanical failure of the plane's cabin pressure control system."

"Yes, that appears to be the case."

"Resulting in the death of 17 people, including the Vice President of the United States."

"The aircraft passed inspection," Ames repeated.

"Are you sure there wasn't any error on the part of your crew?"

"Reasonably sure."

"Reasonably?"

"I'm sure," Ames bristled.

"You can vouch for every member of your staff?"

"To a man."

"Were there any unauthorized personnel in the hangar during the inspection?"

"No … as I've said before."

Agent Clark was silent for a moment, studying Ames, who returned the favor. Then, completely out of the blue, Ames asked, "Who is Hassan Al-Kihan?"

Puzzled, Ames twisted his eyebrows. "Who?"

Agent Clark feigned surprise. "You don't know anyone named Hassan Al-Kihan?"

Ames considered the name, then shook his head. "No."

"You're sure about that?"

"Uh-huh."

"What if I told you that you hired Mr. Al-Kihan for some yard work as recently as last summer?"

Ames sighed deeply and replied, "I would say that I don't know what you're talking about."

"You don't recall hiring anybody to clear your yard last summer?"

"I recall hiring a landscaping crew – Jerry's Lawn Service I think they were called. Or something like that."

"And one of the workers was an Hassan Al-Kihan."

"Yeah. So? What about it?"

"Were you aware that Mr. Al-Kihan was an illegal alien?"

"No, I wasn't aware of that," Ames answered, adding sarcastically, "Although I'm not entirely surprised."

"Mr. Al-Kihan was also a member of a radical modrassa in West New York, New Jersey, where he lived before moving to St. Louis last year."

"Is that right?"

"Do you know what a modrassa is, Mr. Ames?"

"Isn't it some sort of religious school?"

"An Islamic school," Clark corrected.

"What does any of that have to do with me?" asked Ames.

"Perhaps you can tell me," Clark retorted.

"I don't know what you're getting at," Ames retorted impatiently. "What exactly are you implying?"

"I'm not implying anything," said Clark, feigning innocence. "I mean what does one thing have to do with another?"

"I don't know. I was hoping you could tell me."

"Listen, I'm a loyal American," Ames insisted. "I've been working here at the airport for 27 years. I've never been written up for anything, never screwed up once ..."

Agent Clark regarded him with stone cold silence.

"I'm a veteran for Christ's sake!" Ames blurted.

"That makes two of us," Clark casually replied.

"Yeah, well, if you think there's some connection between me and this Al- ... whatever his name is, why don't you just interrogate him?"

"We'd like to, Mr. Ames. But unfortunately, Mr. Al-Kihan hasn't been seen or heard from since the day before Air Force Two crashed." Clark suddenly leaned forward across the desk, as if to drive home a point, then added, "Seems he's vanished ... without a trace."

Riveted, Ames gazed into the agent's unblinking eyes, his face going pale.

"I don't suppose you would know where he is?" asked Clark.

"How the hell would I know where he is?" Ames angrily responded. "I told you, *I don't even know the guy*. What the hell kind of questioning is this?"

"Okay," Clark calmly murmured, leaning back in his chair. "Okay ..."

But Ames wasn't about to be pacified. "Jesus," he muttered through clenched teeth, rubbing his hands together. "Don't you people realize how terrible I feel about what happened?"

Clark raised an eyebrow. "Because you *were* responsible?"

"I'm not responsible!" Ames blurted.

"No, of course not. You just *feel* responsible."

"Wouldn't you?"

"Sure. Especially if I made a mistake."

"There was no mistake!" Ames firmly denied, unable to control his emotions, feeling a great weight bearing down on his conscience. "There was no human error. Not on my part or any of my crew. It was equipment malfunction."

Clark shrugged. "Couldn't be helped."

On the verge of tears, his lower lip quivering, Ames avoided Clark's soulless stare and looked down at his coarse, trembling hands as they lay on his lap.

"Alright," Clark finally said. "That'll be all for now. You're free to go. If we have any more questions … we know where to find you."

But Ames didn't leave the room before Agent Clark. He sat there for awhile, thinking about the sudden unraveling of his heretofore complacent life and what he might have done to have avoided a disaster. He also knew that this was hardly the end of the inquisition.

Chapter 9

If Hunter Davidson knew anything, it was how to run a successful political campaign. The first resulted in his election as eighth grade class president. The second came in his senior year of high school in Youngstown, Ohio when he tied vote-getter Carol Anne McCloskey, the most popular cheerleader in school, and won the class presidency in a best-of-three coin toss. Fortunately, his margin of victory was far greater when he was elected student body president at Kent State University, where he majored in political science.

Davidson's fascination with politics inevitably compelled him to become a volunteer for a variety of state, local and presidential candidates. In fact, he learned more about the process by knocking on doors, handing out flyers, manning the phones, and licking stamps than by listening to professorial lectures and taking notes. After graduation, however, he set his own political ambitions aside to concentrate on consulting and managing the campaigns of others.

He began as an associate at a firm in New York City, where he quickly cultivated a reputation as a resourceful and tireless strategist for clients of both parties. His ability to motivate staff, keep candidates on message, and spin, spin, spin did not go unnoticed. Within a few years and several promotions, Davidson was a full partner.

It wasn't long, however, until he realized that he could be far more influential – and financially secure – as the president of his own firm. No sooner had he opened the doors to H.T. Davidson & Co. than he became known as the political go-to guy. His star had steadily risen to the point that he was profiled in both the *New York Times* and *New York* magazines, often quoted in the dailies, including the *Wall Street Journal*, and occasionally invited to offer his analysis on political TV talk shows. What sealed his celebrity, however, was when Davidson successfully managed the gubernatorial campaign of a certain former Democratic Congressman and state Attorney General from Long Island by way of upstate New York.

Of all the politicians Davidson had ever met, James J. Hartman was the one most worthy of his respect. Although ambitious, Hartman seemed genuinely dedicated to the public welfare. He was also the most scrupulous politician Davidson had ever encountered—wary of lobbyists, beholden to a modicum of special interest groups, and flexible in negotiations but uncompromising in principle – all of which made it that much easier to promote Hartman straight into the governor's mansion in Albany.

Before the inaugural, Hartman offered Davidson a job as his chief of staff, a position which he respectfully declined in order to continue to head his own company and run the presidential primary campaign of Senator Evan Ivers, who never polled more than single digits in a handful of contests. Four years later, however, Davidson was back managing Governor Hartman's victorious reelection bid.

In the interim, Davidson dated and eventually married Melissa Abernathy, a paralegal who had worked as a volunteer on the first Hartman campaign. The couple had their first child nine months later and Davidson's firm expanded to include satellite offices in Chicago and San Diego and twice the amount of staff as when the company was founded.

But Davidson's enthusiasm for campaign management began to wane and he started delegating more and more of those responsibilities to a group of underlings he was grooming to eventually succeed him. He felt the need to move on to the next level, to reach a bit higher. Having successfully navigated most of his clients to their respective political brass rings, he entertained the notion of seeking office himself, or at least a designated political position of some stature and clout.

His opportunity came when Governor Hartman, midway through his second term, invited Davidson, a pregnant Melissa and their daughter Tina up to Albany for the weekend. It was a warm, sunny July in upstate New York, and while Irene Hartman relaxed with Melissa on the veranda of the Governor's mansion, watching Tina frolic in the garden below, Hartman and Davidson strolled the grounds and talked, soon enough addressing the purpose of the weekend getaway.

"Hunt," said the Governor as they plodded the sprawling lawn, "I've decided to run for President."

Davidson had assumed as much and anticipated Hartman's next question: "I wouldn't get into the race unless I intended to win, and I'm convinced that the only way I can do that is if I have a campaign manager who not only knows me better than I know myself, but who can actually sell me to the American people. In case you're wondering," he jokingly added, "that person is you."

Despite Davidson's recent disenchantment with hands-on campaign management, the prospect of a White House run by Hartman – and the opportunity to use it as a stepping stone – had titillated him for some time. Not wanting to sound too eager, however, he replied: "Are you sure I'm your man? The last presidential campaign I worked on never made it to the convention."

"That was just a work-up," Hartman shrugged dismissively. "Besides, you were saddled with Ivers – good man, fine Senator, but a hard sell in the Northeast and to the West Coast progressive wing … not quite ready for primetime."

"But you certainly are," Davidson conceded. "You've got the looks, the energy, and a record that should hold up well."

"My sentiments exactly," Hartman smiled. "So? Are you in?"

Davidson teased his candidate with a moment of quiet reflection. Finally, he said, "I'll do it … on one condition."

"Which is?"

"After we win – and we will win – I'd like an advisory position in the administration."

Hartman bowed his head and pursed his lips, then looked sideways at Davidson and promised, "You get me the nomination and a victory in November, and I'll appoint you White House Chief of Staff. How does that sound?"

Davidson's heart skipped a beat. "Sounds like we have a deal," he replied, pausing to offer his hand.

Hartman stopped walking, brushed Davidson's arm aside and gave him a spontaneous bear hug. "Hunt," he declared, "this is the beginning of a great adventure."

The Monday following the Cabinet meeting, President Hartman held a private brainstorming session in the Oval Office with six members of his staff. Those in attendance included Davidson, National Security advisor Redmond, foreign policy advisor Christopher Hobbs, domestic policy advisor Mark Corcoran, economic advisor Chet Nesbitt and Press Secretary Pauline Cafferty – unofficially known as the Vetting Team. No sooner had everyone settled into comfortable couches and chairs near the unused fireplace than the President got right down to business.

"I'll forego the usual song and dance," Hartman declared. "You all know why we're here. Hunt and I went through this process about three years ago in the weeks leading up to the Democratic Convention, but things were a bit different then. We were looking more for a running mate than a vice president. Now, we're looking for more than just another vice president. Since the rest of you are new to this, I'll let Hunt get the ball rolling."

Glancing at a page of notes resting on his lap, Davidson cleared his voice and began with a bit of historical reference: "Seven U.S. Vice Presidents have died in office," he informed the group. "Well ... eight – if you count Clayton. The last – before Clayton – was James Sherman way back in 1912. In those days, the position was simply left vacant until the end of the President's term. However, in today's world, the country cannot afford to be without a standby chief executive for an extended period of time. In the event of the President's death or incapacitation, someone would be needed to quickly assume power.

"There was a time when the vice presidency was considered a meaningless job. In fact, John Nance Garner, the 32nd Vice President, once said that the office wasn't 'worth a pitcher of warm piss.' Many still hold that belief. However, as you know, recent administrations have gone a long way toward dispelling that notion.

"In addition to a few statutory duties, such as serving on the National Security Council and the Board of Regents of the Smithsonian Institution, the Vice President serves as the President of the Senate, casting a vote in the event of a deadlock and presiding over and certifying the official vote count of the Electoral College. Vice Presidents are also often assigned by the President to chair various commissions, such as the Space Council. They usually serve as the White House liaison with the National Governors Association and the U.S. Conference of Mayors. At the discretion of the President, they also serve as a senior advisor, help draft administration policy, and act as spokesperson for that policy.

"As for eligibility, the vice president must be a natural-born U.S. citizen, at least 35 years of age, and a U.S. resident for 14 years."

"Well, that certainly narrows it down," the President quipped under his breath, eliciting a few chuckles, except for Pauline, whose tense body language suggested she was taking the gathering a bit too seriously.

"Thanks for the Wikipedia briefing," the President teased Davidson. "Ideas, anyone?"

"Well," Redmond was first to chime in, "I think it goes without saying we need someone who can deal effectively with Congress – aside from presiding over sessions of the Senate. Some executive experience would also be desirable, although not a necessity."

"At the same time, we can't afford to relinquish a seat in either house," Corcoran pointed out. "We're already in the minority."

"Then we'll need someone who is either a sitting or former governor or a former member of Congress," Hobbs concluded.

"Or someone who has worked in a previous administration," Nesbitt interjected.

"Or all of the above," Pauline blurted, then immediately looked down at her folded hands, hoping no one noticed her blushing.

"Who fits the bill?" asked the President.

"Well, Harley Singleton immediately comes to mind," Davidson offered. "He's served as both a governor and senator."

"That's a no-brainer," Redmond concurred. "He'd be easy for the Republican leadership to swallow. Lord knows, he voted with them often enough. And he's more or less on the same page as this administration."

"Although he is eight years your senior, sir," Corcoran noted.

The President looked perplexed. "And that's a negative because …?"

"Could look like your Dad."

"Oh, you flatter me," the President muttered.

"He might be too old to lead the party after your second term," Corcoran added.

"Who says he has to succeed me? We've got enough potential presidential timber in the party."

"Which is why you should pick someone younger," Hobbs suggested. "It would cast you in the role of mentor and pave the way for a viable successor."

"Give me a name," said the President.

"Hamilton Caine," Nesbitt offered.

"The rock star?" Hartman replied dismissively, a reference to the California Governor's glamorous image and penchant for attending Hollywood events.

Nesbitt shrugged. "Just began a second term as California governor – by a landslide. Good environmental record – balanced the state budget – doing a good job on immigration."

"What about a woman?" Pauline suggested.

"Or a minority member?" Corcoran interjected.

"You mean, a politically correct choice?" the President smiled.

"Not necessarily," Corcoran replied. "Someone with solid credentials. Someone like …"

"Frank Dawson?" Hobbs ventured, referring to the Mayor of Los Angeles.

"Actually, I was thinking of Congressman Youngblood," Corcoran offered tentatively.

"Hmm," hummed the President, obviously intrigued. He glanced at Davidson, who arched his eyebrows encouragingly.

The President turned to Cafferty, who looked like a deer caught in the headlights. "Which female candidate were you thinking of, Pauline?" he asked.

She hesitated, then stammered, "Uh … A-ambassador Lewis?"

The President narrowed his eyes, considering the choice. "Certainly has a lot of experience under her belt," he thought aloud. "Not bad. Not bad at all."

Gratified, Pauline managed a feeble smile.

"Although …" the President equivocated. "I'm naturally inclined toward a current or former governor. I must say, Paul Gardner looks first rate."

"Oh, yes," Redmond readily agreed. To which everyone else muttered similar enthusiasm.

"Let's boil it down to a short list," the President decided. "The five best candidates. Then I'll need each of you to vet a particular candidate. That'll require obtaining their records – tax returns, medical information, financial holdings, military files. We'll have Treasury and FBI run background checks. In the meantime, we'll interview each of them as discreetly as possible. Hunt has some experience with the process. You can check with him if you have any questions."

"Do we share the list with the press?" Davidson asked. "Float the names to gauge reaction?"

"No," said the President. "That might create certain … expectations. Let's keep the whole effort as close to the vest as possible. Just pull the list together, Hunt, run it by me and we'll take it from there.'

"Very good, sir," the Chief of Staff remarked.

"Well, I've got another appointment in a few minutes," said the President, checking his wristwatch. "Our 'friends' from the Hill. So let's adjourn for now and we'll reconvene soon."

The President took a few moments to freshen up in an adjoining lavatory, then instructed his personal secretary Grace via intercom to send in his guests, which included Senate Majority Leader Henry Howard, House Speaker Pierce Allman, and Majority Whip Bill Bryce.

"Good morning, Mr. President," Howard greeted with a warmer than usual smile.

"Hank," the President acknowledged with a cordial smile of his own and firm handshakes all around. "Bill. Pierce. Please, gentlemen, make yourselves comfortable."

"Thank you for agreeing to meet with us this morning, sir," said Howard, waiting along with the others for the President to sit down before taking his seat. "We know how difficult the last several days have been for you and your entire staff."

"Yes," the President admitted, "it's been a trying time for all of us."

"First, speaking for the entire Congress, as well as myself, may I extend our heartfelt condolences over the passing of Vice President Talbot. It was a great loss for our country and this administration."

"Thank you, Hank," the President replied sincerely. "I appreciate that."

"I assure you, sir," Howard declared, "that during this period of national mourning, the Congressional leadership will do everything in its power to assist you and cooperate as much as possible to provide bipartisan support – for the good of the country."

"I'm glad to hear that," said the President, "and quite grateful. And I'm sure that spirit of bipartisanship and support will extend to the selection and confirmation of a new vice president."

"But of course, Mr. President," Allman gracefully vowed. "We're here merely to offer our advice and suggestions to make the process go as smoothly as possible."

"And what advice would you have?" asked the President, cutting to the chase.

"Well, sir, we believe it would be helpful if your nominee were someone with considerable experience in the legislative process and constitutional law."

"Of course," the President agreed.

"Given the current state of the economy," said Allman, "a fiscal conservative would appeal to many members on both sides of the aisle."

"An individual known for his high moral character," added Bryce, a former Boy Scout, as the President could recollect, and current member of the American Family Association.

"Someone capable of putting principle and patriotism ahead of ideology and petty politics," Howard chimed in.

"Sounds a lot like you, Hank," the President quipped.

There was a round of hearty laughter as the President's underlying sarcasm went unnoted.

"Is that bad?" asked Howard jokingly.

More exaggerated laughter.

"In fact," the President continued the kibitzing, "I'd offer the job to you, but you'd probably think it was a step down."

More laughter as Bryce in particular nearly split a gut.

"In all seriousness, though," said the President, restoring a tone of propriety. "We are actively pursuing a nominee who I hope will meet all of your expectations while being committed to this administration's domestic and international agenda."

That seemed like a mixed blessing to the three legislators, but Howard remained diplomatic. "We're confident you'll exercise reasonable judgment in your selection, Mr. President."

"And what would you consider 'reasonable.' Hank?" the President wondered aloud.

"I'm afraid I don't follow you, sir."

"Well, instead of telling me what type of nominee you would find acceptable, perhaps you should tell me who you might find objectionable. That would make things easier for both of us."

"Well, sir," Allman responded, "I think it goes without saying that a nominee whose philosophy is … oh, firmly to the left might find the confirmation hearings rather long and contentious."

"Duly noted," said the President. "What about gender?"

The three glanced at each other and Allman elected to reply, "We'd have no problem with a female nominee … as long as she's truly qualified."

"What about a minority candidate?"

"Race is irrelevant," Howard claimed, "Just as long as he or she …"

"Is truly qualified and not a left-wing activist," the President finished the Majority Leader's sentence for him.

"Does that mean you're inclined toward a female or minority nominee, sir?" asked Bryce, obviously fishing.

It took all of the President's self-discipline not to laugh. "Not necessarily."

"Word around the Beltway is that you've got your sights set on a former senator from the Lone Star State," Allman declared.

"Right now, my sights aren't set on anyone in particular," the President admitted. "We've only just begun the search."

"Then I guess it's just a rumor."

"The first of many, I suspect," the President replied. "Why? Does that possibility appeal to you?"

"Well," Howard coyly replied. "That nomination would probably sail through the Senate."

The President maintained his poker face.

"Hope I haven't jinxed it," said the Majority Leader with a subtle smile.

"While I have you gentlemen here," the President changed the subject, "what are our chances of getting the energy bill out of committee before the summer recess?"

"Slim to none," Howard candidly replied. "Not unless you give an inch, Mr. President."

"Ah, but Hank, you know that if I give an inch, you boys will take a mile."

"Not if you drop the windfall profits tax."

"Is that all?" asked the President.

"Well, if you'd lift your executive order banning offshore drilling …"

"More drilling isn't going to help us," the President maintained.

"It certainly won't hurt," Howard replied.

The President sighed. "You know as well as I do that if we give the oil companies everything they want, we won't have the incentive to shift to alternate energy sources."

"And if we continue down the path of wealth redistribution, Mr. President, we could end up on a very slippery slope to socialism," Howard countered.

"Oh, save it for the next campaign, Hank," the President advised. "In the meantime, let's try to get something passed in our lifetimes. Shall we?"

"We'll sort it all out just as soon as you get *this* house in order," Howard promised, a calculating smile frozen to his face.

"Well, I thank you gentlemen for your input," said the President, suddenly rising from his chair, signaling an end to the visit. The three legislators automatically sprang to their feet. "I'll keep the Congressional leadership informed and I'll be announcing my nominee in due course. Now, if you'll excuse me, I have some excitable school children to welcome on the South Lawn. Mustn't miss a photo op."

"Well. That was … brief," said Allman in the limousine back to Capitol Hill.

"But informative," Howard replied.

"What was your reading?" asked Bryce.

"He'll do what he usually does," Howard predicted. "He'll toy with a few novel considerations, then settle for the safe, easy choice. This president rarely thinks out of the box, and when he does he always reverts to form. He's a compromiser."

"So you think Singleton has the edge?" Allman surmised.

Howard just smiled.

Chapter 10

The official (i.e. copyrighted) slogan of the *American Observor* was "From K Street to Main Street, we've got it covered." That someone on Madison Avenue was actually paid to come up with that never ceased to amaze Gideon Burnett. In fact, it was the only thing that remotely amazed him anymore. After 18 years in the business, 15 of them on the Washington desk of *AO*, he had pretty much seen everything – from influence peddling lobbyists to whore-mongering Congressmen to wife-beating Senators to drug-dealing diplomatic attaches. If that didn't make you jaded to a fault, nothing would.

Although he had yet to win a Pulitzer Prize, Burnett was nevertheless recognized by his peers as one of the most conscientious – and incorrigible – journalists on the White House/Washington beat. It was he who had exposed the cozy relationship between a previous administration's national security adviser and a Chinese intelligence operative, leading to the former's resignation and a full-scale Congressional investigation. It was he who had established a link between a presidential reelection committee and an elaborate money-laundering operation that proved to be a factor in the outcome of the last national election. And it was he who had forced President Hartman to withdraw his initial nominee for attorney general when he interviewed several illegal aliens who were once employed by the nominee.

Yes, Burnett's reputation as a muckraker was legendary among the current ranks of American news hounds. And yet, it had been some time since he had been able to sink his fangs into a juicy scandal. Covering the White House, although a prestigious assignment, was proving to be a tepid experience ever since the illegal aliens flap. After that one miscue, the Hartman cabal had been painstaking in avoiding the slightest whiff of controversy. In fact, it was downright squeaky clean compared to previous administrations. Oh, how Burnett nostalgically yearned for the good old days of Monicagate and Valerie Plame.

For now, however, Burnett was tethered to his White House beat, a steady gig he thought would provide access to all sorts of juicy gossip, but instead was merely a nest of Democratic policy wonks trying to outmaneuver a Republican Congress angling for a presidential comeback. He had to be content with punching out pithy pieces about the administration's uphill battle to pass any meaningful legislation despite the efforts of numerous special interests intent on ensuring the status quo. Not that Burnett cared who succeeded or failed in this ongoing struggle. He had seen so many politicians come and go, rise and fade from the scene, that he had lost any sense of idealism long ago. Like the hungry lion stalking the elusive antelope, all that mattered to him was getting the big story, the scoop that turns the tide and sets the whole game on its head.

Lately, Burnett's restlessness had become palpable. So, too, was his sudden spurt of motivation in the wake of Clayton Talbot's demise. Greg Paulsen, *AO's* aging but feisty managing editor, sensed that something was up with Burnett, which is why he cornered him one day at his infamously unkempt cubicle.

"So," said Paulsen, straddling the entryway like a wary troll, "how's that piece on Secretary Stanton's upcoming trip to the Middle East coming along?"

"Done," Burnett replied, swiveling from side to side in his squeaky armchair, "in proofing as we speak."

"Good. Next, I was thinking of a feature on the administration's fence mending efforts with the Congressional Black Caucus. I was going to bring it up at the next editorial meeting, but …"

"Put it on the backburner," Burnett advised. "We have a bigger fish to fry."

"We do?" chimed Paulsen, crossing his arms and leaning against the wall. "What have you got in mind?"

"How does an exclusive on the next vice president sound?" Burnett replied, playing the ace up his sleeve.

"You mean an overview of the likely candidates for the nomination?"

"I mean a cover story on the actual nominee – *before* he's announced."

Paulsen's naturally stern, wizened face brightened with mild amusement. "Well, that would be a neat trick. Are you psychic or something?"

"Hardly. I'm talking about a bona fide, 14-karat gold scoop."

"I don't know, Gid," Paulsen sighed doubtfully. "Not much shock and awe in that topic. For one thing, the vice presidency isn't life or death – unless a certifiable, trigger-happy lunatic gets nominated and confirmed. Also, speculation is already rampant. Rumor has it that the President is leaning toward Gardner or Lewis."

"Well, I've got a well-placed source that says otherwise," Burnett bluffed.

"Oh? And where is this well-placed source?"

Burnett leaned forward for dramatic effect and replied, "In the White House."

The look of anticipation on Paulsen's face was priceless. "Inner circle?"

Burnett slowly nodded.

"And who might be the chosen one?" asked Paulsen.

Burnett smiled like the Cheshire Cat, buying time to come up with a name. "Harley Singleton," he finally revealed, merely hazarding an educated guess.

Paulsen's eyes narrowed. "Hmm. The man Hartman passed over three years ago. Interesting. And not even on the radar."

"Not yet," Burnett warned. "Which is why I need to strike while the iron is hot."

"You *will* find a second source to confirm before we go out on a limb?" Paulsen asked rhetorically.

"Of course."

"And you're talking expose here – not *Parade* magazine profile?"

"Warts and all," Burnett promised.

"Okay," Paulsen agreed. "Let's roll."

Flushed with predatory excitement, Burnett turned his attention to his computer and logged on to the Internet, his mind already flowing with ideas. No sooner had he pulled down a list of favorite research sites, however, than his phone rang, the caller I.D. displaying an unfamiliar number with a Texas area code.

"Yeah," he grunted into the receiver.

"Hello? I'm trying to reach Mr. Burnett," said a male voice he didn't recognize. "Mr. Gideon Burnett."

"You found him," Burnett confirmed, slouching in his chair.

"Mr. Burnett, my name is Ross Kayton."

"Mm-hm. What can I do for you, Mr. Kayton?"

"It's not what you can do for me, Mr. Burnett," the caller replied. "It's what I can do for you."

Great, thought Burnett, rolling his eyes – a telemarketer – at work no less. "I'm pretty busy," he said, a trifle impatiently.

"I'm a former employee of Uniplex Industries," the caller informed him. "Are you familiar with the company?"

"I've heard of it."

"I worked there for several years."

"Uh-huh," Burnett murmured, wishing this guy would cut to the chase.

"I am in possession of some records you might find interesting – documents related to Senator Harley Singleton."

Burnett abruptly sat up straight. Was this providential, or what? Yet he coyly replied, "Really? And why would I find them interesting?"

"I have it on good authority, Mr. Burnett, that Harley Singleton is a leading candidate to replace Vice President Talbot. Considering what you've written in the past about the Senator ... and former governor, I would think you'd be interested in knowing who he is covertly associated with."

"Sounds like you have an axe to grind, Mr. Kayton." Burnett noted.

"Not with Singleton."

"Oh? Then with whom?"

"Tate."

Again, Burnett's pulse quickened. Either Kayton was merely a titillating name dropper or he was on to something. "Tate? As in ... Malcolm Everett Tate?"

"That's right."

"What exactly are you suggesting, Mr. Kayton?"

"I'd rather let the documents speak for themselves. In fact, we shouldn't even be talking about this over the phone."

"Well," laughed Burnett, "you're the one who called."

"I know. I had to talk to someone."

"And you chose me. Now why is that?"

"You have access to the President."

"Limited access," Burnett corrected. "I'm just a White House correspondent."

"Well, as I said, you've written in the past about Singleton's close ties to energy lobbyists ..."

"But that's ancient history, Mr. Kayton. Singleton eventually converted into a tree-hugger ever since ..."

"Ever since he left the Senate and Hartman was elected," Kayton interjected. "Yeah, yeah. It's a ruse."

"Really? And you can prove it?"

"I've got the smoking gun."

"Ah-huh. Well, tell me, how did you get a hold of these documents?"

"I knew where they were filed and I borrowed them."

"You mean, you *stole them*."

"No," Kayton begged to differ, "I simply replaced the originals with copies."

"Technically, they're stolen."

"You mean like the Pentagon Papers?"

"I'd hardly compare what you claim to have with the Pentagon Papers," Gideon scoffed.

"If you prefer, Mr. Burnett, I can take them to the *New York Times* or the *Washington Post*."

"They won't pay you, either."

"I'm not interested in money."

"Then what's in it for you?"

Without hesitation, Kayton replied, "The satisfaction of preventing a corporate mole from infiltrating the White House. That and a little payback. Uniplex fired me for questioning certain ... lobbying practices."

"So you want to hang Tate and Singleton out to dry?"

"I'd say they had it coming."

"Okay. Well, how soon can you be here with this ... so-called evidence?"

"I can't travel."

"And why is that?"

Kayton hesitated, then replied, "I may be under surveillance."

Burnett's B.S. meter suddenly pointed toward "paranoid conspiracy theorist." "Uh-huh," he skeptically muttered.

"You'll have to come here," Kayton maintained.

"And where is here?"

"Beauville, Texas. It's just outside of Houston."

Burnett did a double-take. "You want me to fly to Texas based on a phone call from a stranger, claiming to have documents incriminating a former governor and U.S. senator, who believes he is under surveillance?"

Kayton ignored the sarcasm. "Do you have a fax number?"

"Yeah, why?"

"I'll send you one page from the files. No cover sheet. Then you decide if it's worth a trip for the rest of the documents."

What the hell, thought Burnett, divulging his fax number.

"I'll send the document within the next five minutes," Kayton instructed. "Be on the lookout. I wouldn't want it to fall into the wrong hands."

"Tell me something," said Burnett. "If you were being watched, wouldn't your phone be tapped?"

"I'm not calling from home. I'm calling from a friend's place."

"Okay, well … I'll wait for your fax. Then maybe I'll call you back."

As soon as Burnett hung up the phone, his mind started racing. If this was a valid lead, he could have quite an expose on his hands. Just like in the good old days. And if not, well …

While waiting for Kayton's fax, he checked the Uniplex Web site for a contact number and then called the company's human resources department in Houston. Pretending to be verifying previous employment, he confirmed that Ross Kayton was, indeed, a former employee. So far, so good.

Next, Burnett checked AO's archives and Googled as much information as he could about Harley Singleton's ties to various corporations and lobbyists. Except for the usual suspects, he appeared to be relatively clean and had no apparent connection to either Uniplex or any other companies associated with Malcolm Everett Tate. However, upon closer investigation, Burnett did discover a mere two degrees of separation when he stumbled upon a gubernatorial campaign contributor's list that included several Texas entrepreneurs who had served as subcontractors for Uniplex.

Finally, Kayton's fax arrived, transmitted from a different phone number which Burnett quickly traced as the Business Center at a Hyatt hotel in Beauville, Texas. The single page, printed beneath

Uniplex letterhead documented the disbursement of a cashier's check – number 0973-250 in the amount of $250,000 – to what appeared to be an account number in a Grand Cayman Island's bank. It was far from conclusive proof of criminal wrongdoing, but it was enough to suggest an intriguing paper trail existed, one worth pursuing. He was up for a road trip, anyway.

So without further adieu, Burnett trotted over to Paulsen's office, finding his boss at his desk and on the phone. Of course, that didn't stop him. "Hey," he called from the doorway.

"What now?" asked Paulsen, holding the phone receiver to his chest.

"I need to leave town," Burnett announced.

Without missing a beat, Paulsen replied, "I knew it would come to this sooner or later …"

Chapter 11

Mr. L's umbrella was black and quite large – large enough, in fact, to shield two of him from the drizzling rain. He held it upright and steady, never once allowing it to lean in one direction or the other, never resting the handle against his protruding waist, always aloft and rigid against the gusty wind.

He was seated on the same park bench as before, within a short walking distance of the Jefferson Memorial, his squinting eyes set on the drifting Potomac River as usual. Nevertheless, he caught a glimpse of Mr. M approaching with his peripheral vision. Considering he was late, he should have been walking faster, thought Mr. L., who despised tardiness. He waited until the young man took his seat beside him before expressing his displeasure.

"About time you showed up," Mr. L coldly remarked.

"Yeah," Mr. M replied casually, "traffic was a bitch."

"Spare me the excuses."

"That wasn't an excuse. I was being factitious."

"Inconsiderate is more like it. I've been waiting here for half of an hour. The least you can do is apologize."

"For what?" Mr. M scoffed. "Being a little late? Gimme a break."

Mr. L bristled, but held his tongue, his knuckles turning white as he gripped his umbrella handle even tighter.

"Pretty miserable day," Mr. M noted, glancing up at the sky, blinking as raindrops dappled his eyelashes. "I'm really getting soaked here. Do you think we could share your umbrella?"

Mr. L turned his head slowly to scowl at him. "Give me a break."

"Fine. I'll just get wet," Mr. M shrugged. "I don't know what the big deal is. It's not like anyone is going to notice us in this weather."

"Did you pass along the last message?" asked Mr. L, changing the subject and looking away.

"Well, duh," Mr. M responded. "What do you think?"

"I don't know what to think. You don't strike me as being particularly reliable."

"Aw, now I'm really hurt," Mr. M smirked. "Well, if that's how you feel about me, I might as well just walk away."

"Oh, you wouldn't do that," Mr. L assured him. "Not if you want to get paid. Not if you know what's good for you."

"Is that what's known as a veiled threat?" Mr. M smugly retorted.

"You don't take this seriously, do you?"

"Take *what* seriously? Meeting on a park bench in the middle of a monsoon? Swapping coded messages that make no sense to either one of us? Acting like we're doing something *really clandestine*? You've got to admit, this is pretty ridiculous."

"What is ridiculous – aside from your attitude, your hygiene and your wardrobe – is that you don't even have enough sense to carry an umbrella in weather like this."

"I thought we weren't going to get personal? You know, for someone who doesn't even address me face-to-face, you're pretty observant."

"Your inadequacies are hard to ignore."

"What difference does it make to you?"

"Nothing, except that if I have to work with you, I'd appreciate a little professional courtesy."

"You call this work?"

"I can see it's useless to argue with you," said Mr. L with an exhausted sigh.

"You're right about that," Mr. M agreed. "So … do you want today's cryptic message – before I catch pneumonia?"

"What is it?"

"Black rook to white queen four," said Mr. M, glancing at his counterpart's expressionless profile. "Shall I repeat the message?" he asked after a moment of silence.

"That won't be necessary," Mr. L assured him.

"What's with these chess moves, anyway?" Mr. M wondered aloud.

"Never mind," Mr. L replied, rising from the bench. "That'll be all for today."

"Hold on a second," said Mr. M. "There's something I want to discuss with you."

Mr. L sighed, but lingered nonetheless, tilting his umbrella a bit as he turned toward Mr. M. "Well?"

"Could we pick another place to meet next time?" Mr. M requested. "This isn't the most convenient rendezvous point for me. Besides, I'm not the outdoors type. How about some place else, public but private, like a mall or something."

"That wouldn't work," Mr. L maintained.

"Why not?"

"Malls have cameras."

"Oh … well, what about a movie? An early matinee. It's dark … dry … we could split a bucket of popcorn …"

Mr. L glared. "Surely you're joking," he condescendingly replied.

Mr. M kept a straight face as long as he could, then smiled, "Gotcha'."

Mr. L frowned. "We'll meet again next Tuesday," he said. "*Here.* Same time. Do try to be punctual."

"*Okay*," Mr. M consented. He waited for Mr. L to issue more instructions. When none were forthcoming, he sniped, "Am I dismissed?"

Rather than replying, Mr. L and his big umbrella simply left.

Drenched to the bone, Mr. M watched his retreat, bemused. "Stay away from those malls," he sarcastically called after him.

During the course of a rather busy day, Hunter Davidson and President Hartman found the time to meet behind closed doors in the Oval Office to follow up on the vice presidential search project. "Give Lewis to Pauline ... since it was her suggestion," the President instructed, reviewing the short list of five candidates. "Redmond can handle Gardner, Corcoran gets Caine, and Nesbitt can vet Youngblood."

"That leaves Singleton."

"He's all yours," said the President, cautiously adding, "Don't read too much into that. I want each of you to do extensive background checks with the cooperation of appropriate federal agencies. Look for any red flags, anything that would come under intense scrutiny by Congress or the press. If you find anything, let me know immediately. If not, arrange personal interviews here at the White House."

"Are you sure you want to do them face-to-face?" asked Davidson. "Speculation will run rampant throughout the media."

"That's unavoidable," claimed the President, "and doesn't concern me much. But, yes – I'm not about to choose a vice president based on a telephone interview. I want to speak with them face-to-face and eye-to-eye. If that conflicts with anyone's schedule, we can teleconference."

"How soon do you want to conduct these interviews?"

"Let's start next week. One or two per day."

"By the way," Davidson mentioned. "A new Gallup poll has been released."

"Oh?"

"Your job approval has spiked from 42 percent to 58."

"That's not job approval," the President replied dismissively. "It's misplaced sympathy."

"Whatever you want to call it, it's public support and we should make the most of it while it lasts."

"What I need is Congressional support."

"That'll come next year when you're reelected by a wider margin than last time."

"Don't count your chickens before they're hatched."

"Don't worry. We'll have you on the campaign trail later this year – with your new Vice President."

The President did not reply, seemingly lost in a thought.

"You will be running again, won't you?" Davidson inquired.

"Hm?" the President snapped out of his reverie. "Yes, of course. We'll be running again," he emphasized.

Reassured, Davidson smiled.

Later that afternoon, Hartman thought it best to seek the input of an old advisor. Rather than call, he took a walk over to the First Lady's East Wing office, where he was greeted by her secretary, Mrs. Kendall. "Mr. President," she declared, surprised and respectfully rising from the chair behind her desk.

"Please, don't get up," he told her. "Is the First Lady here?"

"Yes, sir," Mrs. Kendall replied, gesturing toward the entrance to an inner office.

"Thank you," the President muttered, proceeding to knock on the door before opening it.

Seated at her own desk, reading letters, Irene was clearly surprised by his appearance. "What is it?" she asked with a hint of curiosity.

The President closed the door behind him. "I wanted to share this with you," he said, handing her a piece of paper like a child presenting his report card to his mother.

"Your short list of vice-presidential candidates?" Irene surmised.

"Mm. What do you think?"

Irene perused the roster, and then handed the list back to her husband. "Well," she replied. "It's certainly diversified."

"Does any name jump out at you?"

"Not really," said Irene. "They're all qualified. Although I wonder how serious you are about Youngblood and Lewis."

"What do you mean?"

Irene hesitated a moment, then plainly remarked, "It looks like you're pandering a bit."

"Why? Because one is black and one is a woman?"

"Yes," Irene bluntly replied. "Because one is black and one is a woman."

"Youngblood is a ranking member of Congress," he reminded her.

"Your governing styles and personalities don't match. It's like ... oil and water."

"And Lewis?"

"She's not a leader," Irene maintained. "She's a contented career diplomat, subservient to a fault."

"What about the rest of them? Gardner, for example."

"More suitable, but a lightweight."

"I disagree," said the President somewhat defensively.

"That is your prerogative," Irene coolly replied.

"Well, that leaves Singleton or Caine."

"The crème de la crème."

"You're keen on both?"

"I wouldn't say I'm keen on anyone," Irene admitted. "But either makes sense."

"Does anyone have the edge ... in your estimation?"

Irene paused to deliberate, and then resolutely responded, "Caine."

"Caine?" Hartman echoed, expressing surprise. "What about Harley?"

"Harley is the safe choice – the workhorse, the wheeler-dealer, the backslapper."

"What's wrong with that?"

Irene shrugged. "Nothing – if you want an enforcer and a 'yes' man."

"A very capable enforcer," the President stressed.

"It sounds as if your mind is already made up," Irene noted.

"Not at all. I just think Harley has a definite edge over Caine."

"You asked my opinion," said Irene pointedly. "I believe I gave it to you." Her feisty but icy glare brought Hartman back to reality. "Anything else?" she asked a tad impatiently. "I have a rather busy schedule today."

The President shook his head, backing off. "Well, then, I'll see you at dinner," he awkwardly muttered as he opened the door and turned to leave.

Irene was about to issue a sarcastic reply, but for some reason refrained. By then the door had closed and it was too late. But was it that she had run out of cutting things to say? Or was she simply tired of waging this unwinnable war? Punishing him with silence, mockery and recrimination certainly didn't make her feel any better. Still …

Chapter 12

If he had accomplished nothing else in his life, Marcus Theolonius Youngblood would have held the distinction of having scored a record 63 points in a game that earned his Michigan State team the NCAA championship. But an even greater source of pride and achievement could be derived from his later career as a six-term Congressman from his native Detroit and the prolific head of the Congressional Black Caucus.

A handsome and frequent fixture on the covers of *Ebony* and *Jet* magazines, an engaging and provocative guest on numerous TV political forums, and an occasional presenter of considerable stature at the annual Image Awards, Youngblood was known throughout the African-American community as a bona fide maverick – or, as he preferred to call it, an "anti-politician." Although he was certainly devoted to his role as a distinguished member of the House of Representatives, rarely if ever missing a vote and considered highly influential, Youngblood made a point of distancing himself from lobbyists, supporting campaign financing and ethics reform, and shunning the elite Washington social scene. Instead, he maintained close ties to his hometown district and religiously forwent many of the perks of a high-powered elected official.

This code of conduct had its roots in Youngblood's earlier role as a community activist. Fresh out of the University of Chicago law school, after his undergraduate stint at Michigan State, he passed the

Michigan bar on his first try and opened his own storefront practice in the Motor City. Often working pro bono, he handled everything from discrimination cases to commercial litigation for local clients who could scarcely afford legal representation.

At the same time, he supported various neighborhood projects and co-chaired several citizens' committees, fearlessly inserting himself into labor disputes and taking a leadership position on educational initiatives, doing whatever he felt was his civic duty to improve the quality of life in his beloved corner of the world. For his tirelessly dedication and quixotic idealism, he was rewarded with a seat in Congress and had earned the unwavering trust of his constituents.

Not that this necessarily endeared Youngblood to a national level. His strong and vocal views on race relations, poverty, immigration and other hot-button issues often ruffled more than a few feathers with public opinion divided between the perception that he was too blunt, too liberal and too combative for higher office and the view that he was a refreshing and forthright change from politics as usual. The one thing everybody could agree on was that he wasn't dull.

Married for 23 years to his high school sweetheart and the father of three young men – one stationed with the U.S. army in Kuwait, another in Harvard Law School and the third currently serving in the Peace Corps in Honduras – Youngblood had the potential to appeal to Main Street as much as he did to Motown. Or at least that's what President Hartman and Chief of Staff Davidson believed up to the moment they welcomed the Congressman to the White House.

"Good morning, Mr. President," he said, striding into the Oval Office with the panache and gravitas of a seasoned statesman, dressed for the part in an impeccably tailored Armani suit and wearing a subtle smile that was as intriguing as the Mona Lisa's.

The two men shook hands firmly.

"Congressman," the President acknowledged. "You know Hunter, don't you?"

"Yes," Youngblood confirmed, shaking Davidson's hand. "We've met on a number of occasions and spoke recently on the phone."

"Please," the President motioned toward the couch, "make yourself comfortable. Care for a cup of coffee?"

"No, thank you, sir. I'm afraid it doesn't agree with me anymore," Youngblood expounded, tapping his stomach.

"Can I offer you something more digestible, instead? Green tea, perhaps?"

"No, thank you," the Congressman again declined, taking his appointed seat.

"Well, then ..." the President muttered, choosing to sit on the couch directly opposite his visitor with Davidson perched to his left. "You know, now that I have you here one-on-one, there's something I've always wanted to ask you."

"And what is that, sir?" Youngblood replied, crossing his legs and folding his hands on his lap.

"How did you get your middle name – Theolonius?"

A wider, mellower smile curled Youngblood's lips. "My Dad was a jazz musician," he revealed. "Bass player. He toured for a time with Monk. They were pretty tight."

"Ah," the President nodded, seemingly impressed. "I assumed as much."

"Are you into jazz, Mr. President?" Youngblood inquired.

"Somewhat. Though I'm more of an R&B kind of guy. Motown ..."

"Uh-huh. Well, that's something we've got in common."

"I'd like to think we have a lot more in common than that," said the President. "Like the same vision for this country."

Youngblood's polite smile became more of a skeptical smirk. "Sounds like a segue into a more meaningful discussion."

Detecting a hint of sarcasm, the President glanced at Davidson, then returned his attention to Youngblood's inquisitive gaze. "I won't beat around the bush," he declared. "I'm looking for someone to succeed Clayton Talbot as vice president. I'm considering a number of people for the position, but you're the first one I'm broaching on the subject."

At the very least Hartman expected Youngblood to be flattered, but instead he blithely remarked, "Saving the best candidates for last?"

The President obliged with a laugh, then realized that Youngblood was not being facetious. "Not necessarily," he replied.

The Congressman scratched the side of his nose and shifted in his chair. "Well, I must admit, I'm a bit surprised."

"Why would you be surprised?" asked the President.

Youngblood tilted his head and looked at Hartman directly in the eyes. "To be frank, Mr. President, you and I are not exactly bosom buddies. In fact, if memory serves, you didn't take kindly when the Congressional Black Caucus supported another candidate for the nomination during the primaries three years ago."

Hartman made light of the thorny memory. "Water under the bridge," he simply muttered.

"Well, that's very magnanimous of you, sir. Still … we haven't seen eye-to-eye on a number of issues over the last two years."

"Are you referring to funding for the Philbin Housing Project, which you slipped into last year's spending bill and which I insisted you remove?" the President suggested.

"For one thing."

"It was a deal-breaker," the President insisted.

"It would have revitalized a key area of my district," Youngblood countered.

"It reeked of pork. Besides, your district already has a disproportionate number of federal projects underway."

"And an unemployment rate that's double the national average."

"Well, Congressman, I guess we'll have to work harder on correcting that. In the meantime, do you have any thoughts about the vice presidency?"

"No, just one question."

"By all means."

"Why – considering our past differences – do you think I may be a worthy candidate? I mean, what are your reasons for including me on the short list – aside from the fact that I'm one of the most competent and charismatic political figures in the nation?"

"Not to mention modest," the President couldn't resist adding.

Youngblood smiled, but persisted, "Well, sir?"

"Excuse me, Congressman," the President responded with a baffled look, "but it's usually the interviewee who makes that case."

"Please … indulge me, sir. Oh, and by the way, you can call me Marcus."

"Alright, then … *Marcus*. As a six-term Congressman and leader of the Black Caucus, you have a strong working relationship with other members of the House. You chair and co-chair two important committees …"

"And?"

"And … you're well known around the country for your human rights and civil liberties activism."

"Ah," said Youngblood playfully, "so it's my resume that made a little light bulb turn on over your head."

"Mainly," the President claimed.

Youngblood's eyes suddenly narrowed. "I think you left something out, sir."

"And what is that?" asked the President.

"I'm an African-American."

"Why would that be relevant?"

"It ought not be. But for your intents and purposes, I suspect it is."

"Beg your pardon?"

"Let's face it, Mr. President. Your relations with the black community are, at best, shaky," Youngblood bluntly asserted. "In fact, in the last election, you drew the lowest percentage of African-American votes for a Democratic presidential candidate since Adlai Stevenson."

Merely listening to the exchange, Davidson found himself squirming uncomfortably in the corner of the couch.

"Are you implying, *Marcus*, that I'm considering you for the vice presidency solely on the basis of your race?" asked the President with a trace of indignation.

"Solely? No. Primarily? Probably."

"Well, you're mistaken. I'm looking for a vice president who can work with Congress to help advance my domestic agenda. I'm also looking for someone who can represent our country more effectively around the globe."

"Including Africa? A continent embroiled in conflicts and crises that your administration has conspicuously ignored thus far?"

"Another mistaken impression on your part," the President replied evenly. "However, it is an area that requires more attention and one where your services would, indeed, be useful. I'm also thinking about the future of the party …"

"Forgive me, Mr. President," Youngblood interrupted. "But I don't believe it's the future of the party that concerns you so much as your own public image and reelection."

The President pursed his lips. "Maybe I'm mistaken, Congressman," he replied, "but it sounds to me that you aren't particularly interested in the vice presidency."

"Oh, you're not mistaken, Mr. President. I'm not," Youngblood admitted. "And if you'll indulge me, I'll tell you why."

"By all means," Hartman invited.

"For one thing," Youngblood explained, "I believe I can accomplish more over the next several years in my current position than as your vice president. If anything, the constraints of that position would stymie my efforts to improve the quality of life for minorities throughout the country."

"On the contrary," the President disagreed. "My intention is to give the next Vice President considerable responsibility for advancing a domestic agenda that will revitalize the inner cities, create jobs, enhance health care and create more opportunity."

"Yeah, I recall your State of the Union address," said Youngblood dismissively. "A lot of lofty goals, vague details and a slither of hope. Truth be told, Mr. President, little of that agenda is going to pass a Republican-controlled Congress regardless of whomever becomes your right hand man."

"That's a rather bleak assessment, don't you think?" the President begged to differ. "Especially coming from someone as involved and committed as yourself. Could it be that you simply lack the ambition for higher office?"

"It's not that I lack ambition, sir. In fact, I would like to seek the presidency one day. But when I do, I'd like to pursue it on my own record … and with my own carefully crafted agenda."

"Without the baggage of a previous administration?" Hartman speculated.

Youngblood's polite silence verified the President's suspicion.

"Well," Hartman sighed, his anger simmering to a lower boil. "I appreciate your candor."

"Please don't think I'm not grateful for the consideration, sir," Youngblood hastened to add. "But I'd be wasting your time and mine if I wasn't totally honest with you."

"Oh, no … I'm the one who's grateful," said the President coldly, rising to signal an end to the meeting.

Youngblood stood and extended his hand. The President looked at it before shaking with a limp grip.

"Mr. President … Mr. Davidson," Youngblood nodded, then turned and headed for the exit.

As soon as he was gone, the President turned to his Chief of Staff and sternly inquired, "What the fuck?"

"I apologize, sir," said Davidson, rising from the couch, red-faced and clearly embarrassed. "I should have felt him out before setting up the meeting."

"*You think?*" the President scolded.

"Honestly, I had no idea he would pull something like this, sir. Really … I'm sorry …"

The President glared for a moment, then took a deep conciliatory breath. "It's alright, Hunt," he said, slapping him on the shoulder. "He was more Corcoran's idea than yours. It was my fault, too," he conceded. "I should have realized who I was dealing with. Oil and water …" he muttered, remembering what Irene had said. "Besides, he may have been right about my motives for considering him. Well, he actually did us a favor. At least it narrows our selection. One down, four to go. Just do me a favor and make sure our next candidate *wants* the job. Eh?"

"Yes, Mr. President," Davidson meekly concurred, breathing a slight sigh of relief.

Pauline and Gideon met for dinner that evening. As usual, she arrived first at their favorite French restaurant and requested the most secluded booth in the place. It was not that she expected complete privacy, she just wanted to ensure that they would not be the most conspicuous couple. Although their relationship was hardly a secret within the Beltway, it wasn't a topic of intense gossip, either, and she wanted to keep it that way.

By the time Gideon finally arrived, however, Pauline's inhibitions had been substantially doused with a dose of alcohol.

"Hi," he greeted with a warm smile. Knowing the rules in public, he limited himself to a peck on her cheek, then took his seat in the booth. "Hope you weren't waiting long."

"I am on my second martini," she informed him, raising the glass to her lips for a sip.

"I was busy making arrangements," he offered as an excuse.

"Arrangements for what?"

"I'm going to be out of town for the next few days," Gideon announced.

"Where are you off to?" asked Pauline, popping an olive into her mouth.

"Texas."

"What's happening there?"

"Following up on a lead," said Gideon matter-of-factly. Then, slyly, he added, "I've got a guy who claims to have some incriminating information about Harley Singleton."

Pauline stopped chewing for a few seconds, then continued, trying unconvincingly to conceal her curiosity.

"Don't you want to know more?" asked Gideon. "I mean, considering that Singleton is on the President's short list?"

"Who says he's on the short list?" Pauline bluffed, looking for a graceful way to dispose of the olive pit in her mouth.

"Come on, sweetheart," Gideon scoffed. "Everyone in D.C. knows that Singleton is the leading contender for the V.P. slot."

Pauline shrugged. "Then you don't need me to confirm or deny."

"Ah-huh. Well, at any rate, if what this source is telling me is true, you and your team of headhunters at the White House might want to hold off tapping old Harley for the job."

"Actually, Gid, we have better sources than you do – the FBI, the CIA, the State Department, the GAO, the Library of Congress, Homeland Security ..." Pauline rattled off. "Our background checks are quite thorough, I assure you. Of course, we're a little deficient in your department – idle and malicious gossip from questionable 'informants.'"

"So you are running a check on Singleton."

"Nice try, Brenda Starr."

"You're being so anal about this," Burnett complained. "I'm not asking you to tip me off on who has the inside edge."

"No, you're just trying to get a peek at the dance card so you can hone in on the likely nominee by process of elimination."

"Exactly. What's wrong with that?"

Pauline flashed a skeptical look. "You're trying to use me for a scoop. Forget how that makes me feel – I could be in hot water for leaking privileged information."

"Why is it privileged?" Burnett argued. "It doesn't involve national security. All it amounts to is a relatively trivial staff change."

"Well, if it's so trivial," Pauline playfully challenged, "then why the intense interest?"

"Look …" Burnett sighed. "I just want to know whether this trip to Texas is necessary or not. I don't want to go off on a potential wild goose chase if it doesn't even matter what kind of shenanigans Singleton has been involved in."

Instead of responding, Pauline took another sip of her drink.

"It matters to you as well as me," Burnett stressed.

Pauline remained tight-lipped, rolling the olive pit from one cheek to the other.

Gideon patiently persisted. "Well? Spit it out."

Pauline did, depositing the olive pit into her hand and placing it on the table. She avoided eye contact, fearful she might buckle under the weight of his intense stare.

"Come on, babe," Burnett cajoled, reaching across the table and caressing her hand. "Throw me a bone."

Slightly tipsy and tingling to his touch, Pauline bit her lip and sighed in frustration. "Texas is a lovely state this time of year," she cryptically replied.

Smiling, Burnett dropped the subject and looked around for a waitress. "I'm starving," he said. "What does it take to get some service in this place?"

Chapter 13

Burnett always traveled light. That way, as soon as his plane landed at George Bush Intercontinental Airport, he simply snatched his carry-on, disembarked and headed straight for the car rental. He settled for an economy vehicle with a GPS unit and was on the road in a matter of minutes. It was twilight as he drove south on Route 59, scanning the local FM radio dial for a decent classic rock station and finally settling for an "oldies" outlet with a limited playlist of 70's and 80's pop hits.

He had been to the Lone Star state a few times before, twice to Dallas, once to Austin, and all three times strictly on business. Aside from making the rounds of a few night clubs and recommended restaurants, he hardly got a taste of the local milieu. There wasn't much opportunity for sight-seeing this time, either. If all went as planned, he'd meet with Kayton, confirm his story, and be on his way back to Washington within the next 24 hours. And if all didn't go as planned and he went home empty-handed, at least he had a short respite from the Beltway grind on the *American Observor's* dime.

Located approximately 37 miles from Houston, Beauville was a small city once known for its textile mills and agricultural and livestock processing plants. But that was before NAFTA sent many of the jobs south of the border. Luckily, however, Beauville was a relatively easy commute from the Houston branch office of Uniplex Energy Systems. That didn't help the blue collar workers in town, but it apparently picked up the slack for a few upscale locals. Aside from a bowling alley, a multiplex cinema just off the highway and a fairly decent motel on the north end, the hamlet didn't strike Burnett as a place where he'd like to spend more than a single night.

His room was hardly as well attended as the suites he was accustomed to when on the road, but at least the carpeting was new, the toilet was clean, the double bed was firm with fresh linen, and the artwork didn't scream provincial. No sooner had he closed the front door than he reached for the remote control and clicked on the television. Reception was good and he was pleased that the selection of programs included all four news channels.

While sitting on the edge of his bed and surfing through the list, he glanced toward the nightstand and noticed that the red light on his room phone was flashing. He lay back on the bed, reached for the receiver and pressed the voice mail button to take his message: "Welcome to Beauville," declared a voice he recognized as Kayton's. "There's a Denny's next door to your motel. I'll meet you there at 8 p.m."

Burnett walked into the restaurant at 7:55 and took a booth at the window overlooking the parking lot.

"Can I start you off with something to drink, hon?" asked a pleasingly plump, redheaded waitress with a cheery disposition and the name "Angel" embossed on her name tag.

"Just regular coffee, please," Burnett smiled, assessing the woman's spacious derriere as she walked away.

Eight o'clock came and went. So, too, did any number of patrons parking their cars and walking through the front door, but none approaching his table. And as Burnett sipped his second cup, he began to wonder if he was going to be stood up. But then a late model Honda pulled into a parking spot and a man of medium height and build and wearing a white, short sleeved shirt, blue jeans and boots got out. It was hard to make out his features from a distance and in the hazy lamplight, but he appeared to be in his thirties with short black hair, and there was something about his cautious gait – plus the fact that he was glancing from side to side suspiciously – that suggested he wasn't just another local.

Sure enough, when the man entered the restaurant and spotted Gideon sitting alone, he moved directly toward his table.

"Mr. Burnett?" he asked.

"Mr. Kayton?" Gideon responded.

The two shook hands. "May I?" Kayton motioned to the empty side of the booth.

"Of course," Burnett replied.

"Thanks for coming. I trust your flight was okay?"

"I travel coach," said Burnett. "It's never okay."

"Well, I can assure you it'll all be worthwhile."

"You're not originally from Texas, are you?" asked Burnett abruptly and astutely. "Your accent …"

"I'm from back East. Maryland. I moved to Beauville a few years ago."

"To work for Uniplex?"

"Yeah."

"How long were you with them?"

"Seven and a half years," Kayton replied with a tinge of bitterness in his voice.

"They fired you?"

"That's right. Escorted me and my box of personal items right out of the building. Just like that."

"So, what are you still doing here in Beauville?"

"I have unfinished business. Not to mention a girlfriend."

"Does she know what you're up to?"

"You mean the matter we discussed on the phone? Not really. I didn't want her to get involved. But she does know where a copy of the evidence is. Just in case something happens to me."

"And where is that?"

"In a safe place."

"I assumed as much. Can you be more specific?"

"Patience. Let me tell you what I've got before I hand it over."

"I'm all ears."

"My position at Uniplex was that of Assistant Vice President of Public Affairs. It was a fancy title for a job that essentially involved doing the dirty work for the Vice President of Public Affairs."

"What kind of dirty work?"

"Intelligence gathering, pay-offs, arm-twisting. I believe those are more polite expressions than blackmail, bribery and extortion."

"Involving whom?"

"Politicians, legislators, regulators."

"For what purpose?"

"What do you think? The bottom line. Favorable legislation and relaxed regulations that would lead to higher profits."

"And you were directly involved?"

"Well … no one is ever *directly* involved. That would be incriminating. Let's just say I had full knowledge of these activities and certain cash transactions."

"Under the table?"

"And off the books. We're talking about a secret, multi-million dollar slush fund ear-marked for bribes and clandestine operations."

"What you're describing is criminal."

"Tell me about it," said Kayton sarcastically. "That's one of the reasons I haven't taken this to the local authorities."

"And the other reason?"

"They're in bed with Uniplex – from the police to the State Attorney General's office."

"Oh, of course," Burnett muttered doubtfully.

"I know you're skeptical," said Kayton, "but when you see for yourself …"

"How far up the Uniplex food chain does this go?" asked Burnett.

"To the top."

"Tate?"

"Absolutely."

"How do you know?"

"Connect the dots. My boss got his marching orders from the CEO, who got his from …"

"But I doubt there's a paper trail from you to the Chairman."

"Of course not. Tate would never put himself in a position where he could be prosecuted. Jail time is for underlings. He meticulously covers his tracks and is always safely ensconced behind multiple levels of deniability. Still, he is the puppet master. He's been influencing public policy for personal gain for decades. You know that better than anyone. He's been a thorn in the side of James Hartman for years … and vice versa. Tate's been trying to derail Hartman since he was New York State Attorney General. He was behind the smear campaign during the last presidential election."

"Which didn't work."

"No, but that hasn't stopped Tate from trying to undermine the administration wherever he could. Only now, the strategy is 'if you can't beat 'em, control 'em.'"

"So you think Singleton is a stalking horse for Tate."

"More than likely. I have proof Singleton has received a considerable amount of laundered cash from Uniplex's slush fund."

"Would you be willing to testify to that?"

"Hell, no. And you can not quote me. Understand? I am strictly an unnamed source."

"Why the anonymity? You've already been fired."

"Because I don't want to end up in a secluded ditch or floating face down in the Rio Grande."

"Is that standard practice at Uniplex, as well?"

"Let's not go there."

"Well, I have a little problem with your reluctance to go public," Burnett confessed. "Without a named source, nothing I write would carry much credibility. And if it did, I could be held liable for any documents stolen from Uniplex. I could even go to jail for refusing to reveal my unnamed source."

"You don't have to write an expose."

"Well, what is it you want me to do?"

"Stop the Singleton nomination."

"And how would I do that?"

"You're a White House correspondent. You have access to the President."

"Whoa. First of all, my access to the President is limited to press conferences and the occasional ride on Air Force One. I don't meet with him one-on-one. Secondly, he may not believe any of this. I'm not even sure I believe it. I mean, Singleton has publicly endorsed the President's energy plan."

"It's a ruse. A way to gain the President's confidence."

"Even so, why would he risk his political career for a few dollars of Tate-tainted money?"

"We're not talking a few dollars here. Singleton has been on the dole for years – both as a senator and as governor. Why do you think Uniplex's corporate offices are located in Houston and many of its facilities – on and offshore – are in Texas? They've got friends in high places."

"There's no guarantee Singleton will be Hartman's pick for vice president."

"No, but the odds are pretty good, wouldn't you say? "

"And even if he is the choice – how much of an influence can he have?"

"Never mind the fact that he would be a chief advisor to the President and would preside over the Senate. As vice president Singleton would be a heartbeat away from becoming Commander-in-Chief himself – *Tate's man in the Oval Office*. Is that something you want to risk?"

"You're not suggesting …"

"Mr. Burnett, I wouldn't put *anything* past these people."

"I would have to corroborate your story."

"With whom?"

"Someone else at Uniplex. Someone else in the loop."

"I would steer clear of Uniplex if I were you," warned Kayton.

"And why's that?"

"I told you – I don't want to end up in the morgue. If they got wind of this, it wouldn't be hard for them to figure out who supplied you with the documents. Who knows what they'd do to me. And it might not be good for your health, either."

"Aren't you being a trifle paranoid?" Burnett suggested. "My boss knows I'm here. It would be awfully suspicious if you and I suddenly met with foul play."

"Foul play?" Kayton chuckled, but his smile soon disappeared. "Accidents happen, Mr. Burnett. Look what happened to Clayton Talbot."

"Where is this evidence of yours?"

"In a safe place," Kayton repeated. "Literally."

"I'd like to see it."

"That won't be possible tonight, but it's doable tomorrow. Here's my address," said Kayton, pulling a piece of paper from his shirt pocket. "Meet me there at noon."

Kayton slid the piece of paper across the table. Burnett scanned it and then tucked it in his own shirt pocket.

"And if I'm not there or something happens to me," Kayton added, "go see my girlfriend. She'll know what to do and will give you what you need. Her name's Janice Reid and she's at 425 West Kendall Avenue. It's just three blocks east of my place."

Burnett reached into his jacket pocket for a pen and notepad.

"No," said Kayton. "Don't write down her address. It's too dangerous. Memorize it. 425 West Kendall Avenue. Got it?"

"Yeah, yeah. 425 West Kendall," Burnett repeated, rolling his eyes.

The two men sat quietly for a moment, Kayton glancing around the restaurant suspiciously.

"Can I get you anything?" Burnett felt obliged to ask.

"No. Got to run," Kayton replied, getting up to leave. "See you tomorrow."

"Yeah," Burnett muttered, watching him head out the door.

A few moments later, Angel finally reappeared with his cup of coffee. "Will that be all for tonight, hon?" she asked sweetly.

Glancing at her ample cleavage, Burnett was tempted to reply, "What did you have in mind?" But instead, he simply answered, "I guess so," took the bill and left an insanely huge tip.

Chapter 14

At the United Nations – and in certain political quarters – Margaret Layton Lewis was known as the "Iron Maiden." Although hardly intimidating in appearance with the refined sophistication and deceiving charm of an old school socialite, she was nevertheless a disciplined, skillful and relentless diplomat with a firm and uncompromising approach to international policy, capable of striking trepidation in the hearts of even her fiercest adversaries while earning their grudging respect.

She was no less assertive yet engaging beyond the milieu of the Security Council. Although relatively short in physical stature (five foot from head to toe) and a bit "frumpy," as one boorish political radio talk show host once described her, she had a commanding, matriarchal way about her with her frosty white hair, piercing gray eyes, Kate Hepburnesque cadence and impeccable fashion sense. In fact, more than once, she had been named to the annual list of the 10 Best Dressed Women in America. And, at 63, she hardly looked her age, thanks to high cheekbones and a finely chiseled face that scarcely sported a wrinkle.

Born Margaret Eloise Layton in Portland, Maine, she was the middle child in a lower middle income family, with an older sister and a younger brother. Her father, a commercial fisherman, called her Peg. Her mother, a local seamstress, preferred to call her Maggie. But her friends and classmates throughout elementary school referred to her as "Brainiac" as she was consistently the smartest student.

In fact, her hunger for knowledge – even at a very young age – was quite insatiable. A fanatical bookworm, young Peg/Maggie would pore through several volumes a week. And when she wasn't reading at home, sometimes by the din of a flashlight in the wee hours of the night, she spent more of her time at a local library than frolicking with her neighborhood chums. Her parents never had to coax her into doing her homework – she applied herself to that task as soon as she got home and always completed her assignments before dinnertime. In high school, she failed to make the cheerleading squad, but did top her classmates for academic honors every single month of her enrollment and was easily elected class president in her senior year. Choosing Margaret Layton as graduation valedictorian was also a no-brainer.

For her academic diligence, Margaret was awarded a full scholarship to Wellesley College where she majored in Education. Living away from home on campus, immersed in a hotbed of intellectual study and political activism, she was challenged in ways she had never been in her previous, provincial environment. Still, her focus was clear. After earning her Masters, Margaret embarked on what she thought would be her lifelong career, accepting a position teaching history at a state college in New Hampshire.

But after two semesters, Margaret began to feel restless. Surely, there was more to life, she thought, than teaching the same class year after year, striving for no loftier goal than tenure. So, to the utter amazement and admonishment of most of her friends and relatives, she abruptly resigned her teaching position and joined the Peace Corps.

She had traveled abroad before, spending an entire summer touring Europe. Now, however, she was committed to a two-year stint teaching in a humble village in Ghana on the West African coast. Happily, the experience was enriching in more ways than one. Not only did Margaret broaden her cultural horizons, but she also met and married Harry Lewis, a business graduate and fellow volunteer from Nashua, New Hampshire.

By the time Margaret and Harry returned to the U.S., they were both ready to conquer the rest of the world. At Margaret's request, the couple took residence in her native Portland, where Harry found work as a junior executive at a footwear company and Margaret a public school board member and an advocate for adult literacy. By the time she was 30, Margaret was elected the state's school commissioner. During her term, student performance standards rose dramatically, despite state and federal cutbacks in aid to education. In fact, Margaret found herself frequently butting heads with legislators in Augusta and Washington, D.C. on the issue. So much so that it compelled her to run as a Democrat for the U.S. Congress – and win. Fortunately, Harry found another executive position with an Arlington, Virginia security systems firm and was able to relocate.

As a new member of the House of Representatives, Margaret struggled at first to become acclimated to the legislative process. Unlike most of her peers, she did not have a legal background. But she was a quick study and gradually mastered the fine arts of parliamentary procedure and Washingtonian wheeling and dealing. Still, she took it upon herself to study law at Georgetown University while maintaining her office and not only earned another degree, but also passed the bar on her first try. As a member of the Committee on Education & Labor and chairperson of the Higher Education, Lifelong Learning, and Competitiveness Subcommittee, she was at the forefront of educational reform.

It was during Margaret's second term that she became pregnant with their first child, a daughter they named Stacey. Four years later, shortly after Margaret was tapped for the position of Peace Corps Director, she gave birth to a second daughter, Kara. Motherhood combined with a prominent career was a challenge, but nothing Margaret couldn't handle. If only she could have said the same for her marriage.

Over the years, Margaret's insatiable commitment to public service and the demands that came with it took a toll on her relationship with Harry. Though proud of his wife's accomplishments and a workhorse himself, Harry increasingly felt incidental in her life, especially as the onset of middle age diminished their desire for intimacy. Rather than prolong the inevitable until their daughters were grown, the couple decided to divorce amicably after 25 years together.

When a new Republican administration came into power, Margaret Layton Lewis found herself back on the job market. She spent those four years of political exile working for a D.C. law firm, litigating workers compensation and discrimination cases. But with the election of James Hartman came new opportunities – first as Education Secretary and more recently as U.S. Ambassador to the United Nations, two high-profile positions that suited her talents.

And now, at the peak of her career, Margaret Layton Lewis found herself invited to the White House for lunch to discuss the possibility of assuming a role no woman had achieved before. Upon her arrival, she was greeted by Chief of Staff Davidson and escorted directly to the Oval Office.

"Margaret," Hartman acknowledged with a beaming smile, taking her hand and giving her a peck on the cheek.

"Mr. President," she responded warmly.

"Thank you for coming on such short notice. I hope you weren't inconvenienced."

"Not at all, sir," Ambassador Lewis assured him. "It's always a pleasure to see you."

"How is your family?"

"Wonderful. Thank you for asking. My youngest daughter has just passed her bar exam."

"Ah, just what the world needs – another attorney."

"She plans on interning this summer for the Senate Judiciary committee."

"Thanks for the warning."

"And my eldest has just informed me that I am going to become a grandmother."

"That's wonderful."

"And you, sir? I trust the First Lady is doing well?"

"Oh, yes," the President smiled without elaborating.

"Please give her my regards."

"I certainly will," the President assured. "Well, then ... lunch awaits. Shall we?"

The party of three repaired to the White House Family Dining Room where, seated at a large cherry wood table, they were treated to shrimp cocktail and lobster salad with stuffed eggs and shared their thoughts on a number of foreign and diplomatic policy issues. Eventually, however, the discussion came around to the real purpose of the meeting.

"As you know, Margaret" said the President, "We've begun conferring with a number of individuals concerning the Vice Presidency. And to my way of thinking, no list of candidates would be complete without you."

"I'm flattered that you're considering me, sir," Ambassador Lewis replied, gently raising her glass of sparkling water to her lips.

"You needn't be. Your service to this country over the years has been exemplary – as an educator, an administrator, a member of Congress and a U.S. Ambassador. ..."

"And don't forget," Margaret gulped, " – occasional pianist at White House state dinners."

"Your versatility is duly noted," replied the President with a smile. "What I'm saying, Margaret, is that you're certainly qualified to become the next Vice President of the United States. I'd just like to get your perspective on the position and how it might play to your strengths."

"Well," she responded with a thoughtful sigh, "the Vice Presidency is a responsibility I don't take lightly, but one that I believe I could manage effectively. Needless to say, I have the international experience that would serve this administration's foreign policy initiatives. In addition, as a former Congresswoman, I know my way around Capitol Hill and can deal with representatives of both parties with the same skills that I have employed with the Russians, Chinese and Iranians."

"In terms of domestic policy, what do you consider priority issues?" asked the President.

"Health care, certainly. However, I think education is just as important. So is social security reform."

"How about energy?" Davidson inquired.

"Yes, of course," Margaret replied. "I think self-sufficiency through the development and use of alternative fuels is a vital long-term goal."

"You do realize that this administration is struggling to pass meaningful legislation in all of these areas?"

"Yes, and I know much of that legislation is currently bogged down in Congress. But I believe these goals can be achieved during your second term, if not before the next election."

"Your confidence and optimism is encouraging, Margaret," said the President, "but it's going to be an uphill battle, regardless of a second-term mandate. I need to know that the person I choose for the Vice Presidency is going to have the ability to take the fight to Congress. In other words, it may take more than mere diplomacy."

"Mr. President, I know how to mix it up with the big boys," Lewis assured him. "I would pull out all the stops necessary – within reason, of course."

"As Vice President, there is also the possibility that you might have to assume my responsibilities at some point," Hartman felt it was incumbent upon him to mention. "What are your thoughts on that?"

"At my age, sir, I have no ambitions whatsoever of seeking the presidency at a future date," Ambassador Lewis answered. "However, in the unlikely event that I had to be sworn in, I would be prepared to assume and faithfully execute my duties as an interim Commander-in-Chief. My foreign policy credentials speaks for itself and I believe I could apply my diplomatic skills toward working with both parties to carry on this administration's domestic agenda."

"How do you think you would fare with the military?" Davidson chimed.

"I am acquainted with the members of the Joint Chiefs, as well as other high-ranking personnel. They may or may not have initial reservations about taking orders from a woman, but I would do everything in my power to earn their respect and loyalty. Frankly, I don't think it would be an issue."

"Pardon me for asking this, Margaret," the President gingerly prefaced, "but is there anything in your past that you'd rather not see come to light in a confirmation hearing?"

"Well …" she briefly reflected, "I was a card-carrying member of the Herman's Hermits fan club back in the day."

Amused, the President glanced at Davidson, then replied, "I'll take that as a 'no.'"

"Seriously, Mr. President," said Lewis. "I underwent confirmation hearings for my ambassadorship. True, those were not as painstaking as this would be, but if there were no red flags then, I don't see why there would be any now."

"How's your health?" Davidson awkwardly asked.

The ambassador stared at him for a moment, as if an old wound had been poked. "Good," she ultimately replied. "Knock wood."

Sensing her discomfort, the President interjected, "You've been kind enough to provide us with your medical records, Margaret. I appreciate that. Unfortunately, it's something that has to be addressed."

"I understand," she insisted, taking another sip of water. "I'm sure all of your candidates are being held to the same scrutiny."

"It's a prerequisite for everyone," the President confirmed. "Anyway …" he said, attempting to change the subject, "let's touch some more on the matter of building Congressional coalitions …"

Later that afternoon in the Oval Office, the President solicited Davidson's feedback on Lewis' viability. "Well? What do you think?"

"A definite maybe," his advisor replied.

"Why not a definite 'yes?'"

Davidson hesitated, then claimed with a sigh, "I'd like to see a female vice president in my lifetime just as much as you. But I'm not sure she's the one. For one thing, it's been years since she's served a constituency. She's a bit out of touch with kitchen table issues."

Hartman cast a dubious look. "That's because she's been building a distinguished career in diplomatic circles. That gives her foreign policy chops."

"Which is wonderful," Davidson conceded. "But we need someone who can whip Congress into shape and help advance our domestic agenda. Her earlier record in Congress was spotty at best. She never authored or coauthored a key piece of legislation."

"But her negotiating skills are undeniable."

"Among foreign ambassadors. The art of diplomacy doesn't always apply when dealing with domestic bureaucrats. There's also the matter of her campaign skills, which are at best rusty. You're facing reelection next year. She's not used to being out on the stump."

"She'd be fine," the President scoffed. "I'd do the heavy lifting."

"Still … a Northeast liberal with a Yankee accent and in a skirt … that might not play well in certain parts of the country. There's also the matter of her perceived sexual orientation."

The President did a double take. "What?"

"There have been rumors …"

"Unsubstantiated," the President noted. "She was married, for Christ's sake. To a *man*. They had two daughters."

"But she divorced 12 years ago and never remarried. Neither has she been associated with any male companions."

"And that makes her gay?

"It makes her fair game. And the fact that her staff is all female doesn't help."

"Please …" the President laughed dismissively. "The woman's in her sixties. She's an international diplomat. She doesn't have time for romance. And even if she were gay, which I doubt, why would it matter?"

"Because perception is everything," Davidson realistically maintained. "Margaret may be admired for her skills and resolve, but it's a two-edged sword. Her toughness has been useful as a U.N. ambassador, but it's a potential liability among voters. It's the old double standard – strong men are perceived as leaders, while strong women are perceived as …"

"Well, maybe it's time to shatter that stereotype," the President suggested, "instead of perpetuating it. Along with the glass ceiling."

"You already have the female vote," Davidson reminded him. "It's white males that elude you in every poll."

"Screw the polls," said the President.

"I wish we had the luxury. But tapping a woman for VP won't persuade more men to vote for you."

"Are those the extent of your reservations about Margaret?"

"Actually, there is another issue," said Davidson. "Her health."

"Are you referring to her brush with breast cancer? That was a good 10 years ago … and she beat it."

"According to her medical records, she has a family history of malignancies. What's to stop a reoccurrence?"

"Any of us could be diagnosed," said the President. "When was the last time you had your colon examined? The point is, she's fit now."

Davidson shrugged his shoulders. "I'm just saying … These things add up."

"So I take it you've already written her off."

"I think she's a great lady and a marvelous ambassador."

"Just not vice presidential material?"

Davidson didn't mince words. "I think we have better candidates to consider," he replied.

The President lowered his head and pursed his lips, as if wrestling with his conscience. "Yeah," he finally admitted with a sigh. "Still …

It would be another blow to equal rights."

"The Vice Presidency isn't a right," Davidson maintained, "You have an obligation to fill the position with the best candidate – not the most politically correct choice."

The President folded his arms and shook his head, "I hate to disappoint her."

"Well," Davidson said at the ready with a suggestion, "there's strong speculation that Supreme Court Justice O'Neill is planning to announce his retirement soon. If so, you could promise Margaret a seat on the Court as a consolation for being passed over for the vice presidency."

"That's not a bad idea," the President admitted. "The Court could use another woman and she'd make a suitable justice."

"She might even prefer the appointment. After all, it is for life."

"All right, then. But I won't break the news to her until I've interviewed all the candidates. I wouldn't want her to think she was rejected out of hand."

"That's very chivalrous of you, sir."

"You know, Hunt, sometimes you're a real smart-ass."

"That's my job, sir."

Chapter 15

The morning after his arrival in the Lone Star State, Gideon Burnett paid a visit to the corporate offices of Uniplex Industries in Houston – this despite Kayton's warning that such a move would be ill-advised. There was no way Burnett was going to run with a story accusing one of the richest men in the world and his corporation of bribing a public official without allowing the suits at Uniplex to respond to the specific allegation – even assuming Kayton's stolen documents proved to be authentic. Unbeknownst to the would-be whistleblower, Burnett had arranged an interview with Kayton's former supervisor before flying to Texas, although the true subject of the interview had not been disclosed.

Prior to his trip, Burnett had researched Uniplex Industries online to obtain a little background information. According to the sources, Uniplex provided a variety of services and products to the energy industry and United States military. The company operated under a pair of divisions – a Completion and Production segment, and a Drilling and Evaluation segment. Under these two divisions, the company facilitated the exploration, development and production of oil and gas by national and independent companies throughout the world. Several years earlier, Uniplex had acquired RTC Energy Services Limited, a provider of process, pipeline, and well intervention services with more than 76,000 employees and operational bases in northern Europe, North Africa, the Middle East and the Pacific Rim. It also acquired the intellectual property, assets and existing business of an Alberta-based energy firm named Megastar Services Corporation. All told, Uniplex earned an annual income of $3.5 billion on annual sales of $19.4 billion.

The five-sided corporate headquarters of Uniplex in Houston resembled a cross between the Pentagon and an ultramodern shopping mall. There was a bit of a gauntlet to gain access to the facility – a security gate leading to the visitors and employee parking lot and a metal detector at the main entrance – no doubt because of the company's association with numerous defense contractors and its status as a frequent target for protestors. Burnett navigated both checkpoints with relative ease and found himself in a huge atrium lobby that resembled an airline terminal.

"Good morning," greeted a cheery, mature lady in a red suit behind the reception desk. "May I help you?"

"I'm here to see Mr. Mayfield. My name's Gideon Burnett."

Still smiling, the lady checked her roster, then replied, "Do you have photo I.D., Mr. Burnett?"

Gideon produced a driver's license, which the receptionist glanced at, then returned to him. "Please take a seat," she suggested.

As Gideon settled into a nearby chair, the receptionist placed a call.

While cooling his heels, Burnett took visual inventory of the various individuals that entered and left the inner sanctum beyond the reception area. Nine out of ten were men dressed in tailored business attire, mostly Caucasian and mostly north of 40 years old. The one exception was a tall, sleek young blonde woman in a navy blue lady's business suit and rather attractive legs – surely a former prom queen or Miss Texas contestant – who emerged from the glass doorway from the inner offices, paused to peruse the waiting area and, spotting him, unhesitatingly approached, her high heels clacking on the marble-tiled floor. "Mr. Burnett?" she asked with an inquisitive smile.

"Yes?" he replied, staring up at her.

"Hi," she drawled, offering her hand. "I'm Cindy Hastings, director of public relations. Welcome to Uniplex."

"Hello," Burnett replied with a faint smile, rising to shake her hand.

"Would you follow me, please?" she requested.

"I'd be delighted."

Swiping her security card, Cindy opened the glass door and held it while Burnett passed into the executive wing. As they proceeded along an adjacent, carpeted corridor, Cindy made small talk. "How was your trip from Washington?" she asked with a perkiness that made Burnett bristle.

"Fine," he responded without elaboration.

"And your stay in Houston?"

"Actually, I'm staying in Beauville."

"Oh, really? And how are you enjoying your visit?"

"So far, so good."

They eventually entered a small conference room with a round table. Cindy closed the door behind them and offered Burnett a chair. He sat down and watched while Cindy pulled up a chair and sat facing him. Confused, he asked, "Will Mr. Mayfield be joining us?"

"Actually," Cindy chimed with an apologetic smile, "Mr. Mayfield is out of town on business."

"Out of town? You must be mistaken. I made an appointment with Mr. Mayfield through his assistant just the other day."

"Yes, well," Cindy explained, "something suddenly came up and he had to fly to Vancouver."

Burnett eyed her warily. "Well, someone should have called and informed me. Don't you think?"

"I do apologize," Cindy cringed theatrically.

"Then, how about Mr. Carter," Burnett suggested, "Mr. Mayfield's assistant vice president?"

"He's unavailable as well," Cindy claimed. "So I'm afraid you're stuck with me. But I'm sure I can answer any questions you may have."

"Uh-huh," Burnett muttered doubtfully.

"May I ask what sort of story you had in mind? I can provide you with a ton of information about the company ... its products and services ... affiliates ..."

"Ms. Hastings," Burnett interrupted.

"Hm?"

"This is not a fluff piece," he informed her. "It's an expose."

Cindy stared for a second. "An ... an expose?"

"That's right, concerning some activities ... some allegations ... that the company may not necessary want the public to know about."

"Oh," Cindy replied guardedly. "Oh, I see."

"That's why I wanted to speak with Mr. Mayfield or Mr. Carter," Burnett explained, as if talking to a child. "Is there anyone else in management who would be an appropriate interview? Mr. Benoir, perhaps. Or ..."

"What publication did you say you were from?" Cindy abruptly inquired.

"The *American Observor*. Have you heard of it?"

"Oh, yes," Cindy replied, her eyebrows slightly raised. "Yes, I have. In fact, if I'm not mistaken, your magazine did quite a hatchet job on Mr. Tate some time ago."

"I wouldn't categorize it that way but, yes, we profiled him. It was during the last presidential campaign when Mr. Tate was believed to have circulated some unsubstantiated rumors about James J. Hartman. I'm sure that story went over like a lead balloon here at Uniplex."

Cindy had no response, just a frozen stare that got icier by the moment.

"Anyway," Burnett continued. "I've come across some new information involving senior management here at Uniplex and I would really like to give your company the opportunity to respond to some serious allegations."

"You know what," Cindy suddenly replied, rising from her seat, "I think we're going to have to cut this meeting short."

Burnett regarded her with dull surprise. "Really? No guided tour of the facility? No PowerPoint presentation on Uniplex's quest for energy solutions? How about a few press releases about the company's tax deductible charitable contributions?"

"Mr. Burnett ..." said Cindy, suddenly depleted of her perkiness. "Perhaps you should make other arrangements."

"Fine. Can I at least make an appointment to speak with Mr. Mayfield or Mr. Carter at a more convenient time?"

"I doubt they would want to speak with you," Cindy replied with a haughty little guffaw, "given your biased approach to the company."

"My biased approach?" Burnett replied indignantly.

"You obviously have an agenda and ..."

"An agenda? Well, *Cindy*, with all due respect, I think it's Uniplex that has an agenda. Don't you? Or is it Mr. Tate who has the agenda?"

Ms. Hastings' icy expression became an impenetrable glacier. "Please leave, sir," she sternly intoned.

"Look, this has nothing to do with you," Gideon attempted to mollify. "Just hook me up with someone in Public Affairs, so I can get to the bottom of ..."

"*Mr. Burnett*," said Ms. Hastings firmly. "I've asked you to leave. Do I need to call security?"

Burnett glanced away and laughed in disbelief. "No. You don't need to call anybody. Actually," he said, slapping his thighs and rising from his chair, "you've been very helpful."

As soon as he left the room, Hastings retreated to her neighboring office, picked up the phone and dialed the front desk. When Burnett reached the reception area, he was greeted by two burly guards. "This way, sir," one of them directed, placing his beefy hand on Gideon's arm.

"Thanks, fellas," he replied, jerking his arm away and heading for the front door. "I know the way out."

But the guards followed him through the revolving doors and out toward the parking lot. "You're escorting me to my car?" asked Gideon incredulously. "Well, that's a first, even for me."

Not only did they tail Burnett to his vehicle, but stood nearby and watched as he opened the door, got in, started his engine and backed out of his space. He waved goodbye as he drove off, then made a beeline for the interstate.

Heading back toward Beauville, Burnett realized it was only 9:45 a.m. He had plenty of time to kill until he was scheduled to meet with Kayton again, so he decided to go back to his motel room to check for messages, make some calls and update his notes. Along the way, he thought about Kayton's warning and how fearful the informant had been about his own safety. He briefly wondered about his own well-being, but quickly dismissed that notion. He was a renowned journalist, for Christ's sake. He had covered war zones and military juntas, dealt with foreign dictators and underworld crime figures, visited crack dens and bombed-out neighborhoods over the course of his 20-year career – all without sustaining a single scratch. Even if Kayton's fears were justified, it would be rather foolish for a bunch of corporate thugs to try and intimidate him – or worse.

When he arrived at his motel, Burnett pulled into a parking spot, turned off the car's engine and reached into his pocket for his cell phone. He placed a call to his editor, but had to leave a voice mail message: "Hey, Greg. It's Gid. I just paid a visit to Uniplex in Houston and got stiffed on an interview. I'll have to follow up with them later. I've got a meeting at 12 with that source I told you about. I'll have a better idea then if this is a fishing expedition or the real deal. I'll follow up with you this afternoon, so keep your powder dry in the meantime. Later ..."

Burnett closed the phone, stashed it in his shirt and got out of the car. But no sooner had he locked the door and turned toward the curb than he heard footsteps rushing up behind him. Before he had a chance to turn around, he felt a sudden pressure against his back and then a crippling jolt of electricity. He crumbled to the pavement, unable to move. For good measure, the assailant rolled him over, placed the taser against his neck and gave him another convulsive jolt.

Totally dazed and paralyzed, Burnett helplessly watched as two men in ski masks lifted him off the ground and quickly transported him to the open side door of a nearby van. Once he had been deposited inside, one of the men climbed into the vehicle beside him and shut the door, while the other raced to the driver's seat and cranked the ignition. As the van sped off and made a sharp turn, Burnett rolled onto his side, unable to look up at the captor who was hovering over him, removing his mask. Instead, he stared at a tattoo on the man's forearm – a skull and crossbones. *That can't be good*, thought Burnett as he slipped into unconsciousness.

Chapter 16

When Paul Edwin Gardner first ran for a seat in the United States Congress, he did so "not as a Democrat, not as a Republican, but as the proud son of a West Virginia coal miner."

Pitted against the Ivy League-educated offspring of a multimillionaire who spent nearly three times as much money (most of it on negative ads belittling his opponent's hairstyle and credentials as a former trial lawyer), Gardner spent his time campaigning door-to-door in his district, often with his pregnant wife Sissy at his side. Against all expectations, he won by a veritable landslide.

It was no small feat for a man of such humble beginnings. Born into a family of seven, Paul was the middle child between two older brothers and two younger sisters, all raised in the town of Whitesville in the Coal River Valley. While their father often worked the night shift in various nearby bituminous shafts, their mother toiled as a seamstress in a local clothing factory. It was enough to make ends meet – barely.

Like many Appalachian households at the time, the Gardner residence was a modest , one-story wood-frame structure with an attic crawlspace on a crabgrass-riddled plot of land with only three bedrooms, one of which was shared by the three brothers, a small kitchen, one bathroom and a living room that served as a veritable shrine to John and Robert Kennedy. Appliances were simple and often in disrepair, electric baseboard heating compensated for drafts in the winter, and a 20-year old, 19-inch color television with fickle reception was considered a luxury – but it was home.

Unlike his brothers, who barely made it through secondary school and promptly joined their father in the mining industry when they came of age, Paul showed an aptitude for academics that justified his ambition to become an attorney when he grew up. Of course, the family's economic circumstances precluded such lofty aspirations, so Paul took the initiative. The day after his high school graduation, he enlisted in the U.S. Army. After a two-year stint, mostly stationed at Fort Knox, Kentucky, he returned to West Virginia and took advantage of his veterans' benefits and obtained a scholarship to the University of Charleston. Upon graduation, and while holding down a part-time job working in a fast food franchise, he enrolled in the West Virginia University College of Law. There he studied personal injury litigation with the intention of representing disabled miners and other industrial laborers.

After passing the bar, Gardner joined a practice in Huntington in dire need of new blood. Specializing in medical malpractice cases, the firm provided the young attorney with valuable experience and an income that helped pay his lingering student loans, as well as the rent on an upscale townhouse. But when Paul's father suddenly suffered a fatal heart attack and his mother's meager wages failed to meet the mortgage payments on the family homestead, he felt obligated to offer financial support. So Paul downsized to an apartment, provided his mother with a monthly stipend and even paid for his sisters' community college tuition.

A few years later, Gardner was offered a job at the U.S. Attorney's Office for the Southern District of West Virginia, which he eagerly accepted. As his reputation as an effective public defender grew, so did his interest in politics. He flirted with the idea of running for Mayor of Charleston, but convinced himself that he should aim higher. It was during this period that he met, courted and married Sissy Landreau, a legal secretary from a lower middle class family who shared his aspirations for a more fulfilling life. In short order, the Gardners got to work on conceiving a family and a future. Two months after Paul won his Congressional seat, their son Josh was born.

Three terms – and another child, daughter Amy – later, Paul Gardner was considered a rising star in the Democratic Party. So much so that desperate party officials convinced him to run for governor of West Virginia. Defeating the incumbent seemed a tall order, especially at a time when Republicans ruled the roost both in the state legislature and throughout the entire South. But once again, Gardner referred to his roots and scoured every VW hall, factory, mill and waffle house in the state, and, sure enough, his populist approach helped eke out a narrow victory.

By the time he, Sissy and their two young children, moved into the governor's mansion the following January, politicos across the country were already measuring Gardner for bigger and better things. With his clean-cut good looks, down-to-earth demeanor and Southern charm, he was bound to be mentioned as a possible national candidate. But when approached to seek the Democratic nomination for president, Gardner balked, citing his desire to focus on his growing family. Besides, he was only in his early forties then – there was plenty of time to consider a White House run. Instead, he ran for reelection as governor and won handily, while James J. Hartman became the national standard bearer and won the presidency.

Now, two and a half years later, in the aftermath of the Talbot tragedy and in the midst of the ensuing vetting for a new vice president, Gardner was summoned to the White House for a private meeting in the West Wing with the President, Chief of Staff Davidson and Security Advisor Redmond. Dressed in his "lucky suit" – the dark blue Brooks Brothers outfit with a starched white Arrow shirt, red striped tie and American flag lapel pin that he had worn when he announced his candidacy for governor – Gardner arrived by limousine at 1600 Pennsylvania Avenue promptly at 9:30 a.m. He was greeted outside the Portico by Davidson, who escorted him directly to the Oval Office.

"Paul," smiled Hartman, extending his hand.

"Mr. President," Gardner replied, making sure his grip was firm. "It's good to see you again. It's been awhile."

"A year ago last February," the President recalled. "At the National Governors Association Conference."

"You have a good memory, sir."

"Yes ... and it occasionally serves me well," the President ribbed.

After some more cordial chit-chat, the four men seated themselves and got down to business.

"Well, Paul," said the President, crossing his legs and folding his hands on his lap. "You know what this is all about."

Gardner squinted his eyes judiciously and coyly replied, "Unless I'm mistaken, Mr. President, it's a job interview."

"And an important job at that," Hartman remarked, " ... despite what you may have heard to the contrary."

"Oh, I take the vice presidency quite seriously, sir," Gardner assured on cue with a slight drawl.

"What I'm looking for primarily," the President explained, "is someone who can provide substantive counsel and work to advance the administration's agenda on Capitol Hill."

Gardner nodded thoughtfully. "Well, I believe I'm certainly equipped to do that. For one thing, I have this administration's best interests – as well as that of the entire nation – at heart. Also, I have had considerable experience working with legislators of both parties on the state level."

"Although dealing with the West Virginia legislature couldn't possibly be as treacherous as dealing with the U.S. Congress," Hartman wryly interjected.

"Well, I don't know about that, Mr. President," Gardner laughed, glancing at Davidson and Redmond. "Those reps in Charleston keep me pretty busy. For example., we've got plenty of pork barrel projects on the backburner and so far I've managed to keep them there to rein in spending and maintain a balanced budget. I know that's one of your goals here in Washington."

"That and the Energy Bill," Davidson chimed in. "You've supported the administration on a wide range of issues, but you've been noticeably reticent about that."

"For purely political reasons," claimed Gardner in his defense. "The coal restrictions that are a part of that bill don't sit well with many of my constituents. I had to distance myself from the measure to ensure re-election."

"And now?" asked the President.

"As vice-president, I wouldn't have any concerns."

"But could you help sell the bill to Congress?" Davidson persisted. "We would need your whole-hearted, unwavering support."

"And you'd have it," Gardner promised.

"On the other hand, I'm not looking for a 'yes man,'" the President hastened to add.

"*No*, sir," Gardner concurred with an earnest smile, adding, "If or when I disagree on an issue, I'll state my case. I think that's important. But so is loyalty and solidarity. I wouldn't agree to come on board if I couldn't pledge both."

The President glanced at Davidson, who raised his eyebrows to signal approval.

Redmond cleared his throat, drawing Gardner's attention. "Governor," he said, "as executive of a relatively small state, your foreign policy expertise is … shall we say … limited."

"Ah, but don't forget I served six years in the United States Congress," Gardner readily pointed out. "Although I was not a member of the foreign relations committee, I did vote on any number of bills dealing with foreign trade, military appropriations and international policies."

"How many foreign countries have you actually visited?" asked Redmond.

"Why, you know the answer to that, Sam," Gardner replied jovially. "I'm sure it's in my dossier. I spent a little time in Europe one summer during my college days. I also went to China … oh, about five years ago … trying to drum up business for my state. Does Canada count? Spent a week in the Rockies on vacation last year with Sissy and the kids."

Gardner grinned just to make sure they all realized he was being facetious. They obliged him with polite smiles.

"Other than that," he continued, "I admit I haven't strayed too far from my own backyard. To be honest, if you asked me who the prime minister of Nepal is, I'd be stumped. But I could certainly find Nepal on a map and I'm sure that as vice president I'll have the opportunity to broaden my horizons. My education in foreign policy would be swift and thorough … That would be your job, Sam," he added with a wink.

The President suppressed a smirk and asked, "How would you feel about moving your family to Washington, Paul?"

"I'd have no problem with that, Mr. President, and I doubt my wife would, either. It's just a hop, skip and a jump away from Charleston. I trust the public schools here are up to par?"

The President looked a little perplexed. "Wouldn't you rather send your kids to private school? Most government officials do."

"Sir, as the son of a coal miner and a factory seamstress, I am a product of the public school system," said Gardner with appropriate humility. "I have always been supportive of public education and, as governor, made a point of sending my children to public school. Helps to keep them grounded, unspoiled. Plus, I think it sets a good example."

Davidson and Redmond exchanged glances. The President simply pursed his lips and nodded. "That's … very commendable." Still, he couldn't resist asking, "Would you have any reservations about living in Blair House?"

"No, sir," Gardner replied. "I'm sure my family would be quite comfortable there."

"Well," the President sighed, "I must say that I have been impressed with your record as Governor of West Virginia. You've run a clean administration, free of any … embarrassing revelations."

"Yes, well, I think moral leadership and personal integrity are important factors in successful government operations," Gardner staunchly maintained.

"Forgive me for asking this," the President nonetheless inquired, "but … is there anything we need to know … anything about your past that could come back to haunt you or embarrass the administration going forward?"

"You mean any skeletons in my closet? No, sir," Gardner scoffed. "I'm a church-going, law-abiding public servant who loves his wife, his children, his family and his country. I don't even smoke or drink. Now, that might make me boring, but that's just me."

"Boring is fine with me," the President assured him. "Boring is the least of my concerns."

"What are your concerns, sir? If I may ask …"

The President was blunt. "I just wonder if you're prepared to step into my shoes if necessary."

It was Gardner's cue to sell himself and he made the most of the opportunity. "Mr. President," he calmly and thoughtfully declared, "I know you consider the vice presidency more than a ceremonial position. Well, so do I. I understand that, in order to be a valuable member of this administration, I would need to take a proactive role in helping craft policy and in building bipartisan Congressional support. As a former member of Congress and current second-term governor, I know that I have the appropriate legislative and executive skills and experience to help this administration realize its domestic agenda and foreign policy initiatives. Following in Clayton Talbot's footsteps, the next vice president must be fully engaged and totally dedicated to improving the quality of life of all Americans." Without batting an eyelid, Gardner resolved, "And I'm prepared to make that commitment."

President Hartman maintained his poker face, then responded, "Thank you, Governor. I appreciate your time this morning. It will be at least another few days before I make my decision. In the interim," he said, rising from his chair, prompting the others to rise as well, "if I have any further questions, I will call you directly."

"Thank you, Mr. President," Gardner replied, extending his hand. "As always, it's been an honor."

After Gardner left, the President turned to Davidson and Redmond. "Well, he seems eager enough," he remarked. "What do you think?"

"A real boy scout," Davidson replied.

"Is that good?"

"Well, it isn't bad."

"He'd sail through confirmation hearings," Redmond predicted.

"But is he up to the task?" the President wondered.

"He's no Talbot or Gore," Davidson offered. "But he's no Quayle, either."

"He's experienced enough to handle the job," Redmond concurred, "and green enough to stay out of your hair for another five years."

"How did his background check go?" asked the President.

"So far, so good," said Redmond. "But we're still working on it. Why?"

"You know the old expression -- if it's too good to be true ..."

Redmond and Davidson exchanged glances.

"We'll continue interviewing other candidates," said the President. "But so far, I'd say Paul Gardner is our top contender."

Chapter 17

Burnett awoke with a start.

Panicking at first, he slowly regained control of his breathing as well as his bearings. He was indeed alive, certainly conscious. The only problem was that he was also in total darkness and, for some reason, didn't have the use of his arms or legs.

Focus. Feel. Realize, he told himself. He was in the dark, seated, his wrists bound behind him with his arms wrapped around the back of a wooden chair. His ankles were tied to the legs of the chair.

Okay. But where was he? He listened intently and heard only the constant hum of a mechanical device. It sounded like an HVAC unit. A utility room? Peering straight ahead through the darkness he detected the faintest horizontal beam of light, no doubt the bottom of a door about ten feet away. His rapidly beating heart began to slow down, but then skipped a beat as the door abruptly opened.

A sudden burst of light made him squint, and all Burnett could see were two shadowy figures framed in the doorway. They entered the room and ominously closed the door behind them. Utter darkness again. Only the sound of the air handler. Burnett's heart began to race again.

Then someone flicked a switch and a glaring spotlight stabbed at his eyes. He turned his head to the side and heard soft, slow footsteps approaching him. The two visitors paused a few feet away, but despite their proximity, Burnett couldn't make out their faces because of the damn light.

"Where am I?" he demanded to know.

There was no response, so he repeated, "I said, where am I?"

"The last place you wanna' be," replied a deep, drawling male voice. His male companion chuckled.

"You do know kidnapping is a felony?" said Burnett, squinting in their direction, but only seeing spots before his eyes. It was merely a sarcastic remark, but it obviously rubbed his captors the wrong way because one of them suddenly punched Burnett in the face, a blow that caught him in the left cheek bone and made him see stars instead.

"We ask the questions," the chuckler who hit him declared.

"Of course," Burnett muttered, wincing.

He refrained from saying anything else and merely awaited his interrogation. Something similar had happened to him when he was a bureau correspondent in Lebanon. He had been "detained" at gunpoint, along with several other Western journalists, for a couple of days by what he assumed were members of Hamas. It was a dicey situation, but it didn't involve being bound to a chair in a dark room and pounded in the face for being impertinent. In that case, being fully cooperative proved helpful. In this case, Burnett had his doubts.

"Identify yourself," the drawling captor commanded.

Burnett was tempted to tell him that he already knew who he was. Surely they had checked his wallet for I.D. Instead, he played along. "My name is Burnett ... Gideon Burnett. I'm a journalist. I work for …"

"We don't give a shit who you work for," the interrogator interrupted. "What are you doin' in Beauville?"

Burnett hesitated, then answered, "Following a lead."

A long pause followed, the humming of the air handler seemingly louder. And then came another bruising punch to the face.

"Ahhh!" Burnett gasped, taking this one on the chin. He tasted blood and realized it was coming from the corner of his mouth.

"Don't be cute with me," the interrogator warned in a sneering voice. "I asked you what you're doin' down here."

"Research," said Burnett, straightening up in his chair. "For a story."

"A story about what?"

Burnett hesitated again and swallowed hard. "Politics."

"Politics?" the interrogator repeated with a scoffing tone. "Politics?"

"Basically, yeah," Burnett confirmed with a nervous titter.

"Who have you been talkin' to ... about *politics*?" asked the interrogator.

Great, thought Burnett, either name my source or get the crap kicked out of me. "Oh, lots of people," he replied, stalling for time.

"Would one of those people be a man named Ross Kayton?"

Burnett feigned bewilderment. "Huh?" He expected another blow to the face, but instead of lashing out, the interrogator reached for a pack of cigarettes in the breast pocket of his short-sleeved shirt. He lit up with a blue, disposable lighter without offering a smoke to his companion and took a deep drag. "Ross Kayton," he repeated, exhaling slowly and tossing the pack and lighter on a folding table just to the right of Burnett's chair. "Does the name ring a bell?"

"I ... I don't seem to recall," Burnett stammered.

"Really?" said the interrogator softly. "Dark hair. Medium height. About 35 years old. Used to work for Uniplex. I believe he was a junior executive of some kind. Sound familiar now?"

Burnett looked up toward the ceiling, as if racking his brain. "What did you say his name was?"

Then he watched as the interrogator leaned in toward him, his features still too fuzzy to make out distinctly in the glaring light. He paused within a feet of Burnett and then casually applied the burning tip of his cigarette to Burnett's left cheek.

"Yaaa!" Burnett recoiled, struggling in vain to loosen his wrists. "Ah! God damn it!"

"I got a whole pack of Marlboros," the interrogator informed him. "And you know what they say – smoking can be hazardous to your health." He paused to grin at his sniggering companion, then turned back to Burnett. "So why don't you stop bullshitting us and tell me what it is you and Ross Kayton were talkin' about."

"Look," said Burnett. "I don't know who you guys are and, frankly, I don't want to know. I didn't come here looking for trouble."

"No, but you sure as hell found it, didn't you?" the interrogator replied, taking another drag of his cigarette and blowing the smoke into Burnett's face.

"Be that as it may," Burnett continued. "If I crossed some sort of line coming to Beauville, I apologize. No story is worth this kind of hassle. If you'll just … just let me go my way, I promise to leave town and forget about the whole thing."

The interrogator took another puff of his cigarette, glanced at his partner, and started to laugh. "Boy," he chortled, "you sure did cross a line … and I'm afraid there's no goin' back." He took the cigarette out of his mouth, held it between his fingers and inspected the burning tip. "Now, are you gonna' tell me what you and old Ross were discussin'?"

Burnett sighed. This was like something out of a Tarantino movie and he suspected it wasn't destined to end well no matter what he told them. There was a difference between spending time in a jail cell for protecting a source and withholding information from a pair of sociopaths in the middle of nowhere. The truth, however, might get both himself and Kayton killed. So he said nothing at all.

"Suit yourself," shrugged the interrogator, moving toward him again with the cigarette in hand.

"Hold on a minute," said the accomplice, advancing from the shadows. "I got a better idea. It's gonna' save us a lot of time."

As he menacingly approached, Burnett tensed up apprehensively, the knot binding his wrists behind him seeming to get tighter and the cigarette burn on his cheek stinging sharply as a bead of sweat trickled down from his temple. The accomplice removed something from his trouser pocket. With a flick of his wrist, it retracted – a switchblade knife.

Catching his breath, Burnett got a better look at his assailant. He was totally bald with a craggy face and a Satanic red moustache and goatee. There was also an elaborate tattoo of indistinguishable reptilian form on his neck and the skull and crossbones Burnett had noticed earlier on his forearm. The demonic illustrated man brought his face within inches of his prey and stared at him with dull, merciless eyes.

Don't piss yourself, thought Burnett, frighteningly aware that his legs were spread apart and could not be closed. He stiffened as the blade of the knife was suddenly pressing against the crotch of his trousers. "I'll slit you, boy," his tormentor leeringly hissed. "Make you bleed like a pig. Take away your manhood. Ain't nobody gonna' hear you scream, neither."

His foul breath forced Burnett to turn his head to the side and gulp.

"What's it gonna' be? Huh?" Tattoo Guy demanded, applying pressure to Burnett's groin. "You gonna' talk? Huh? Huh?"

"Whoa!" Marlboro Man suddenly intervened, grabbing his accomplice by the arm and tugging him away. Blocking the light, he came into focus as lean but muscular with a brown ponytail and a craggy, pockmarked face. "Let's not be too hasty. We ought to give our guest a little time to consider his situation."

Burnett took a deep breath and shivered. His heart was pounding so hard he thought it might burst from his chest.

"We're gonna' leave you in here for a little while. But we'll be back," warned the Marlboro Man. "And when we are, you better start talkin' or you ain't never gonna' see the light of day."

Reluctantly, Tattoo Guy closed his knife and put it back in his pocket for the time being. Then he and Marlboro Man exited the room, leaving Burnett alone with the glaring light and the humming air handler. "Jesus Christ," he muttered to the ceiling. When he caught his breath, he again tussled with the ropes binding him to the chair, but it was useless. He was no Harry Houdini and his tugging only made the knot tighter.

He looked to his left and right, searching for some means of escape. To his amazement, he discovered that Marlboro Man had left his cigarettes and the lighter on the table. Okay, he thought, this wasn't going to be easy, but it was worth a try. Better to try and fail than wait for them to come back and torture him. With his feet planted on the floor, he was able to tug and move his chair closer to the edge of the table. There he could lift himself up enough to feel for the lighter with his hands. After struggling for a few minutes, he located it and settled back into a sitting position.

Just don't drop the lighter, he told himself, flicking it a few times until the flint produced a flame. Craning his neck to look over his shoulder, he fretted and fumbled, trying to direct the flame toward the rope. Eventually, he succeeded, but not without allowing the flame to get too close to his skin. "Oww!" he winced, lifting his thumb from the tab, losing the flame. He flicked the lighter again, straining his neck to watch what he was doing. But this time he was able to burn enough of the rope to weaken its grip. Finally, tugging hard, he broke free.

Acting quickly, Burnett untied the knots binding his legs and rose to his feet. He patted his pockets, but found them empty. The bastards had taken his cell phone and wallet, and without credit cards or cash it would be hard to get anywhere – provided, of course, he could even get out of the room.

But when Burnett tried the door, he found it was unlocked. He opened it slowly, poking his head outside to see if the coast was clear, and discovered an eerie, narrow mortared corridor illuminated by a row of ceiling lights in what appeared to be a basement. He listened for any sound of human activity before venturing from the room. Hearing none, he proceeded cautiously, heading toward the right as his captors had, hoping to find the nearest way out.

The subterranean chamber with its endless L-shaped passageways reminded him of a dark labyrinth in a horror movie. There seemed to be no end to this dank concrete maze and who knew what he'd find around the next corner. But eventually he came to a stone staircase that led up to a metal door and the promise of daylight. He ascended one step at a time, a bit fearful of what might await him on the other side, then paused apprehensively before finally reaching for the handle.

Chapter 18

Hamilton Tyler Caine was born into wealth, raised in a 42-room mansion on a 16-acre estate in the Pacific coastal community of Newport Beach, California – but no one could hold that against him.

That was because his father, industrialist and Orange County social magnate Roger Caine, made it clear to his son and only heir at an early age that, despite the family fortune, no special privileges would be afforded to him, no nepotism would be extended toward him, and no trust fund would await him when he reached 21. Instead, he would have to create his own prosperity, a challenge his father was convinced would build character and purpose – just as it had done for him.

True to his word, Roger sent Hamilton to public school and had him work weekends and summers. Deprived of even a meager weekly allowance, young Hamilton earned his own cash throughout his adolescence by mowing lawns, delivering newspapers, bagging groceries, picking lettuce and hustling pizzas. Family vacations – to such exotic locales as Santa Catalina, Palm Springs and Lake Tahoe – were rare and always cut short to accommodate Roger Caine's busy business schedule. If Hamilton wanted to see the world, he would have to wait until he was adult and do so on his own dime. Which probably explained why, at the age of eighteen, he chose to attend college at the University of Hawaii on Oahu.

However, it became clear that by his sophomore year, the only thing

Hamilton had learned was how to surf, having cut classes regularly and saddled with a mediocre grade point average. That was when Roger Caine decided to modify his master plan for Hamilton and offered a proposition. If Hamilton applied himself, graduated with honors and earned gainful employment, he would ultimately inherit the entire Caine fortune. But if he failed to rise to the challenge, he wouldn't receive one red cent. It was all or nothing.

Up for the dare and with an enticing goal as incentive, Hamilton put his surfboard aside, cracked the books and exceeded his father's expectations by graduating summa cum laude with a Bachelor of Business Administration degree. His performance and references then enabled him to earn his MBA at Stanford University. Finally recognizing his son's potential, Roger offered Hamilton a mid-level management position at one of his companies – which he surprisingly but graciously declined.

It seemed Hamilton had the notion of starting his own firm – a software company no less at a time when computer technology had yet to capture the public's imagination. Roger thought it was a foolish idea – until he read Hamilton's detailed business plan. Believing it was worth the risk, Roger offered to finance a portion of the start-up. His leap of faith did not go unrewarded. In fact, over the next few years, not only did Roger see a sizeable return on his investment, but also Hamilton became a self-made multi-millionaire while still in his twenties, seeing his fortune more than quadruple when he eventually sold his company to a major software manufacturer in Washington State.

Wealth agreed with Hamilton and he spent it wisely. Not that he didn't enjoy partying with a wide circle of friends that included the Hollywood elite and the Silicon Valley noveau riche. In fact, it was during his playboy days that he met and married Sara Kay Clark, an exceedingly attractive yet wholesome model and would-be actress. But instead of investing in the usual vices of the rich and infamous, he sowed more productive seeds by contributing to the campaigns and causes of various influential California politicians, intent on currying their favor for future business ventures.

However, his activism on behalf of the environment and promoting small business in the Golden State gradually turned Hamilton Caine toward another career. It was one thing to donate money to political action committees and another to have the actual power to facilitate change. Once he realized that, he set his sights on the Governor's mansion in Sacramento. But first he settled for a seat in the State Senate, where he established his public credentials crusading for green technology, tax reform and both labor and consumer rights.

Then, when the opportunity arose, he parlayed his experience and political cache into a successful bid for Lieutenant Governor. If nothing else, Hamilton was a patient man, but as fate would have it, he realized his ultimate goal when his predecessor resigned the governorship half way through his term due to illness. One man's cancer proved to be another's good luck as Caine took charge and swiftly put an ambitious agenda of executive reform into effect. His strategy was to reverse the trend toward insolvency by running the state "like a business" with a CEO keenly focused on the bottom line. The gambit paid off in the form of diminishing budget deficits, rising employment and increased property values and tax revenues.

Admired for his brains, ingenuity, style and celebrity, Hamilton won election in his own right by a plurality of nearly two million votes. Overnight, he became a media obsession – the wunderkind from the O.C., the liberal Ronald Reagan from Central Casting and Democratic heir apparent to James J. Hartman. Surely, at the age of 44, he was destined for even greater things. Certainly his was a force that could not be ignored by national party leaders and an American electorate invariably drawn to a charismatic figure.

Which is why, despite his initial reluctance and lingering doubts, the President of the United States agreed to include Hamilton Caine on his short list of vice presidential prospects. The scheduling of a formal face-to-face meeting, however, proved a bit problematic. So, rather than settle for a phone interview or have the Governor of California fly all the way to Washington, D.C., the vetting team decided on a teleconference held in one of the White House briefing rooms.

Promptly at 11 a.m., Eastern Daylight Savings Time, Governor Caine appeared on the large screen looking rested, robust and impeccably groomed in a dark pinstripe suit. He had a face for television, as many had often said, with his handsome features, jet black hair, piercing blue eyes, jutting jaw and elegant smile. Seated at a desk with his hands folded and the state flag and insignia propped behind him, Caine looked mighty presidential. Shrewd, thought Hartman.

"Good morning, Governor," the President greeted.

"Good morning, Mr. President," Caine responded with a slight nod.

"Can you see and hear me all right?"

"Loud and clear, sir."

"Great. Thank you for making time this morning."

"My pleasure, sir."

"I'm joined today by Chief of Staff Davidson and National Security Advisor Redmond."

"Gentlemen," Governor Caine politely acknowledged.

"I'll try to make this as brief as possible …"

"I'm completely at your disposal, Mr. President," the Governor graciously replied. "Please take as much time as you feel necessary."

"Let me begin by congratulating you on the work you're doing out there in California. I understand that the state is now operating with a balanced budget and is ranked number one in the nation in terms of educational standards and quality of health care."

"Yes, sir," Caine proudly confirmed. "Actually, we have a budget surplus this year, much of which has been earmarked for tax cuts and improvements in infrastructure. Might I also point out that our literacy rate has increased dramatically, employment is up, the crime rate down and the number of citizens with health insurance is on the rise."

"Very impressive," the President remarked. "Sounds like you're doing a fine job as governor. Perhaps too good – I would hate to disrupt that progress by offering you a job here in Washington," he teased.

"Well, you know, Mr. President," Caine smoothly countered, "what we've accomplished in California is a testament to the strength and resourcefulness of our entire administration. I am particularly blessed with an able Lieutenant Governor. If, for any reason, I were to resign as Governor, my successor and staff would be well equipped to carry on without me."

Touché, thought Hartman.

"Also," the Governor added, "I believe many of the progressive programs we've initiated in California could be effectively adapted to the country as a whole."

"Such as?" the President wondered.

"Such as affordable housing and redevelopment, education reform, green job creation, alternative energy development …"

"Speaking of which," the President interjected, "you're a vocal proponent of my energy bill."

"I am, sir. I think it's vitally important that our nation take aggressive measures to lower greenhouse gases, promote renewable and alternative energy sources, and drastically reduce our dependency on foreign oil. I believe your bill sets us on that path."

"That's good to hear," said the President. "But given the opportunity, how would you help me convince Congress?"

"The same way I convinced the state legislature – by aggressively focusing on the economic benefits of the policy. It's not just a moral issue. Quality of life should be the determining factor, but regrettably it's not when it comes to the bureaucratic mind. We need to show irrefutable evidence that adopting the measure and converting to clean, renewable energy will result in substantial profit for American industry. That would be my approach. And with my credibility and cooperative relationship with many in the private sector, I believe we can forge new alliances with special interests to gain the support we'll need to pass this legislation."

Satisfied with the answer, the President turned to Redmond. "Sam, I believe you have a question for the Governor."

"Yes," said Redmond, shifting in his chair and addressing the screen. "Governor, how would you assess your breadth of experience and ability to deal with foreign governments in an official capacity?"

"As both a private citizen and a public official, I have traveled extensively to more than 30 foreign countries," Caine informed. "As governor of the most populous state in the union, I have had a cordial relationship with the President of Mexico and I have had successful dealings with business leaders from Japan, Korea, China, Singapore, Canada, Brazil, and many European nations. There are thousands of international companies with offices and other facilities in the state of California and I would like to think I have played an instrumental role in improving that ongoing commerce."

"In terms of national security," Redmond followed up, "do you believe you're qualified to assume a leadership role if that were necessary – especially in terms of commanding the military?"

Without batting an eye, Caine replied, "First of all, California's contributions to the national security effort during my administration have been considerable. We've beefed up safety measures at our major airports, provided enhanced border patrol, and assisted the federal government in improving cargo inspection at our ports. In respect to interacting with the military, I have utilized the National Guard in a number of situations, notably in securing the lives and property of citizens in the southern part of the state during a wave of wildfires last summer. I have also overseen the renovation of several Army and Marine Corps bases and worked with the legislature to improve conditions at various Veterans Administration hospitals statewide."

Davidson cleared his throat, then posed a question of his own: "Governor, having served as a chief executive both in public and private life, how would you feel about assuming a role that is – for want of a better expression – subordinate to that of the President?"

Caine's smile never wavered as he replied, "Well, as you know, managing a state the size of California is like running a country. It takes dedication, resourcefulness and savvy. It also takes the ability to work tirelessly with a corresponding legislative and judicial branch to govern effectively. But it also takes a measure of humility, the realization that the decisions you make will affect the quality of life of millions of citizens. I believe the record shows that I have been a successful governor with the requisite executive skills to lead. But it also shows my commitment to causes greater than my own personal interests and a willingness to assist and support my president in any way I can."

Obviously impressed, the President gave Davidson and Redmond an approving glance before turning back to the screen. "Thank you, Governor," he said. "We'll be in touch."

Chapter 19

As Burnett emerged from his dungeon, he had to shield his eyes from glaring sunlight. He staggered forward, then paused and turned back to see where he had come from. It appeared to be some kind of abandoned, brick warehouse with several broken windows and no identifying signs. There were no other facilities in the immediate vicinity either – only surrounding woods and a tree-line dirt road that led out of the place to who knows where.

He started walking at a brisk pace in that direction, hoping it would lead to civilization or at least a paved roadway. Judging by the sun's position directly overhead in the blue, cloudless sky, it was noontime. He estimated the heat index at somewhere in the 90's and he broke out into a sweat just half a mile down the road. He kept looking back to see if anyone was after him until the road veered to the left and the building disappeared behind the bend.

To his concern and disappointment, the air was eerily still; there was no sound of a distant highway, no sound at all except his own footfall on the bumpy, dusty path. He couldn't even tell if he was heading east or west. But seeing as this was the only road out, he stuck to it. That is, until he suddenly heard a familiar sound – a vehicle was approaching down the road and around another bend.

His first instinct was to stay put and flag down whoever came driving by. But what if it was *them*? Acting swiftly, Burnett traipsed to the side of the road and concealed himself behind a thick oak tree.

As the vehicle – a dark, late-model Chevy van – came ambling by, he took a peek and caught sight of his captors in the cab.

Great, he thought. As soon as they got back to the warehouse and found him missing, they'd surely pursue. If he continued along the dirt road, they'd catch up with him in no time in their van. But if they followed his footprints, they could also see where he left the path if he decided to take to the woods. The idea of being hunted in the wild gave him the chills. But maybe he was giving them too much credit. After all, they did unwittingly provide him with the means to escape. Were they even capable of tracking him? Burnett decided to take his chances in the woods.

Swiftly forging his way through the dense, overgrown thicket, Burnett tried to focus on what he would do once he got wherever he was headed. Without his wallet, cell phone or car he couldn't get far. If he found a gas station or a convenience store, he could have the proprietor call the police. But recalling what Kayton told him about the local authorities, he wasn't sure that was a good idea. At the very least, they could detain him. He needed to locate Kayton, get his hands on the Uniplex files and get the hell out of Texas as fast as possible.

Eventually, the woods came to an end, replaced by an expanse of open prairie. Scanning the horizon, Burnett caught sight of a roadside café adjacent to a county highway about a quarter of a mile away and headed straight for it. As he got nearer, he knew the restaurant was open by the smoke billowing from a chimney stack and the smell of barbecue wafting through the air. Sure enough, there were numerous cars in its parking lot. His heart racing, he hurried to the front door.

No sooner had Burnett entered the café than he drew the attention of everyone present. Several patrons at various tables looked up from their lunches and a few others seated at a counter turned their heads to stare. Sheepishly, Burnett approached the cash register, where a stocky, middle-aged waitress with tinted red hair and a bit too much makeup greeted him with a glossy smile. "Can I help you?" she drawled.

"I sure hope so," he replied. "Do you know where I could find a phone?"

"There's one outside," she answered, her smile fading as she noticed the bruise and cigarette burn on his face.

"Really? I didn't see it on the way in," said Burnett, trying to keep his voice low.

"It's around the side of the building," the waitress elaborated, eying him suspiciously. "On the right."

"On the right?" Burnett pointed.

"On the right," she repeated impatiently, as if instructing a moron.

"Okay. Thank you."

"Mm-hm."

Feeling more eyes on the back of his neck, Burnett hastily departed through the front door. He walked around the side of the building and spotted the public phone station. Digging into his pants pocket, he extracted a few coins and was about to deposit them when he suddenly caught sight of a familiar vehicle veering off the highway and into the café's lot.

Burnett hit the ground and scurried to hide behind a parked car. Peering cautiously over the hood, he spotted Tattoo Guy and the Marlboro Man hopping out of their van and heading for the café entrance, leaving the motor running. Panic seized him. Why would they do that unless they were in a hurry and had only gone inside to inquire whether anyone had seen a stranger in the area? The waitress would tell them he just stepped outside to use the phone. There was nowhere to run or hide. He was trapped. Except … *they left the motor running*.

Instinct overcame reason. Burnett bolted for the van. By the time he got into the cab and slammed the door shut, his pursuers were on their way out of the café. When they saw him behind the wheel, they froze for a second, as did Burnett. Then they began to holler and charged the vehicle. *No time to buckle up*, thought Burnett as he locked the doors and shifted into reverse. He hit the gas pedal and the Chevy lurched backwards. His adrenaline pumping, Burnett slammed the brake and turned the wheel at the same time, swerving the van around to face the highway. He paused to turn around to look out the back windows and saw the two men running frantically toward the vehicle. If either one managed to hop aboard, he'd have a problem, so he put the transmission into drive, stomped on the accelerator pedal and peeled away, kicking up a cloud of dust and barely missing a head-on collision with a honking motorist coming in the opposite direction on the two-lane blacktop.

Catching his breath and glancing nervously in the rearview mirror, Burnett reduced his speed once he was safely away. But he knew he had only bought himself a head start. In minutes, his grand theft auto would be reported to the police and the big, bulky Chevy stood out like a sore thumb. He had to find out fast where he was and decide where he was going. Fortunately, he soon spotted a sign indicating that Beauville was just three miles away. All he knew was that he had to get to Kayton's place.

Despite the short distance, the ride seemed to take forever and was not without a moment of sheer panic. Along the way, Burnett spotted an oncoming vehicle with flashing lights on its roof. As it got closer, he heard its wildly warbling siren and held his breath. Speeding along the highway in the direction of the café, it passed him. Gripping the steering wheel, Burnett watched the sheriff's car in the driver's side view mirror, hoping it wouldn't stop, turn around and pursue him. To his relief, it kept going until it faded in the distance. Pressing his luck, he increased his speed until it challenged the limit. It wouldn't be long before police had a description of the stolen van, so there was no time to waste.

He reached Beauville, jumped a few traffic lights, and parked the Chevy a block away from Kayton's apartment complex. As inconspicuously as possible, he strolled to the address, climbed the concrete stairs to the second floor landing and rang the doorbell of 2C. When no one answered, he turned around and looked over the balcony. A car he recognized as Kayton's was parked below. He rang the doorbell again, but there was no answer. Then he rapped on the door, only to discover it was ajar. "Hello?" he called out from the doorway into the apartment. "Mr. Kayton?" No response. Glancing to his left and right to make sure no one saw him, Burnett reluctantly crossed the threshold and closed the door quietly behind him.

Turning around, Burnett was startled to find the living room in shambles. The coffee table had been overturned, cushions from the sofa ripped up, and books and paper strewn all over the carpeted floor. Cautiously, he ventured deeper into the apartment, bypassing the kitchenette and moving tentatively toward the bedroom, making sure he didn't touch anything. His impulse was to call out for Kayton again, but he thought better of the idea, especially when he reached the bedroom doorway.

The room looked like a cyclone had passed through, leaving the contents of ransacked dresser drawers and a wardrobe – clothes, jewelry, luggage and other personal belongings – scattered in its wake. Even the bed had been stripped and its mattress tossed aside and ripped to shreds. Whoever did this was pretty desperate to find something.

How desperate, Burnett didn't realize until he turned toward an adjacent bathroom. Using a knuckle, he flicked on the bathroom light. At first, nothing looked out of the ordinary – the floor, sink and toilet were spotless, the medicine cabinet undisturbed. But the closed shower curtain gave him an uneasy feeling. Biting his lip, he extended his forearm and slowly brushed the curtain aside. Startled, he jerked up and accidentally sent a small rinsing glass crashing into the sink. The tub was splattered with what looked like human blood.

Hastily, Burnett fled the apartment, nearly tripping as he descended the concrete staircase, and rushed onto the street. He started walking back toward the van, paused and tried to collect his thoughts. Janice

Reid – Kayton had told him that if anything happened to him, go see Janice Reid. 325 West Kendall. Just three blocks east.

Burnett started walking, not too slowly but not too fast. Few people were out in the midday sun in this residential neighborhood, but the few who were paid him more than a passing glance, noticing a stranger in their midst. He refrained from acknowledging them and cautiously made his way to the white clapboard house with an aluminum awning on West Kendall.

When he arrived at his destination, Burnett stood on the sidewalk and looked both ways to make sure no one was watching. Then he climbed the front steps to a wooden porch and, failing to find a buzzer, knocked gently on the front door.

"Who is it?" a female voice behind the door eventually demanded.

"Hi," said Burnett. "I'm looking for Janice Reid."

"And who are you?"

"My name is Gideon Burnett. Ross Kayton gave me this address, told me to ask for Janice. Is that you?"

"Maybe," Janice all but confirmed. "Have you got some I.D.?"

"Well, actually, no. I had a run-in with a couple of guys," he tried to explain. "Well, it's a long story. I don't have my wallet."

"Uh-huh," the wary homeowner replied dubiously. "Then how do I know you're who you say you are?"

"I guess you'll just have to trust me."

"Yeah, right," Janice scoffed. "Well, you better find your wallet, mister, because I ain't openin' this door."

"Ah … have you got a computer?" Burnett asked, thinking fast. "Access to the Web?"

"Why?"

"If you go to American – hyphen – observer dot com and do a site search for Gideon Burnett, it'll bring up one of my columns. There's a picture of me."

Janice was silent for a moment, then replied, "Okay. I'll check."

"While you're doing that, may I come inside?" asked Burnett.

"No," she firmly insisted. "Wait there."

Burnett nervously paced the porch, looking in both directions along the street for any sign of his pursuers or the police. For all he knew, Kayton's girlfriend was calling the cops while he cooled his heels. He expected wailing sirens any minute now. But after what seemed like an interminable length of time, Janice finally opened the door .

She was a rather comely young woman of about thirty with bleached blonde hair and blue eyes, wearing a University of Texas T-shirt and jeans. "That's a lousy picture of you," she commented, standing aside to let him into her modestly furnished living room.

"Do you know where Ross is?" asked Burnett as she closed the door.

"No," Janice replied. "In fact, I've been trying to call him, but I keep getting his voice mail." Her blank expression suddenly turned anxious. "Do I need to worry?"

"I don't know. Do you?"

"What do you mean?"

"What I mean is, did Ross tell you he was in any danger?"

"Danger?" She suddenly looked alarmed. "What kind of danger?"

"The kind where people are after you," Burnett bluntly responded. "The kind where they'll hurt you to get something you might have."

"Oh, God. Do you think he's hurt?"

"No, no. I'm sure he's alright," Burnett lied, realizing it wasn't a good idea to fan the flames of mutual paranoia. "I just think he may be laying low."

"But why?" asked Janice. "Does it have anything to do with the stuff he gave me for safe keeping?"

"Maybe."

Now Janice looked genuinely frightened. "He told me to give it to you if ... if ..."

"I'm sure he's alright," Burnett tried to reassure her. "But I also think you'd better let me have what you're holding."

Janice obviously agreed. She promptly headed for a corner of the room, fell to her knees and lifted the edge of a worn Persian area rug. She then opened a door in the wood floorboards concealing a built-in safe. She started turning the combination lock, but hesitated, self-conscious of Burnett's attention. He rolled his eyes and turned his back to afford her privacy while she opened the safe.

When he turned around, she was standing before him with a thick, sealed Manila envelope. "Here," she said, hastily handing him the package. "Get this thing out of my house."

"Have you read the contents?" Burnett asked.

"No!" she emphatically replied. "I don't want to know what's in there. All I care about is Ross. Why hasn't he called me?"

"I don't know, but I'm sure he will."

"What if the people who are after him come after me?" Janice fretted, wringing the bottom of her T-shirt with both hands.

"I don't think that'll happen," said Burnett. "But if someone does come by ..."

"Oh, Jesus!" cried Janice, putting a hand to her mouth.

"I'm just saying ... if someone comes by, you don't know anything."

"Oh, yeah? Well, I'm not hanging around here. I'm gonna' leave town for awhile."

"That might be a good idea," Burnett agreed. "By the way, have you got a car?"

"Why?"

"I could use a ride."

"Are you kidding?" Janice gaped. "Just go, okay?"

"But I don't have any money and I need to leave town myself."

"Well, that's your problem. How did you get here in the first place?"

"I ... I borrowed a van," Burnett awkwardly explained.

"Well," said Janice, "you'll have to borrow it again. Now will you please leave?"

"You sure I can't hitch a ride?" Burnett suggested.

"Go!" implored Janice, pushing him toward the front door.

"Well, can I at least borrow a screwdriver?"

"What?"

"Please."

"Oh, for God's sake," Janice muttered.

A half a block away from the Chevy, Burnett paused to scope out the area. The street was as quiet as he left it – no sign of a police car or even a pedestrian. Approaching the van guardedly, he scanned both sides of the street for another full-size vehicle and spotted a Jeep Grand Cherokee nearby. As inconspicuously as possible, he removed the screwdriver from his pocket, crouched behind the SUV, and began loosening its license plate. Once he removed the tag, Burnett hastened to the Chevy, unscrewed its license plate and replaced it with the other tag, discarding the original in a nearby sewer grate. He then climbed into the van, removed the manila envelope from the waist of his trousers, placed it on the seat beside him and started the engine. But before he pulled away from the curb, Burnett checked the glove compartment, hoping to find a map or anything else that might assist him in his escape, as well as registration that would confirm the identity of at least one of his captors and their association with Uniplex. All he found instead was an utter surprise – his missing wallet.

He checked the contents and was relieved to find all his cash and credit cards. Things were looking up, but he was still not entirely out of the woods. He had to get as far away from Beauville as possible and back to Washington as quickly as he could. But that posed another problem. Did he dare show his face at the nearest airport? Hopping a train or bus posed a similar risk and would take him too long to get back to D.C. But he also had to ditch the van as soon as possible. The best option, he determined, was to take his chances at GBIA in Houston and fly out from there.

PROCESS OF ELIMINATION

Traffic was heavy en route to Houston and no less so when Burnett finally arrived at the airport. He found a spot for the Chevy in long-term parking, where he left the engine and air conditioner running while he sat in the cabin, opened the manila envelope and inspected the documents within. It was all there – just like Kayton had said – copies of receipts, cancelled checks and correspondence between then Governor Harley Singleton and various mid-level officers of Uniplex.

Now, the dicey part. His rented car, luggage and return flight airline ticket were back at the motel in Beauville. No big deal. He could call the rental car company and have them pick up the vehicle when he got back to D.C. He could also arrange to have his personal belongings sent to him later. For an additional charge, he could switch flights. It was just a matter of clearing security.

Tucking the envelope under his left arm, Burnett finally turned off the engine, left the keys on the front seat and got out of the van. He then walked for several lanes until he reached the busy thoroughfare separating the garage and the main terminal. Blending into a bustling crowd of travelers, he traversed the crosswalk and entered the building, then took an escalator up to the second floor. Seeking out his airline ticket counter, he paused for a moment to scan the electronic board of imminent departures and was pleased to see there was a flight for D.C. leaving within the hour. If necessary, he would fly first-class, anything to get the hell out of Dodge ASAP.

Burnett proceeded toward ticketing feeling more relieved by the second, easing up his grip on the envelope as he got nearer to the counter. But then suddenly, he froze in his tracks. Peering into the distance, he noticed a familiar face in the crowd and it sent a shiver through his body. Fearing he would be noticed as well, he sidestepped to a nearby telephone kiosk. Concealed behind its circular metal frame, he peeked around the bend to make sure his eyes had not deceived it. If only they were. Standing sentinel at the service line was Tattoo Guy, vigilantly scanning the area like a lone wolf patiently awaiting his prey.

Okay, thought Burnett, keeping his wits about him. *I'll just book with another airline.* Surreptitiously, he headed in the direction from which he came, toward the other side of the terminal, holding the envelope tighter and closer to his side. He kept telling himself that he had been in more precarious positions before. Compared to those, this was just a walk in the park.

But Burnett's bravado abruptly evaporated when he suddenly noticed another familiar face scoping out the terminal. Just a hundred feet away, pretending to be reading the jacket of a book at a concession stand, was the Marlboro Man. Just before the thug could catch sight of him, Burnett slipped into a gift shop where he could watch his pursuer through a window without being detected and assess the situation.

Whatever doubts Burnett may have had about Kayton's story and the authenticity of the documents he was carrying were laid to rest in light of his predicament. He was on to something big. Big enough to be kidnapped, tortured and stalked. It had obviously been foolish of him to head straight for the airport. That was the first place they would look for him. But what could they do to him in a high-security, public place? Pull a gun? Taser him? Yet, did he dare to force the issue? Then again, it probably wasn't him they were after, but the contents of the envelope he was carrying, and that could be wrested away rather easily if they caught him.

The question was how to elude them. Surely they had not just arrived. They must have been waiting for him for some time now. How much longer would they stay? Perhaps if he just waited them out before making a move … But that could take hours and he had to get on a plane as soon as he could. And what if they weren't alone? What if there were other operatives posted throughout the terminal looking for someone who fit Burnett's description?

"Damn it," he muttered, drawing the attention of a nearby shopper, a white-haired businessman who eyed him suspiciously.

Sheepishly, Burnett slunk away, heading back out into the terminal and toward the nearest escalator down. If he wanted to get back to Washington, he'd have to take a flight from another airport and that required immediate transportation. Forget the van he had left in long-term parking. For all he knew, it was equipped with an anti-theft device and had been tracked all the way to the airport. He wouldn't put anything past these people.

So when he reached the first floor, he followed signs to the first rental car booth. Fortunately, a serviceable compact was available and in no time at all, he was back on Route 10, heading east for Louisiana.

It was already late afternoon, so the plan was to reach New Orleans later that night and catch a red eye out of Louis Armstrong International. But Burnett was famished, so he stopped for a bite to eat about 30 miles west of St. Charles and killed another hour. That was okay, he reasoned. Once he had crossed the Louisiana state line, he felt practically home free and the sense of urgency had abated. At least he was miles away from trouble and all in one piece. Chalk another one up for the Beltway Bloodhound.

Night had fallen when Burnett got back on the road. He drove for another hour or so intent on reaching his destination. But after what felt like the longest day of his life and on a full stomach, he was feeling drowsy, barely able to keep his drooping eyelids open and mesmerized by the seemingly endless stretch of highway. To play it safe, he pulled into a rest area, parked close to the public rest rooms, and shut off the engine. *Just a quick catnap,* he decided, adjusting the car seat to the reclining position and closing his weary eyes. *Then I'll be on my way ...*

Chapter 20

Harley Singleton was something of a political anomaly. Although born and raised among the East Texas oil fields, the product of religious private schools and an avid hunter from the age of 12, the former governor and senator from the Lone Star state was a moderate Democrat who publicly supported gun control, stem cell research, a woman's right to choose and the Hartman administration's controversial energy bill.

The son of a Smith County judge and hospital administrator, Harley spent his youth in a suburb of Tyler where he excelled in both academics and athletics. The former enabled him to attend South Methodist University, majoring in law. The latter landed him a spot as a wide receiver on the SMU football team. Not only was Singleton near the top of his graduating class, but his gridiron performance attracted several offers from the NFL. On the advice of his career counselors and family, he passed up any pro ball aspirations for a lucrative position as a corporate lawyer for a major oil company in San Antonio.

Within a few years, Harley established himself as a successful attorney and slowly expanded his sphere of influence as a community activist and fundraiser for the Democratic Party. He also took a bride, Melanie "Sissy" McArthur, a debutante whose family made a fortune in drilling and rig equipment and whose Lone Star State roots dated back to the days of Sam Houston. Harley and Sissy made quite a power couple on the local social scene, hosting affairs and hobnobbing with prominent homegrown millionaires. It was just a matter of time until Harley saw the advantage of applying his social skills to a more prestigious pursuit.

He started by running for Congress at the age of 29. Five terms and 10 years later, he was elected Governor of Texas and served two terms. Then, it was back to Washington, this time as a U.S. Senator, serving two six-year terms. During that period, Singleton chaired the Ways and Means Committee and broadened his national exposure as a vocal and formidable member of the Loyal Opposition. As a governor, he had been perceived as right-of-center – pro-business, fiscally conservative, anti-illegal immigration - but as a United States Senator, his views noticeably moderated and his voting record reflected a more progressive inclination.

Some speculated there was an ulterior motive to this miraculous conversion. In fact, when Harley Singleton announced his retirement from the Senate – at the relatively young age of 59 – it was assumed he would run for President. After all, he had won every local and statewide election of his career handily and was well-known throughout the country as an energetic, articulate, and skillful executive and legislator. Like the late Clayton Talbot, Singleton was a Southerner who could garner support in traditional Democratic quarters up north and out west. Tall and silver-haired with the widest and whitest smile west of the Mississippi, he was a Democratic pollster's dream candidate and every Republicans worst nightmare.

But instead of hitting the campaign trail, Singleton defied expectations by opting for work in the private sector with the prestigious, Houston-based Haskell and Dekker law firm. Compared to the rigors of Austin and Washington, D.C., it was a cushy, well-paying job and one that allowed him to spend more time with his family and to moonlight as a political guest or commentator on cable news. There had been buzz about his vice-presidential chances when presidential nominee James Hartman was in the market for a running mate, but that didn't pan out. Neither did speculation about a cabinet position – possibly Attorney General – when Hartman was elected.

Nevertheless, in the minds of many, Singleton remained an elder statesman in waiting. All it would take was the right opportunity for him to step back into the political arena and it seemed that the perfect opportunity had arisen.

Upon his arrival at the White House, Singleton was escorted through the West Wing lobby to the Roosevelt Room where he was joined by Chief of Staff Davidson and National Security Advisor Redmond for a preliminary meeting. An auspicious sign, thought Singleton, unaware that Davidson and Redmond were merely stalling for time while the President concluded some unfinished business. Eventually, Mrs. Garrett arrived to inform them that the President was ready to receive them in the Oval Office across the hall.

"Harley," President Hartman warmly greeted, walking around his desk to shake the hand of his old colleague.

"Mr. President," smiled Singleton, touching Hartman's elbow while gently pumping his hand.

"You're looking good," Hartman observed enviously. "Is that what private life does to a man?"

"Evidently," laughed Harley. "You ought to try it someday."

"How's Sissy and the family?"

"Doing fine, sir. They send their regards."

"It's a pretty nice day today," the President noticed, glancing at the windows overlooking the Rose Garden. "Why don't you and I take this outside for a change?" he suggested, signaling to Davidson and Redmond that their presence was no longer necessary for now.

Strolling the central lawn side-by-side, flanked on either side by a stunning array of crabapple trees, tulips, primrose and hyacinth, Singleton and the President casually chatted before getting down to the crux of the discussion.

"Thought I might be hearing from you," said Singleton. "How unfortunate it has to be under these circumstances."

"Yes," admitted the President with a sigh. "We're still trying to get a grip on things since Clayton's death."

"I was just a teenager at the time," Harley reminisced, "but I distinctly remember how it was when JFK was taken from us. Especially in Texas. I was an admirer of Lyndon Johnson and despite what anyone might say about him today, I was sure glad he was on hand to take the reins of government in the wake of that tragedy."

"Mm," the President tacitly concurred. "It just goes to show how important the vice presidency can be. Which is why I asked you here today."

"I had hoped you would have considered me for the job three years ago, Mr. President," Singleton couldn't resist commented. "You would have carried Texas."

"I did consider you, Harley. But back then, we didn't see eye-to-eye on as many issues. Clayton was a better fit."

"Oh, don't get me wrong," Harley hastened to elaborate. "Clayton was the right choice. Definitely a political asset and a fine Vice President to boot. He just wasn't as good at arm-twisting as I was … and still am. Let's face it, Mr. President, what you need up on the Hill is someone who can get legislation passed. Someone who can win votes both here in Washington and in the next general election."

"And you're my man?"

"I'm your best shot," Harley boldly maintained.

"Convince me," Hartman challenged.

"Hell, you know how long I've been in public service," Singleton replied. "I've had a hand in every facet of it from the local level to state and federal. I was a five-term Congressman, a two-term governor and a two-term Senator. I served on the Armed Services and Ways and Means Committees. I helped pass scores of bills, signed dozens more into law. I've been to more than 40 countries on official business. I've dealt with labor," he rattled off, counting on his fingers, "I've dealt with the military, I've dealt with corporations, I've dealt with farmers and doctors and civil rights leaders. I've had more experience and ..

shoot … I've made more friends and fewer enemies than anybody else in this town."

"That you have," the President acknowledged, suddenly pausing to face his last remaining contender. "Of course, all that experience and prestige begs one question."

"Which is?"

"Would you be content as number two?"

"Huh," Singleton scoffed. "If you're asking whether I can be a good soldier to your general, the answer is an unequivocal 'Yes, sir.' I'd be whatever you wanted me to be – your right arm man, your legislative enforcer, your whimsical sidekick … However, if it ever became necessary, you can rest assured that I'd be ready to step into the driver's seat on a moment's notice."

"Let's talk specifics," the President proposed. "As you know, I've got an energy bill that's going nowhere in Congress."

"I support it."

"Well, that's all well and good, Harley. But I need more than your support. I need a full court press that's going to push that bill through both houses."

"And you need it before next year's election," Harley presumed.

"Preferably," said Hartman. "How persuasive do you think you can be?"

"Well, as I see it, you've got holdouts in both parties – a handful of conservative Dixiecrats and a handful of closet moderates on the Republican side of the aisle. A few owe me favors, a few could be seduced with enticing political perks and the rest – well, I could make a nuisance of myself and wear them down."

"I'm not expecting miracles," the President cautioned.

"Good. That way you'll be overjoyed when we succeed."

"What else do you bring to the table?"

"How are relations with military brass?" asked Singleton.

"Could be better," Hartman conceded.

"I daresay it could. Slashing the defense budget with a

war on terror still in effect didn't make you the most popular Commander-in-Chief. Oh, I know the statistics are on your side – we've got leaner and meaner forces, but it's still a hard pill for the brass to swallow. I've got lots of friends in every branch. I could definitely cool down the chicken hawks and put smiles on the faces of the Joint Chiefs of Staff."

"That I'd like to see," the President quipped.

"I'm not selling you a bill of goods, Mr. President," Singleton earnestly asserted, looking Hartman directly in the eyes. "I'm the real deal." The President did not reply, but his silence all but confirmed that he agreed.

Later in the day, Hartman met with Redmond and Davidson in the Oval Office with the intention of relating his discussion with Harley Singleton. But by the look on Redmond's face, something was amiss. "What's wrong, Sam?" asked the President.

"It's about...Gardner," Redmond said with an unusually hesitant tone.

"What about him?"

"Well, for the most part, he came up clean in the preliminary background checks."

"But?"

Redmond regarded Davidson before answering. "Buried in his military records is an item about an inquiry during basic training at Fort Bragg."

"An inquiry pertaining to what?"

"An allegation that Private Paul Edwin Gardner had engaged in... shall we say ... inappropriate sexual conduct with a fellow recruit."

The President leaned against the edge of his desk and folded his arms. "What was the outcome of the inquiry?" he asked.

"Charges dismissed."

"Well, there you go. He was cleared."

"Mmm," Redmond concurred coyly.

"So?"

"Well, sir, something else came up in our research. As recently as a year ago, a Charleston newspaper was approached by a man claiming to have had a liaison with the Governor one night in his limo."

"Did he have proof?"

"No, which is why the paper never ran the story. They couldn't corroborate the source's account. However, several other anonymous sources maintained that the Governor was 'seen' at a gay bar in Chicago."

"Chicago? What would he be doing there?"

"Attending the National Governors Conference."

"We are talking about Paul Gardner, the Governor of West Virginia, right?" the President wondered skeptically. "I mean, the man is the closest thing we have to a family values candidate in the Democratic Party. Do you expect me to believe that he is a closet homosexual?"

"No, sir, I don't expect *you* to believe it," Redmond responded. "But I do expect the press and the public to question it if it's put out there."

"You think a Senate committee would touch this?"

"I wouldn't put it past them," said Davidson cynically. "And it wouldn't matter whether it was true or not. Simply raising the allegation could be devastating."

"Shit," the President muttered, putting a hand to his brow and massaging his temples. "I was counting on Gardner as my alternative to Harley Singleton."

"I don't think you'll need your alternative," Davidson advised. "But if you do, there's always Governor Caine. One thing's for sure – we can't afford to risk a media feeding frenzy over Gardner. Besides, it's not as if his nomination were absolutely necessary."

"Fine, fine," the President agreed with a hint of aggravation. "That boils it down to Singleton and Caine."

"For what it's worth," added Davidson. "I think those two were our best choices all along. Either one would sail through confirmation and prove to be an asset to the administration. It's your choice, but whichever way you go, you can't lose."

"I suppose not," said Hartman, staring at the presidential seal emblazoned on the carpet before him. "But I need time to think about this."

Davidson and Redmond exchanged glances. "Of course," they said in unison.

Following the meeting, Davidson returned to his office to find a surprise guest.

"Mrs. Hartman …"

"No need to be so formal, Hunter," the First Lady replied. "After all, we've known each other for quite some time."

"To what do I owe the pleasure of this visit?" asked Davidson.

"A personal matter," said Irene, discreetly closing the door and turning to face him. "There's something I need to ask you." She paused and pursed her lips, finding it difficult to broach whatever was on her mind. "It's about … Shannon Cole," she revealed.

Suddenly, Davidson found it hard to maintain eye contact.

"Were you aware," asked the First Lady, "that my husband actually *did* have an affair with that woman?"

"Irene …" Davidson demurred. "Why go there? It was three years ago …"

"Please answer my question. Did you know?"

Squirming on the spot, Davidson bit his lower lip, then admitted, "Yes."

"When did you know?"'

"Shortly after it happened."

"Before the story broke?"

"Yes," Davidson replied, hastening to add, "I found out and I confronted Jim about it."

"You told him to break it off because it could ruin his campaign," Irene surmised.

"Something like that," Davidson reluctantly confirmed.

"So you knew before I did."

"Yes, I did."

"So he confessed to you, but not to me. Instead, the two of you lied to everyone – including me – and denied it."

"In fairness to the President," said Davidson, "he wanted to tell you the truth, but I was the one who discouraged him. I knew you'd be hurt and there was no way he could be honest about what happened. The press would have crucified him … and humiliated you in the process."

"No," Irene begged to differ, her eyes glaring like burning coals. "He waited until the election was won. It was all about protecting his candidacy."

"Irene … hasn't he paid enough for his mistake?" Davidson feebly cajoled. "You want a bad guy? It's me. Hate me, not your husband."

A corner of Irene's mouth stretched into a sad smirk. "I don't hate you, Hunter," she replied. "I'm just disappointed. I considered you more than just a campaign manager, more than an employee. You were a family friend."

Sincerely humbled, Davidson offered, "For what it's worth … I'm sorry."

Irene crossed her arms and gazed off reflectively. "He's going to run again, isn't he?"

"More than likely," Davidson speculated. "I certainly hope so. But I guess that'll depend on you."

She looked at him quizzically. "On me?"

"Your support means more to him than any other factor."

"I doubt that," Irene scoffed. "Jim has a mind of his own. Always has. By the way, any idea who he'll pick to succeed Clayton?"

Davidson hesitated, more out of uncertainty than the vetting team's code of silence.

"It's Singleton, isn't it?" Irene deduced cynically.

Davidson shrugged. "It's the logical choice. Don't you think?"

"It doesn't matter what I think, Hunter," she replied. "It never has."

Before Davidson could disagree, Irene opened the door and walked out, leaving him with much to consider–and much to regret.

Chapter 21

For their "third date," the punctual Mr. L had decided to arrive later than usual, whilst Mr. M made a half-hearted effort to arrive sooner rather than later. Consequently, both men met up at virtually the same time. It was a pleasant spring day for a change – scarcely a cloud in the sky and only a light breeze that barely rustled the trees and sent subtle ripples across the Potomac. Mr. L waited until he had settled on the park bench and passersby were out of earshot before he spoke. "I take it traffic has improved," he quipped.

Expecting a barbed retort, he was surprised when Mr. M failed to take the bait and instead took his place beside him, raised his face to the bright sunshine and replied, "Yeah, life is good."

"Lovely," Mr. L acerbically concurred, hardly in the mood to stop and smell the roses. "Well, since you're here on time for a change," he said, "we can make this short and sweet ..."

"Before you continue," Mr. M interrupted, "there's something I'd like to talk about."

Mr. L glanced at him curiously. "Well?"

Mr. M hesitated, then said, "Look, I know you don't want to talk about what we're doing ..."

"That's right," Mr. L replied with a condescending sigh. "I don't. As I've explained before, there's nothing to talk about. Ours is a very simple process. No reason to complicate things by discussing it."

"Still, you've got to wonder," Mr. M persisted, "why we're being paid so well to do what we're doing."

"But you see, I *don't* wonder about it," Mr. L insisted. "It's not my job to wonder about it. My job – and yours – is simply to exchange messages, nothing more and nothing less."

"But what do these messages mean? What is their significance?"

"Why do you care?"

"Because I do. Because it's human nature to be curious. I'm also concerned."

"Concerned? Concerned about what?"

"The ramifications," Mr. M replied. "For all we know we could be passing state secrets to a foreign power. Or unwittingly engaging in industrial espionage. Or … or … some kind of plot."

Mr. L bowed his head and chuckled. "The ramifications …" he muttered. "As I told you from the outset – the last thing you want to know is the ramifications. They're just words. Leave it at that."

"When I was a student at Georgetown …" Mr. M declared.

"Uh-uh-uh …" Mr. L cut him off, raising a hand in protest. "I told you, I don't want to know anything about you. So just hold your tongue and listen …"

"No!" Mr. M snapped. "You're going to listen to me."

Paying no heed, Mr. L announced, "Today's message is 'black bishop to white pawn four.'"

"As I was saying," Mr. M sternly retorted, "when I was a student at Georgetown …"

"I'm not listening," Mr. L grumbled, rising from the bench and starting to walk away. "Good day."

"I won't pass along the message," Mr. M threatened.

Mr. L paused and turned on his heels to face him. "What was that?"

"I won't pass along the message," Mr. M repeated. "I won't pass along the message unless you sit down and listen to me."

"Don't be ridiculous," Mr. L scoffed derisively. "You have no choice. You have to pass the message along."

"I do … and I won't," warned Mr. M. "Instead, I'll tell Mr. N that you never showed up for our meeting. That would disrupt things, wouldn't it?"

"You really are a rank amateur," Mr. L balked.

"If you want me to pass along the message," Mr. M obstinately persisted, "you'll sit down and listen to what I have to say."

Mr. L looked toward the river, bristling with anger. Who did this boy think he was? Why was he being so difficult? He had a mind to report him. But what good would that do? It would only disrupt the flow of information. God, how he hated complications. Grudgingly, Mr. L returned to the bench and sat down.

"When I was a student at Georgetown," Mr. M said once again, "I never thought I would become involved in this type of work. One minute I'm just an average sophomore struggling to maintain his grade-point average, and then I'm suddenly approached by a guy in a two thousand dollar suit and offered a job as a 'special courier.' He made it sound so intriguing – certainly a lot more interesting than my boring little life – and Lord knows, I needed the money, especially with the student loans I've been piling up. I thought, what the heck. So here I am, sitting on a park bench with you, playing telephone. Only neither one of us has a clue what's really going on … or what it's leading to."

Mr. L remained silent. It was enough that he had to tolerate Mr. M's self-indulgent soul-searching – there was no need to bear his sullen soul as well.

"How about you?" asked Mr. M. "How did you get into this business?"

"I'm not about to divulge any personal information," Mr. L tersely replied.

Mr. L rolled his tongue in his cheek, then playfully inquired, "What was that message again? White knight to black queen?"

"Black bishop to white pawn four," Mr. L corrected.

"Oh, right. White queen to black rook," Mr. M teased.

Mr. L turned his head and glared at him. "I could have you reported …"

"To whom? Mr. K?"

"This is not how it works."

"Tell me one personal thing about you," Mr. M persisted, "and I'll let you off the hook."

"This is absurd."

"I'll make it easy for you. Just answer this question – where are you from? Where were you born and raised?"

Mr. L hesitated, but seeing as he had no choice and had to tell Mr. M something, he finally replied, "Sacramento, California."

Mr. M smiled. "You're lying."

"How would you know?"

"Your accent," Mr. M replied. "I was a speech major at Georgetown. My specialty was linguistics. That was probably one of the reasons I was recruited for this job."

"Well, if that's the case," Mr. L challenged, "why don't you tell me where I'm really from?"

"Midwest … originally," Mr. M surmised. "Southern Ohio. Cincinnati, I would imagine. Although you've got a trace of northern Virginia. That's probably where you live now. Alexandria, I'll bet."

Mr. L's stunned silence confirmed Mr. M's suspicions.

"I was born in Wisconsin myself," Mr. M offered, "in a suburb of Milwaukee."

"You're overstepping the boundaries," Mr. L insisted uneasily.

"Am I?" wondered Mr. M. "And why is that? Because too much information is a dangerous thing?"

Mr. L refrained from answering what he dismissed as a rhetorical question.

But Mr. M was relentless. "I don't suppose you'd tell me why you're a part of all this?"

Indeed, Mr. L would not, stoically avoiding eye contact.

"Actually, you don't have to tell me anything," Mr. L mused. "I'm a fairly good study of people. For example, I'll bet you were once married, but now you live alone."

Mr. L stiffened. Was he that much of an open book or was Mr. L that shrewdly observant?

"Widowed or divorced?" Mr. M considered aloud. "Hmm. I'm guessing divorced."

"Are you quite finished?" said Mr. L in awkward exasperation, picking imaginary lint off his trousers.

"Almost," said Mr. M with a merciless smile.

"What makes you such an expert on people, anyway?"

"It's quite simple," Mr. M contended. "The more one conceals, the more one reveals."

That got at least a fleeting glance from Mr. L, who was beginning to see his counterpart in a different light.

"Black bishop to red pawn four?" said Mr. M, finally relenting.

Mr. L nodded and looked away. While he sat and gazed at his favorite monument, Mr. M surreptitiously disappeared.

After several moments of quiet reflection, Mr. L did the same, wandering along the river walk for a spell before leaving the park. *How did I get into this business*, he briefly wondered before dispelling the thought, thankful for being blessed with a selective memory.

At the conclusion of his daily national security briefing, President Hartman gratefully dismissed Redmond and summoned Hunter Davidson to the Oval Office. As the Chief of Staff entered the room, he found the President sitting pensively in his favorite chair by the bare fireplace.

Looking up, Hartman flashed a quick, thoughtful smile. "Hunt, I've reached a decision on Clayton's replacement," he unceremoniously announced. "I wanted you to be the first to know."

Without saying a word, Davidson crossed the room and sat down on the couch opposite the President. He leaned forward, folded his hands and rested his forearms on his knees, awaiting the final verdict.

"I must admit that I was impressed with Governor Caine's performance in his recent interview," said the President. "In fact, I may have underestimated him. He's bright, articulate and his executive skills certainly qualify him for higher office. I have no doubt he'll be a political force to reckon with in the years ahead. However ..."

Davidson hung on the dramatic pause.

"Weighed against Harley Singleton's experience and gravitas," the President continued, "I don't think Governor Caine quite measures up. I don't think anyone on the horizon does at this particular time."

Davidson withheld comment. Instead, he continued to listen, allowing the President to explain his choice.

"I've never been a risk taker, you know that," Hartman rationalized. "Choosing Hamilton Caine would certainly shake things up. It would generate great press and probably energize the party in the short term. But for the long haul, I think Harley is more prepared and equipped for the role of Vice President. He has the depth of congressional, foreign policy and military experience that we need. He also has the temperament for the job ... and mine, if necessary. It's a safe move for this administration and, I believe, the right thing for the country. As far as I'm concerned, he's our man. Do you agree?"

Davidson nodded solemnly. "Yes, Mr. President. I do."

"Any misgivings?"

Davidson shook his head. "None. All things considered, it's a slam-dunk."

"Alright then," the President sighed, rising from his chair, obviously relieved. "I'll place the call to Harley later this afternoon and extend the formal offer. If he accepts – which we both know he will – we'll make an official announcement tomorrow. In the meantime, you can share this with the other members of our search team, but with strict instructions not to leak it to anyone."

"Yes, sir," said Davidson. Then, with a smile, he stood up, reached over and extended his hand. "Congratulations, Mr. President."

Savoring the historic moment, the two men shook on it.

But no sooner had Davidson left the room than Hartman caught sight of Irene's framed photograph propped on a nearby end table and found himself pondering. The picture had been taken several years earlier, back before the presidential campaign, back when she was younger and happier, back when they shared more than a festering secret. It was enough to make him wonder for a moment if, indeed, he was doing the right thing.

Chapter 22

In his dream, Burnett was back in high school, anxiously combing endless, empty, interconnected hallways lined with identical lockers, searching in vain for Mr. Padella's homeroom where he was already late for his algebra final. He had been absent from the class all term and if he didn't take the examination and pass, he wouldn't graduate. Desperation was beginning to set in and the more urgently he plodded, the longer the distance and slower the pace, until he turned a corner and found himself at a dead end. He paused and swirled around and around, lost and confused, wondering where that knocking sound was coming from.

The next thing he knew his eyes fluttered open and he was looking up from a reclining position at the deadpan face of a highway patrol officer tapping on his car window. He abruptly brought his backrest up to the sitting position and hastily rolled down the window.

"Good morning," said the cop sarcastically. "License, please."

Barely awake, Burnett fumbled for his wallet. "I just stopped to rest," he explained. "This is a rest area, isn't it?"

"Actually, you've been here all night," the officer informed him. "You were spotted at about 11 p.m., then at 4 a.m. and now at 8:15. Yeah, it's a rest area .... not a motel."

Burnett handed him his driver's license. "I was pretty exhausted," he said. "I didn't want to drive while drowsy, so I pulled in here. I just meant to be here for a half hour or so. I didn't expect to sleep through the night. Honestly."

"What brings you to Louisiana, Mr. Burnett?" the officer inquired, noticing his D.C. address.

"I was on a business trip. I'm on my way to New Orleans."

"Ah-huh," said the cop, handing back the license. "Well, then you'd best be on your way."

"Yes, officer," Burnett agreed, buckling up and starting his engine. "Thanks for the wake-up call."

The officer smirked, then walked off toward his own vehicle parked nearby.

In a minute, Burnett was back on the highway, cruising in the right lane at five miles per hour under the speed limit. He glanced at his rearview mirror and noticed the patrol car following and maintained his lawful velocity. After a few miles, however, the patrol car veered off an exit and Burnett was free to burn some rubber and make up for lost time.

Skipping breakfast, he reached the outskirts of New Orleans by 10 a.m. But that's where he ran into heavy traffic around some roadway construction sites. The congestion of gridlocked vehicles continued for several miles, killing more time and sending Burnett's anxiety level to a new threshold. "Come on!" he snapped at one point, honking like a madman when a van in front of him allowed several other cars to merge into a single lane.

But once the final roadblock had been circumvented, the highway expanded once again into multiple lanes of traffic, allowing him to speed to his destination. He delivered the car at the appropriate airport drop-off point just before noon, then hastily headed for the nearest ticket counter. He purchased a ticket on a flight leaving for Atlanta in less than an hour with only a half an hour stopover until a connecting flight to D.C. After clearing security, he had just enough time for a hot dog and beverage before boarding.

But when Burnett arrived in Atlanta at 2:30 p.m., he discovered that his connecting flight, along with many others, was delayed due to severe weather in the South East. With no choice but to wait, he plopped himself down on a seat near the boarding gate and watched the newscast on an overhead television. He tuned out a series of reports on a shooting spree in North Dakota, a political demonstration in Chile and an insider trading scandal on Wall Street, but his ears perked up when attention was focused on a more relevant topic:

"Fox News has confirmed that Former Texas Governor and Senator Harley Singleton met yesterday with President Hartman at the White House, raising speculation that Singleton will be the President's eventual choice to replace the late Vice President Clayton Talbot. According to an unnamed White House source, Singleton's nomination is almost a certainty and may be announced as early as tomorrow …"

"Oh, great," Burnett muttered, springing to his feet and searching for the nearest telephone bank.

When he found a vacant unit, he directly dialed a number in the West Wing of the White House. "Pauline?"

"Gid?" she replied brightly. "Is that you?"

"Yeah."

"Where are you?"

"Atlanta. I'm waiting to board a flight back to D.C. Listen, I need your help."

"What is it?"

Burnett took a deep breath. "I need a one-on-one with the President."

There was a pause on the other end of the line. "What? Are you joking?"

"I'm afraid not. I need to talk with the President face-to-face."

She sounded puzzled. "And … why would you need to do that?"

"I have some information he needs to hear and some documents he needs to see."

"Can't you run it by me or Davidson?"

"We don't have time," Burnett insisted. "I need to meet with the President as soon as I get to Washington. This evening. And you need to arrange it."

"*Tonight*? Are you crazy? I can't just …"

"Pauline!" Burnett cut her off. "This is urgent. I'm serious." He lowered his voice and practically whispered into the phone so no one around him could hear. "If the President chooses Harley Singleton for the VP spot, he'll be making a disastrous mistake."

"But it's a done deal," Pauline revealed. "The President has already offered the job and Singleton has accepted."

"Well, I'm afraid it's going to have to be undone."

"What's this all about, anyway?" Pauline demanded to know. "At least tell me that."

Burnett hesitated, then explained, "Singleton is linked to Uniplex and Malcolm Everett Tate. He's knee-deep in all sorts of corruption."

"Come on, Gid," Pauline scoffed. "If that were true, it would've come up in the vetting process."

"Not if the parties involved kept a tight lid on it. Look, I have the evidence he needs to see, but it's for his eyes only and I'm the only one who can show it to him. Please! I need you as the go-between."

"But I'll have to go through Davidson," Pauline fretted.

"Then, *do it*," Burnett firmly advised. "It's either that or I go straight to press after the nomination is announced and the administration will have a scandal on its hands that'll make Watergate, Iran-Contra and Monica look like sideshows."

"Gid," said Pauline, plainly uneasy, "you're putting me in a dangerous situation."

"You're putting the President in a dangerous situation if you don't do what I ask," he replied. "As soon as I get to D.C., I'm heading for the White House. Just make it happen."

Before Pauline could say anything else, Burnett hung up. She lowered the receiver and stared anxiously at the digital clock on her desk. Only Hannah Goodwin's sudden appearance in her doorway startled Pauline out of her reverie.

"Excuse me," said Hannah. "Just wanted to remind you of my dental appointment at four. Unless you need anything, I'll be leaving now."

"No," Pauline replied. "That's fine."

"Is everything okay?" asked Hannah, sensing Pauline's anxiety. "Are you alright?"

Pauline tried to compose herself. "Yeah, I'm fine," she said. "You'd better get moving for your appointment. I'll see you tomorrow." Then she gathered herself and headed for Davidson's office.

He looked surprised to see her. "What's up?" he asked.

Pauline took a deep breath, stepped into the office and closed the door behind her. Turning to face Davidson, she said, "We need to talk."

"Where to?" asked the cabbie, a middle-aged, bearded man of Jamaican descent who had spent a half an hour in queue waiting for his next fare when his conversation with a fellow driver had been brought to an abrupt halt by an airport passenger who curiously was not carrying any luggage.

"1600 Pennsylvania Avenue," Burnett replied.

The driver scrutinized him in his rear view mirror.

"*Tonight*," Burnett stressed.

The cabbie rolled his eyes, then turned on the meter and pulled away from the curb.

Traffic was relatively light that evening. Within minutes they were out of the airport and on the interstate. Only then did the cabbie regard his passenger in the mirror again and noticed how tense and unkempt he looked. Feeling a bit uneasy himself, the driver inquired, "You alright, man?"

Looking out the window at cars passing in the opposite direction, Burnett muttered, "I hope so."

Neither one of them said anything else for the rest of the ride.

When the taxi reached the outer perimeter of the White House, Burnett told the driver to pull over. He handed the cabbie a hundred dollar bill and got out on the street. Then, clutching the envelope close to his chest, he walked several hundred feet to the guard house at the front gate and presented his press credentials. He was informed that Pauline had authorized his after-hours visit. *Good girl*, thought Burnett.

After undergoing a routine search, he was then escorted by security personnel up the long driveway to a side entrance into the building. Once again, his press credentials were reviewed, his body scanned with a magnetic wand and sent through a metal detector while jewelry, keys and the envelope were sent through an X-ray machine. On the other side, he retrieved his items from the conveyer belt, attached his press pass to his lapel and was then escorted by a uniformed guard through the corridors to the West Wing.

It was the first time Burnett had actually been in the Oval Office and he was surprised that it seemed a bit smaller than it appeared in photographs and on television. Of course, he didn't have much time to survey his surroundings, for his attention was immediately drawn to President Hartman himself and Chief of Staff Hunter Davidson who stood in the middle of the room, hands at their sides, awaiting his arrival with serious expressions on their faces.

"Mr. Burnett," Hartman acknowledged.

"Mr. President," he replied with a quick nod. "Mr. Davidson."

"What happened to you?" asked the President, noticing the stubble on Burnett's face and what looked like a bruise on his chin and a burn on his cheek.

"Please excuse my appearance," the journalist self-consciously murmured. "It's been a rough 36 hours."

"I've been told you have something rather important to share with us," said the President, wanting to dispense with any pleasantries and get right to the point.

"Yes, sir," Burnett confirmed, clutching his envelope a little tighter. "Thank you for allowing me the time … I know this is rather unorthodox," he admitted, "but … I have come into possession of certain documents related to Harley Singleton, who I understand has been offered the Vice Presidency."

The President tried to maintain a poker face, but was obviously startled by Burnett's assertion. "I can neither confirm nor deny that," he automatically replied.

"Yes, well, assuming he is *one* of your choices, I think it's critical you see these documents," said Burnett, offering the envelope to Davidson, who reluctantly accepted it.

"And why is that, Mr. Burnett?" asked the President.

"Because, sir, these documents indicate that Singleton is beholden to Uniplex Industries. The Chairman of that corporation, as you well know, is Malcolm Everett Tate, who has worked vigorously in the past – and is probably working now – to undermine your administration."

Burnett tried to read the President's inscrutable expression. He was either skeptical or had been genuinely blindsided and trying not to look like a gullible fool. Either way, he was not betraying his immediate reaction.

"What makes you think Harley Singleton is even in contention?" asked Davidson, curious as to where Burnett got his information.

"I have my sources," Gideon replied.

"I'll bet you do," Davidson frigidly remarked. "I don't suppose that source would be Ms. Cafferty?"

"That shouldn't be your concern at the moment," Burnett responded. "What's important is that a man you're about to entrust with the second most important job in our government is associated with your shrewdest – and most treacherous – political enemy."

The President glanced at Davidson, then back to Burnett. "Okay, you have my attention. Let's see what you've got."

Davidson opened the envelope, removed the contents and handed them to the President. As Hartman examined the evidence and then handed it to Davidson for his review, Burnett watched intently as the President's countenance became more transparent, shifting from intense scrutiny to dull realization to seething suspicion.

"Where did you get this?" asked Davidson.

"From a former employee at Uniplex," Burnett honestly replied.

"And how did *he* get it?"

"He was involved in the operation and had access to restricted files."

"So he stole it?"

"What difference does it make?"

"Well, actually, Mr. Burnett, it makes a lot of difference. This material wasn't obtained legally. If it's real, it might not be admissible in a court of law."

"That's not the point, *Mr. Davidson*," Burnett sharply replied. "This isn't about indicting anybody. It's about informing the White House of a serious conflict of interest. Would you have rather seen this *after* the President nominated Harley Singleton or after he was confirmed by the Senate?"

"Who's to say this is authentic?" Davidson challenged. "The FBI and other agencies did background checks on Singleton and they didn't come up with anything. But we're supposed to take the word of a former employee of Uniplex? A disgruntled one, I take it."

"You're missing the big picture here," Burnett maintained. "I'm not 100 percent sure this is real, either. But I can tell you that since I got involved in this, there have been people out to stop me from getting this information into your hands. Now why is that?"

"All I'm saying," Davidson argued, "is that all of this could have been forged or doctored by someone who has a grudge against Harley Singleton."

"Oh, come on," scoffed Burnett. "If you have your doubts, run it by the FBI or whoever can verify its authenticity."

"Oh, don't worry," Davidson assured him. "We will, Mr. Burnett. And while we're at it, we'll have the Bureau take a close look at you and your recent activities."

"Hunt," the President interceded.

The room was quiet for a moment, then the President asked, "The alleged whistleblower who supplied this information ... what is his name?"

"I can't disclose that, sir," Burnett replied.

"But you did a background check?"

"I verified his employment, yes. He was a highly-placed executive at Uniplex."

"And what were you planning to do with this information, Mr. Burnett?'

"Sir?"

"If true, it's highly incriminating for Senator Singleton – not to mention a potential source of embarrassment for this administration."

"Ha, you think?"

"Disclosure wouldn't serve any useful purpose."

"Sir," Burnett replied. "You have no idea what I've gone through to obtain this evidence. I have literally risked my life to get the story and … mind you … I came here to warn you. I didn't have to do that, Mr. President. I could have gone straight to my editor."

"I understand," said the President obligingly. "And I appreciate that you came to me first. However, I would appreciate it even more if this … revelation never left the room."

"Mr. President, I am a journalist," Burnett pointed out. "I have an obligation to my readers. And you have an obligation to the American people. Burying this story would compromise both of us. I can't …"

"So, what is it that you want?" the President bluntly inquired.

"Excuse me, sir?" Burnett did a double-take.

Hartman stepped forward and looked him in the eyes. "How can we … accommodate you in return for your … indulgence?"

"Well, Mr. President …" Burnett chuckled uneasily. "It'll take a lot more than getting the first question at a White House press conference."

"How does an exclusive sound?"

"What kind of an exclusive?"

"You can break the story of our eventual choice for Vice President. We'll let you know hours before the official announcement. That ought to be worth some bragging rights."

"Well," Burnett mused. "That would be a start."

"What else do you want?" Davidson asked with an edge of irritation.

"The first interview with the VP designate," said Burnett without hesitation.

Davidson looked to the President. "Agreed," said Hartman.

"Thank you," said Burnett, suppressing a smile of smug satisfaction.

"So you won't use this?" Davidson nervously confirmed, raising the documents in both hands.

Burnett shook his head. "It'll be your dirty little secret."

"Is there anything else we need to discuss?" asked the President, anxious to bring the meeting to a close.

"No. I think that'll do for one night," said Gideon. "May I ask when you'll be making your final decision on Vice President Talbot's replacement, sir?"

"Shortly," the President replied, adding solemnly, "and you'll be among the first to know."

"Well …" said Burnett, backing away. "Good night, gentlemen." Then he turned and left the room.

As soon as the door closed, Davidson turned to the President. "This can't be real," he insisted, referring to the documents. "How could we have missed it in the vetting process? This has got to be a set-up from someone opposed to Singleton."

"Well, there's only one way to find out," the President responded.

"I can give it to Wyler at FBI. If anyone can verify the authenticity – and be trusted to keep the whole thing quiet – it's him."

"I was referring to Harley," said the President. "He needs to be confronted with this accusation."

"What makes you think he'll be forthcoming? Even if the evidence is real, he'll just deny it. We should at least verify its legitimacy."

"I don't want to share it with anyone else," the President declared, relieving Davidson of the documents. "I don't want to risk a shred of this going public. I just need to talk to Harley again. I'll know if he's guilty or not."

Meanwhile, Burnett found Pauline waiting for him outside the Oval Office. "Hey," he acknowledged.

She put a finger to her lips to caution silence, then beckoned him down the hallway to her office. There, she hastily closed the door and leaned against it looking breathless. "You look like hell," she observed.

"Well, that's a fine how-do-you-do," said Burnett, having expected a more empathetic greeting.

"How did it go?" she asked.

"The meeting? It went well … under the circumstances."

"Did they question you about me?"

"You? No, it wasn't about *you*."

"Thank God," Pauline sighed, only marginally relieved. "When I told Davidson why you needed to meet with the President, he had this look on his face …"

"What are you talking about?"

"He knows about us, our relationship …"

"Of course he does. So what?"

"So I'm sure he's convinced I told you Singleton was the President's pick for vice president."

"Which you did," Burnett playfully pointed out.

"So what does that make me?" Pauline agonized.

"The White House snitch?" Burnett teased.

"This isn't funny, Gid," she warned.

"Relax," he told her, taking her in his arms for a reassuring hug. "Davidson and the President have more pressing matters than who said what to whom. Actually, you did them a favor by confiding in me."

"How do you figure?" Pauline asked, her head nestled against his chest.

"You and I just saved them from making a catastrophic choice."

Chapter 23

The next day, Harley Singleton arrived at the White House promptly at 10 a.m. Summoned by the President through Chief of Staff Davidson, he assumed the get-together was to prepare for the imminent announcement of his nomination for the vice presidency. Buoyed by that assumption, he entered the Oval Office with a broad grin on his face only to find the President standing behind his desk, staring out the window.

"Good morning, Mr. President," Singleton cheerfully greeted. But when the President failed to respond, his toothy grin slowly dissolved.

"Tell me about Uniplex," Hartman intoned, turning to face his visitor.

Singleton wasn't sure he had heard correctly. "Excuse me?" he asked.

"Uniplex Industries," the President distinctly repeated. "What is your relationship with that company ... and Malcolm Everett Tate?"

Singleton looked bewildered. "I don't have a relationship with either," he evenly maintained.

"Never accepted a campaign contribution from them in your long political career?"

"Not that I recall."

"Never met Tate?"

"Oh, I've met him, all right," Singleton conceded. "Long ago at a conference in Dallas when I was governor. Exchanged a few words. That was about it."

The President bowed his head and arched his eyebrows. "Was it?"

"Was it, what, Mr. President?"

"Was that all?"

Singleton looked convincingly befuddled. "I'm sorry, but I don't understand what you're getting at, sir."

"You've been in public service for decades," the President noted, sauntering around his desk and drifting toward Singleton. "You've dealt with thousands of people in government and the private sector," he said, pausing when he was eye to eye, "and you're telling me you've never been associated with Uniplex or Tate?"

"Well," Singleton replied with an awkward snicker, "we've all had our share of corporate contributors and dealings with various lobbyists – it comes with the territory. If Uniplex legally donated to one of my campaigns and I wasn't aware of it … "

"I'm talking about something considerably more intimate," the President clarified. "I'm talking about an arrangement – money laundering, influence peddling, bribery."

"Hell, no!" Singleton exclaimed, looking righteously offended.

The President relented for a moment, pivoting toward his desk to retrieve a certain stack of papers. Turning back to Singleton, he said, "Then perhaps you can tell me what this is all about," slapping the documents against his chest.

Startled, Singleton took possession of the papers and curiously reviewed them. In short order, his puzzled expression transformed into one of pale apprehension. There was page upon page of communiqués, e-mails and photocopied checks. The dated messages were between high-level executives and Singleton's gubernatorial and Senate offices, the checks made out to cash and deposited in the same offshore account. "Mr. President …" he managed breathlessly. "I don't understand …"

"Oh, I think you do," Hartman begged to differ. "The evidence is right in your hands."

"I'm telling you, I am in no way associated with Mr. Tate or any of his companies," Singleton maintained. "This material must have been falsified."

"That's what I suspected at first," said Hartman, "but we dug a little deeper. You just so happen to own a condominium a block away from the bank where these checks were deposited."

"That doesn't prove anything."

"*And*," the President added, "the dates of these payoffs approximately coincide with key votes involving energy policy and military appropriations in the Texas state legislature and the U.S. Congress."

"Circumstantial at best," Singleton scoffed. "This is … this is hogwash!" he declared, dumping the documents on the President's desk. "Someone's doing a hatchet job on me."

"Then perhaps we should turn this information over to the Justice Department," Hartman suggested.

Singleton's face suddenly turned livid. "Justice?" he balked. "W-why involve them?"

"Why not? I'm sure they could get to the bottom of all this. Or is that what you're afraid of, Harley?"

"No, no," Singleton insisted. "It's just … it'll just open a can of worms. And if any of this gets out, I'll be found guilty by implication."

The President looked deeply into his eyes and saw something he had seen many times back when he was a prosecutor. Unable to conceal his disappointment, he took a cleansing breath and sadly declared, "Harley, I will not be placing your name in nomination for the vice presidency."

Singleton smiled feebly and blinked several times. "I- I don't understand," he stammered.

"It's not necessarily the payoffs that disturb me, Harley," the

President explained. "It's the duplicity -- passing yourself off as a reborn environmentalist while all the while being in bed with Tate."

"But that was all in the past," Singleton contended. "I publicly came out in support of your Energy Bill more than a year ago."

"Yes, you did. However, the key word here is 'publicly.' How do I know where your true allegiance lies?"

"Mr. President, you have my word …"

"*Your word*?" the President angrily responded. "Your word means nothing to me now! You were less than honest with me from the outset about your affiliations. But what I find most unforgiveable, Harley, is that you've put me in a truly untenable position. Now I have to withhold information not only to spare your reputation, but to spare this administration from ridicule. Do you know how that makes me feel? Like a cheap, common politician!"

Seething, Hartman crossed the room to pour himself a glass of water.

Jolted, Singleton struggled to maintain his composure. Grasping at straws, he pleaded, "Don't you find it a bit odd, Mr. President, that this information should find its way into your hands at this particular moment?"

"You mean, in the nick of time?" Hartman wryly retorted.

"Has it occurred to you, sir, that someone may be deliberately trying to besmirch me and influence your decision?"

"What has occurred to me, Harley, is that you've been less than forthcoming with me and my vetting team, not to mention the American people."

"I never meant to deceive you, Mr. President," said Singleton, sounding genuinely remorseful. "What I did … or may have done … in the past does not reflect who I am now … and who I will be in the future."

The President took a drink. Then he replied, "Be that as it may, I cannot risk entrusting the vice presidency to someone with ties – direct or indirect – to this particular group of corporate criminals." He paused to reflect, then added, "What a pity. At least you would have been a competent vice president."

"Yes, I know," Singleton immodestly agreed. "Which is why I think you're making a huge mistake."

"My mistake," the President coldly replied, "was in even considering you for the job. Consider yourself lucky that you get to walk away with your legacy intact."

"Well," said Singleton, hardly disguising his bitterness, "that's awfully big of you. You know, this is the second time you've pulled the rug out from under me. I'm beginning to see why you have so many enemies, *sir*."

"Good day, Harley," the President bid. "And goodbye."

Marshalling what remained of his dignity, Singleton turned on his heels and left the room, slamming the door behind him.

A few moments later, Davidson entered unannounced.

"That was one of the hardest things I've ever had to do," the President conceded.

"You had no choice, sir," said the Chief of Staff.

"It's just a shame it had to come to this. If only I had listened to Irene."

"Sir?"

"She tried to dissuade me from choosing Harley. Of course, I did the contrary. I should have trusted her judgment."

Davidson noticed the documents on the President's desk. "What would you like to do with this?" he asked, organizing the papers into a neat pile.

The President shrugged. "It's not like we can put them back where we found them, can we? What do you suggest?"

"Our options are safekeeping or shredding. Unless we'll need them for leverage at a later date …"

"Shred them," Hartman said without hesitation.

"Are you sure?" asked Davidson.

"It's the lesser of two evils," Hartman rationalized. "Also, it's time to put all this unpleasantness behind us and move forward."

"Speaking of moving forward, sir ..."

The President raised his hand to halt Davidson in mid-sentence. He then moved to his desk and pressed the red button on his phone console. "Grace," he instructed, "get me Governor Caine on the phone."

"Yes, Mr. President," his personal secretary responded.

"And, Hunt," said Hartman to his Chief of Staff, "tell Pauline to schedule a press conference for tomorrow morning at 10 a.m."

Chapter 24

Hamilton and Sara Caine left the Governor's Mansion in Sacramento the next morning and boarded a private jet bound for Washington, D.C. No sooner had they been airborne than rumors started flying over the airwaves that the White House would shortly announce a new pick for Vice President.

Before their arrival, the inner circle of the Hartman administration hustled to make arrangements. Yet, unbeknownst to Press Secretary Pauline Cafferty, who was busy drafting the statement concerning Caine's nomination, another announcement would soon have to be prepared.

"Excuse me, Pauline," said Hunter Davidson in an uncharacteristically polite tone, suddenly standing in the doorway of her office. "The President would like to see us."

Seated at her desk, reviewing the final draft, Pauline glanced up. "Now?" she asked.

"Now," Davidson replied in a somber tone that struck Pauline as odd. She paused in her task to try and read his face. The fact that he was avoiding eye contact set her intuition into overdrive. Hesitantly, she rose from her seat and moved slowly to the front of the desk. Watching him, she realized that Davidson was deliberately inexpressive, usually a sign that something was amiss. But before she could ask what was wrong, he took off, forcing her to follow.

They didn't speak along the way to the Oval Office, which only fed her mounting sense of dread. Expect the worst, Pauline told herself. It was an old trick she had employed since childhood. If you always expected the worst, things wouldn't turn out so badly.

But when they reached the presidential anteroom and Davidson opened the door to the Oval Office without knocking, Pauline's pessimism seemed truly justified. Holding her breath, she entered the room, came to an abrupt halt and quivered when she saw the President standing at the front of his desk with his arms folded.

As Davidson closed the door behind her, Pauline slowly exhaled, her eyes fixed on the President's. "Please sit down, Pauline," he requested, his face an expressionless mask, his gaze cold and distant.

Pauline hesitated, unable to move. She noted that the President had not encouraged Davidson to sit. "If you don't mind, sir," she replied tentatively. "I'd rather stand."

Hartman pursed his lips and bowed his head, as if wrestling with a difficult decision. "Pauline," he eventually declared, "I'm afraid I'm going to have to ask you to tender your resignation as White House Press Secretary."

The initial shock made her feel lightheaded. Then, as the words resonated, Pauline's body began to quiver. Although not entirely unexpected, the moment seemed surreal. It took all of her intestinal fortitude to hold it together. "Sir …" she barely managed to reply.

"As you know," Hartman interrupted, "all conversations that take place within these walls are confidential unless otherwise authorized by the President. Whatever we discuss in here – however incidental or trivial it may seem – is privileged information. There's a reason for this policy. And you, of all people, should know that reason. You violated that policy. You violated my trust."

Pauline took a deep breath. "Sir," she responded, "if this is about Gideon Burnett, I can explain …"

"I don't want an explanation, Pauline," the President brusquely cut her off. "I'm well aware of your relationship with Mr. Burnett. Knowing that, I probably made a mistake in allowing you to be part of the vetting process. But I did make it clear that our discussions regarding Clayton's replacement were not to be shared with anyone else – especially a member of the press. You ignored that directive."

"Sir, I did not run to Gideon with this information," Pauline defensively maintained. "He knew you were leaning to Senator Singleton ..."

"Because you confirmed his suspicions."

Pauline looked toward Davidson, hoping for some support, some sympathy, but none was forthcoming. "Sir," she said, turning back to the President. "If Gideon hadn't come to you with what he had learned about Senator Singleton, you might have made a disastrous decision."

"I understand that," the President conceded. "Nevertheless ... I can not have a Press Secretary who can't keep a secret and lacks discretion."

"It was wrong," Pauline admitted, trying not to sound desperate. "But it did no harm. I apologize. I made a mistake in judgment. I assure you, it will never happen again."

"No, it won't," Hartman agreed ominously.

"Please, Mr. President," Pauline pleaded, her knees practically knocking. "My job means a lot to me. I think I've done it well for the last two and a half years. I ask your indulgence. Please, give me another chance."

As Pauline held her breath, the President's stoic expression seemed to soften. There was definitely a trace of regret and second-guessing. Perhaps he realized Pauline's long-standing value to his administration, or felt empathy for her situation having suffered his own share of ill-conceived acts of judgment. Surely his innate compassion would force him to reconsider. He glanced up at the ceiling and sighed, then looked into Pauline's imploring eyes and replied, "I'm sorry."

Pauline suppressed a whimper. Tears began to well in her eyes, but she promptly winked them away.

"Please submit a letter of resignation by the end of the day," the

President instructed. "Deputy Press Secretary Goodwin will assume your responsibilities starting tomorrow. We will issue a statement indicating that you resigned to pursue other interests. That'll be all."

Devastated, Pauline barely had the ability to turn and leave the room. But somehow she did. As she wandered through the corridors of the West Wing toward her office, she was oblivious to every person she passed. She didn't even hear Burnett calling out and hustling to catch up with her. When he grabbed her arm and turned her around, she jerked it away.

"What is it?" he asked, noticing her shell-shocked, pallid expression.

"I've been fired," she sullenly replied.

"*What*?" Gideon gaped. "Why?"

"Why? Because I leaked information. Because I confided in *you*."

"But that's crazy. If you hadn't confided in me …"

"I would still have my job!"

Pauline stormed off, but Burnett followed her straight into her office and away from any eavesdroppers.

"Do me a favor, Gid," she angrily said, turning on him. "Leave me alone."

"Look," he responded, trying to calm her down, "I know you're upset, but I'll talk to Davidson and …"

"No! You've done enough damage as it is."

"Seriously," he insisted. "I can fix this."

"I don't want you to … to fix it!" she shouted. "I just want you to leave. Okay? I never want to see you again. Ever."

"You don't mean that," Burnett scoffed, reaching out to take her in his arms.

"Don't!" she warned, pushing him away. "Don't … touch … me."

"Come on …" he murmured. "You know I care about you."

Pauline's glare transformed into a pained expression. "No, you don't," she declared. "You never did. You don't care anybody. Not even yourself. It's time we face the fact that there's nothing meaningful about this relationship."

"Aw, for Christ's sake," Gideon muttered, suddenly at a loss for words. Feebly, he extended his arms again.

"Just go," said Pauline, turning her back to him. "Please."

It's okay, Burnett told himself. *Just give her a little time and space. Let the dust settle and she'll come around.* So he did as she asked.

But as she listened to his retreating footfall, Pauline knew she was listening to him walking out her life for good. And with no one there to see it, she allowed herself to cry ever so softly and ever so briefly.

Chapter 25

As usual, Mr. L was early for his appointment. But much to his surprise, so was Mr. M.

There he was, slouched on the park bench, wearing a black parka, of all things, on a warm and sunny day, staring out at the drifting river as if mesmerized. Apparently, all of Mr. L's cajoling had finally gotten through to the young punk. It was an unexpected pleasure to see him cooling his own heels for a change. But why on earth did he look so glum?

"Been here long?" asked Mr. L, sidling down beside Mr. M and leisurely crossing his legs.

Mr. M slowly turned his head and stared at him for a moment. Then, snapping out of his peculiar reverie, he looked back at the river and replied, "No. No, not long. Not long at all."

"Well, at least you're on time for once," Mr. L smugly observed. "Is it too much to hope that you're finally getting the hang of this?"

He waited for the usual sarcastic answer, but Mr. M didn't respond. Perhaps he thought it was merely a rhetorical question.

"Well?" Mr. L persisted.

"Hm?" said Mr. M, again as if his mind were miles away.

"Nothing," Mr. L sighed. He, too, focused instead on the flowing river and the way the midday sun glistened on its choppy waves. What was the point of needling the young man? People are who they are, thought Mr. L, and all the criticism in the world wouldn't change them. Besides, maybe Mr. M was right – maybe this was nothing more than a fool's errand, exchanging coded messages whose significance they would never know – and in chess moves, no less. If so, then in the grand scheme of things, they were merely pawns in an elaborate and incomprehensible game.

A full minute passed in silence. During the lull, Mr. L regarded Mr. M from the corner of his eye. His profile was as fixed and rigid as a statue's, his arms obscured and apparently folded under his parka, everything about his body language suggested he was either lost in a trance or heavily sedated, which wouldn't surprise Mr. L in the least. Mr. M's behavior was worse than odd; it was downright uncharacteristic.

They would have stayed like this forever, Mr. L assumed, unless his impatience prompted him to finally remark, "I believe it's your turn today. Do you have a message for me?"

Mr. M turned his head to look at Mr. L, but said nothing.

Eventually, Mr. L looked his way as well, bewildered by the austere expression on Mr. M's face. "Well?" he asked. "What is it?"

Mr. M swallowed hard, then quietly said, "Checkmate."

Mr. L knitted his eyebrows in befuddlement and bemusement. Surely that couldn't be the message. "Check ..." he started to repeat, but paused abruptly as something jolted his ribcage, accompanied by a muted yet distinct popping sound.

Looking down, he noticed a hole in Mr. M's parka that was emitting a winding wisp of white smoke. Then he felt a sharp pain in his chest and a strange wetness oozing from his side. It took several seconds for him to realize what had happened, but when he did, he gazed at Mr. M with an expression of astonishment, then anger and, finally, sadness.

"Sorry," Mr. M muttered with genuine regret, his dark eyes boring into Mr. L's. "Orders," he lamely explained.

Of course, thought Mr. L, gasping for air and struggling to remain conscious. The chain had to be broken somewhere along the line.

No linkage, no accountability. But why him and not M or K or N? Why had he been deemed the most expendable to the operation? And who decided this? Didn't anybody value experience and competence anymore?

A moment later, his eyes grew heavy and slowly closed as he faded into the abyss of unknowing. His head slumped forward, but his body remained in a sitting position, making him look like a well-dressed vagrant napping in the park. All in all, not a bad way to die.

Remarkably calm, despite the fact that this was his first kill, Mr. M took a moment to reflect, as if he owed Mr. L at least that. Then, without further adieu, he rose to his feet and casually walked away from the bench and toward the nearest park exit.

There was no need to hurry. Besides, there were some things you just couldn't run away from. But he didn't look back and he didn't dwell on it. What's done was done, although he'd never be able to look at the river again in quite the same way.

Chapter 26

Confirmation hearings for Vice-President Designate Hamilton Caine began promptly at 9 a.m. on the third Monday in June. Testifying before the House Judiciary Committee and the Senate Rules Committee, Caine did a masterful job of clarifying his positions on a wide range of issues, justifying his actions as California governor, and deflecting any criticism without alienating any of the Committee members.

Spread out over a period of two weeks, the hearings proved to be both enlightening and entertaining viewing for political junkies and average citizens alike with moments of notable candor, eloquent dissertation and even refreshing levity. Caine certainly had a face for television and enough personal charm to disarm even the most hardened and argumentative member of the loyal opposition. Sufficiently satisfied with his testimony, both Committees unanimously approved confirmation, sending it to the floor of the Senate for a perfunctory vote. Just before recessing for the 4th of July holiday, the Senate approved the nomination by a vote of 99-1.

Later that day at a White House ceremony, Chief Justice Orrin Sanford administered the oath of office to the new Vice President, flanked by his wife Sara, the President and the First Lady. Following Justice Sanford's instructions, Caine placed his left hand on the Bible, raised his right hand and repeated after him:

"I, Hamilton Tyler Caine …"

"I, Hamilton Tyler Caine …"

" … do solemnly swear …"

" …do solemnly swear …"

" … that I will support and defend the Constitution of the United States …"

" … that I will support and defend the Constitution of the United States …"

" … against all enemies, foreign and domestic …"

" … against all enemies, foreign and domestic …:

" … that I will bear true faith and allegiance to the same …"

" … that I will bear true faith and allegiance to the same …"

" … that I take this obligation freely …"

" … that I take this obligation freely …"

" … without any mental reservation or purpose of evasion …"

" … without any mental reservation or purpose of evasion …"

" … and that I will well and faithfully discharge …"

" … and that I will well and faithfully discharge …"

" … the duties of the office on which I am about to enter."

" … the duties of the office on which I am about to enter."

"So help me God."

"So help me God."

As assembled guests and members of the press applauded, Caine shook the Chief Justice's hand, then turned to kiss his wife on the cheek. He did the same to Mrs. Hartman, then firmly shook the President's hand.

"Congratulations," said Hartman with a gracious smile. "Now, let's get down to work."

"Thank you, Mr. President," Caine replied, beaming. "I'm looking forward to the challenge."

As the two posed for more photos, Senate Whip Bill Bryce and Majority Leader Henry Howard stood in a corner of the room, maintaining their frozen smiles. Bryce leaned toward Howard and quipped, "Talk about *raising Caine*. Well, at least he's no pit bull like Harley."

"No, he's not," Howard quietly agreed through his clenched teeth. "He's just the better half of a political dream ticket."

"That'll wear thin in no time," Bryce predicted cynically. "After you're nominated next year ..."

"After I'm nominated," Howard interrupted, "I'll be lucky to carry a dozen states. Thanks for the encouragement, Bill, but I'm nothing if not a realist. Take a good look," he suggested, motioning to President Hartman and Vice President Caine. "Now tell me that 50.1 percent of the American people wouldn't vote for that."

Later that evening, the President and First Lady held a supper in the State Dining Room of the White House in honor of Vice President and Mrs. Caine with various members of Congress, the administration and their spouses in attendance. Once they were seated at the head of their table, amid the chatter of their guests, the President leaned toward his wife and quietly told her, "You're looking especially lovely tonight."

Ordinarily immune to flattery, Irene turned her head to look at her husband. "Well, thank you, Mr. President," she replied with an uncharacteristic hint of whimsy. The trace of a smile on her face warmed his heart.

"Are you pleased?" he asked, adding, "With the choice of Hamilton, that is." His tone suggested that it was important that she approve.

Irene's smile widened. "You made a wise decision," she replied.

Hartman hesitated, then conceded, "I wouldn't have done it without your advice. You always were a good judge of people, Renie," he said sincerely. "I'm glad I listened to you."

He held his wife's gaze for several meaningful moments, long enough to compel her to place her hand on his, which he interpreted as a gesture of forgiveness. It reminded Hartman of a similar moment, many years before, early in their relationship, when he and Irene had quarreled over something trivial. He was quite sure that he was right, but it was he who apologized first. Irene had touched his hand then the same way -- with tenderness and acceptance. Only this time, it wasn't about something trivial, and the touch of Irene's hand – and the look in her eyes – meant much, much more.

Then, realizing where they were, who they were and whom they were with, the President and First Lady turned their attention back to their distinguished guests, although for each the sublimeness of the moment lingered.

"What are you looking at?" asked Doris Ames.

Startled by her sudden presence, Pete flinched. "Huh? Oh. Nothing," he replied, standing by the living room bay window, his finger caught between two Venetian blinds. "Our neighbor ..." he claimed, fumbling for an explanation. "The one with the big Doberman … He's out walking his dog on our front swale. I'm watching to make sure he picks up after him."

"Are you going to report him to maintenance if he doesn't?" his wife angrily inquired.

"Yeah," Ames muttered. "I'll take care of it."

"Honestly, some people have no respect for other people's property," Doris bristled, shaking her head and leaving the room.

As soon as she was gone, Ames parted the blinds wider and peered through the slit again. What he observed, however, was not an inconsiderate neighbor, but a late model black sedan parked two doors down across the street. He clearly saw two men in suits sitting in the front seat, barely moving, simply watching his house. It was the same vehicle he had noticed the other day as he left the airport on his way home from work. It was waiting for him in the employee parking lot and as soon as he got into his car and drove off, the vehicle followed.

Obviously, he was under surveillance and part of him welcomed the scrutiny. *Let them watch. They'll see I had nothing to do with the crash, he told himself.* But for how long would they continue spying on him and to what extent? Were they watching his *every* move? And is that all they were doing? Did they have a lengthy dossier going back to the day he was born? Were they aware of every small transgression he had made in the course of 47 years? Were they questioning friends, acquaintances, neighbors from the past and the present? Were they also prying into the lives of his family – his wife of 25 years, his son stationed in Kuwait, his daughter in her sophomore year at the University of Missouri?

Shuddering, Ames stepped away from the window and paced the room nervously, his imagination getting the best of him. He wondered, *why me? I did everything by the book. And every inspection of the plane done by my crew checked out fine. Why won't they accept the fact that it was just a freak accident? No one was to blame. Why are they doing this to me? Why?*

And then, he abruptly stopped pacing. *They need a fall guy, he realized.* The idea kept him momentarily rooted to the spot. *That's it,* he convinced himself. *They're building a case against me, circumstantial or completely fabricated evidence – like that Al-Kihan nonsense. Guilt by association. Like that guy who was mistakenly connected to the Olympic bombing in Atlanta – the one whose life was turned upside down even though he had nothing to do with it. That's what they have planned for me.*

Ames' head was swimming. He felt trapped, unable to breathe. Then he felt angry. *They can't do this to me, Goddamn it*, he vowed. He had to take action. He had to fight back. He had to talk to someone. But who? Maybe he needed a lawyer. Better yet, a watchdog group of some kind. The only thing he could think of was the ACLU. At the very least, they might be able to advise him on where to turn.

The notion sent Ames scurrying to the Yellow Pages, where he eventually found a toll-free number. Emboldened, he grabbed the phone and dialed. But as the number was ringing, he heard several mysterious clicks on the line and froze. "American Civil Liberties Union," a female voice chimed. "How may I direct your call?"

Ames hesitated, fearful that someone else was listening on the line.

"Hello?" said the receptionist.

Instead of answering, Ames hastily hung up, convinced his phone was tapped. His heart and mind were racing. First, he had been reassigned to a "less demanding" schedule at work. Then, he had noticed the men in the dark car. Now, the phone. What else were they doing? Intercepting and reading his mail? Monitoring his credit card purchases? What if … what if they planted video cameras in his home?

Ames wanted to be away from all this – far, far away. But where could he go? Now that they had him in their sights, there was no place to hide. Still, he needed air, so he trudged from the living room to the hallway and out the door to his backyard.

There, standing on his deck, he reached into his shirt pocket and fumbled with a crumpled pack of cigarettes. It took several frantic flicks of his lighter to spark a flame, but soon he was cupping his shaky hands and drawing smoke deeply into his lungs. As he exhaled, he gazed at the trees in the dense woods beyond his backyard fence. Their leaves were rustling in a warm breeze that made it seem as if they were alive. It was if even the trees were suspiciously watching him. *Good Lord*, he thought, shuddering. *What am I going to do? What am I going to do?*

Chapter 27

Claire McNally, the U. S. Ambassador to the Philippines, was awoken from a sound sleep at 3:47 a.m. on the morning of July 23 by a persistent knock on her bedroom door.

"Coming ... coming ..." she groggily muttered, groping in the dark for her robe, then trudging wearily across the room to answer the urgent summons.

On the other side of the door stood Robert Jennings, the American Embassy's Legal Attache. He was wearing a white shirt, dark blue dress slacks and a pair of black loafers, as if he himself had been roused from his bed and dressed hastily.

"What's going on?" asked Ambassador McNally, only half awake.

"Forgive the intrusion," Jennings replied, "but this is important."

"I should hope so," sighed McNally, running a hand through her short, tousled blonde locks.

"The hostages ..." he said.

McNally was suddenly quite alert. "Oh, God," she shuddered.

"They're alive," Jennings hastened to assure her.

"They've been found?"

"Well, actually they found *us*. All five of them turned up at the front gate about 10 minutes ago."

"So they escaped their captors?"

"Apparently they were released – driven to a neighborhood about a mile away – blindfolded – and left on the street. One of them knew the way to the Embassy."

McNally looked confused. "And that's it? Held for three months with no demands and then suddenly released? It doesn't make sense. Where are they?"

"Downstairs – under Marine guard," said Jennings. "I thought you'd want to be present while they're debriefed."

"Yeah," McNally agreed. "I'll get dressed and be down in a moment. In the meantime, make them as comfortable as possible. Do they need medical attention?"

"No. They're in good shape."

"Are they hungry? Thirsty?"

"We've got that covered."

"Has the White House been notified?"

"Not yet. I thought you might want to handle that, too."

"What time is it there?"

"Almost 4 p.m. ..." Jennings calculated. "Yesterday."

"This is good news," McNally acknowledged, managing a smile. "This is very good news."

On the morning of August 25, President Hartman boarded Air Force One at Andrews Air Force base, along with several junior staff members, more than a dozen members of the press, and a larger than usual detail of Secret Service agents, and flew directly to Kansas City. With the start of the presidential campaign season just months away, the trip was intended to shore up Hartman's sagging support in Missouri, an important swing state in his reelection bid.

Upon his arrival at Kansas City International Airport, the President was greeted by the governor of Missouri and a few other state officials who rode with him by motorcade to a breakfast hosted by the city's Chamber of Commerce at a five-star hotel in the city's business district. There, as the featured guest, the President addressed attendees and spoke of the need for America to regain its competitive edge in a global economy. The key, he said, was to spark a "renaissance of responsible capitalism" by providing small business owners with new government incentives, which went over well with the hopeful entrepreneurs in attendance, who often greeted his remarks with spontaneous applause.

After the speech and a few bits of breakfast, President Hartman bid the governor and his other hosts farewell. He was then escorted from the dais and, surrounded by Secret Service agents, worked his way through the crowd, shaking hands, signing autographs and exchanging cordial remarks.

He was then led through the hotel kitchen to a loading dock that served as a rear exit and his waiting limousine, which was parked in an adjacent alley. Along the way, he paused briefly to chat with several workers, each of whom were thrilled to press flesh with a bona fide Commander-In-Chief and swore their undying support.

Once the President was safely ensconced in his bulletproof vehicle, the motorcade proceeded on its prearranged course to the town hall meeting at the Baylor Auditorium half a mile away. Traffic had been diverted from the route, manhole covers sealed in advanced, with numerous police cars posted at each intersection to ensure the President's safety. Except for a group of vocal but peaceful World Trade Organization protestors wrangled behind barricades across the street from the civic center, the ride went off without a hitch. Avoiding the crowd, the motorcade proceeded to the center's underground delivery facility, where the President entered the building and was whisked upstairs to the main auditorium.

There, before a packed house of some 2,000 supporters, coordinators and press, Sharon Lockhart, head of the state's Democratic Party committee was in the midst of a rousing warm-up speech. Receiving her cue that the guest of honor had arrived and was waiting in the wings, she concluded her remarks and then ceremoniously announced, "And so, my fellow Missourians … it is with great pride that I introduce to you a man of vision and integrity. Ladies and gentlemen … the President of the United States."

As the P.A. system blared *Hail to the Chief*, James J. Hartman strode out onto the stage to a thunderous standing ovation. Light bulbs flashed and miniature American flags waved and the decibel level of the applause, hooting and whistling, was almost painful as the President beamed and waved back at a sea of adoring, smiling faces. He paused at the center of the stage to give Sharon Lockhart a hug and plant a kiss on her cheek, then turned back toward the assembled throng which had started to chant, "Four more years! Four more years!"

Overwhelmed and gratified by the reception, President Hartman placed his hand on his chest and patted it several times in appreciation. Then he lowered his arm to his side and just stood there, basking in the glow. He had attended many a rally and town hall meeting before where the response was equally as welcoming, but for some strange reason, this moment resonated like none before. It was as if this were some kind of epiphany, the realization of something so profound and gratifying that it rooted him to the spot.

Suddenly, his entire life flashed through his mind – memories of childhood, remembrance of personal milestones mingling with visions of his family, his friends, his colleagues, Irene. Images and events and precise emotions flooded his consciousness in one massive, overwhelming wave. But why? And then it occurred to him – slowly but surely. *Oh, God*, he thought, shuddering with intuitive awareness. *This is it. This is the moment.*

And then, there was something akin to a bolt of lightning and a clap of thunder. He scarcely heard the cheering turn to screams of unimaginable horror. The world itself seemed to be imploding, crumbling, falling apart, as a massive avalanche of debris rained down, crushing him beneath its weight.

It happened so quickly, so inexplicably, so devastatingly that his Secret Service protectors had no time to reach him, no time to shield him – or themselves. They, too, perished in what seemed like a blink of an eye. But before any of them could feel the pain … they were all enveloped in utter darkness.

"Someone!" a voice, female and wounded, desperately cried out in the flaming rubble. "Anyone! Help us! Help …"

The faint sound of moaning amid the crackling of an isolated blaze.

The pungent odor of sulfur in the air.

Dense smoke and suffocating dust. Hellish.

"Out of the way!" a frantic male voice angrily shouted. "Out of the way! Out of the way!"

"Look out!" another man bellowed. "We need to get through!"

"Lord Jesus! NO!"

"How many in there? What about the President? *What about the President?*"

"This is unbelievable … How could this happen again?"

"I don't know, but we need every first responder in the city … and every ambulance available."

Static … inaudible gibberish on a transceiver.

"Stay back! Please! Stay back!"

"My crew is inside!"

"You can't go in there!"

" CNN! CNN! Here's my press pass! We were taping the event in the van outside, but I have two camera people and a sound technician inside …"

"I don't care who you are … you can't go in there! It's too dangerous! Now back off and let us do our job!"

"Rick! Danny! Over here!"

"Fucking terrorists! Motherfuckers! They hit us again! They hit us again! Awww, Jesus!"

"What was it? An explosion?"

"Yeah, big one! The entire roof caved in!"

"We got to reach the survivors!"

"Shit, I don't know … Lucky if anyone survived …"

Faint sounds of moaning and sobbing.

"This is a nightmare."

"Watch out! Don't climb on that. It might give way."

"God, the smell. I can't breathe."

"I'd stay back if I were you. Debris' still falling. Wait until the Haz-Mat people arrive."

"We can't wait. There are some people still alive in there. We've got to try to get them out."

"How? God damn it!"

"What's that?"

"You don't want to know."

"Jesus … this is horrible …"

"Look! Over there! Is that an arm?"

"Yeah …"

"Can you reach him?"

"Yeah, I think I can."

"Watch yourself."

"We're gonna' need some heavy equipment in here."

"But in the meantime, we can start moving some of the rubble …"

"With what?"

"I don't know! Our bare hands, god damn it! Come on!"

"Christ … this is going to change everything …"

Chapter 28

The assassination of James J. Hartman and the deaths of 647 other Americans in Kansas City on August 25th would come to be regarded as a seminal moment in both the history of the United States and that of the 21st century with political and social ramifications that would be felt for decades to come. However, the actual shock of the tragedy was relatively short-lived.

After all, this was an age of senseless violence where sudden death and carnage were a common occurrence. The 24-hour news cycle, with its repetitive spin and over-analysis of the latest momentous event, actually dulled the impact somewhat. And the proliferation of movies and television shows in which such acts of collateral damage were routinely served up as entertainment added to the sense that such things were to be expected. Certainly, the talking heads and Sunday morning pundits never stopped to ask the critical questions: What really happened on August 25th and who was responsible?

This much was certain: James Hartman was the fifth American president to be assassinated and the first to die as a result of an apparent terrorist act. Unlike the other four, he was not the victim of an assassin's bullet but instead crushed, along with hundreds of other people, beneath the debris of a collapsed ceiling demolished when a guided missile launched from the rooftop of an abandoned warehouse located several miles away struck the dome of the Baylor Auditorium.

A pre-event security sweep of the venue had failed to detect a small homing device that had been attached to the dome's upper rafters, allowing the missile to find its target. Heads would roll and conspiracy theories would abound on the Internet in the months to come, but in the meantime federal law enforcement combed the blast sight and the entire Kansas City area in search of answers. The launch site of the missile was discovered just beyond the radius of the Secret Service's security perimeter for the President's visit. Also found was the actual missile launcher, left behind by the perpetrators of the attack, which was quickly identified as a weapon manufactured in a predominantly Muslim breakaway republic of the old Soviet Union and apparently sold on the black market to an Islamic nation believed to harbor terrorist training camps.

Then came a recorded message phoned into the *Washington Post* by an alleged offshoot of Al Qaeda called Jambiya, claiming responsibility for the attack. *"A silver dagger has been thrust into the heart of the infidel,"* declared the caller. Suddenly, once again, it was the season of fear with calls for retribution.

However, it was also a time for reflection and soul-searching with its own share of indelible scenes that would linger in the national consciousness – Vice President Hamilton Caine being sworn in as president, his poignant and reassuring address to the nation shortly thereafter, the somber procession of mourners through the Capitol rotunda, Mrs. Hartman laying a single long-stem rose on her husband's casket – all vaguely familiar to those old enough to remember a similar event half a century earlier.

Immediately following the funeral, President Caine held a series of meetings with members of the Cabinet, the Joint Chiefs of Staff, and representatives of the Congressional delegation. Within a few days, with a surge of support from an angry American populace and the approval of NATO allies, the U.S. launched surgical strikes against suspected terrorist camps in Pakistan, Afghanistan, Indonesia, Somalia and Sudan.

Shortly thereafter, despite token objections from United Nations Security Council members Russia and China, the President issued an ultimatum to several Middle Eastern nations believed to be harboring Al Qaeda and Al Saba terrorists calling for their full cooperation in bringing the organizations' hierarchy to justice. Unable or unwilling to comply, a few of the implicated nations provided a pretext for U.S. attacks and one outright invasion and occupation that was swift, brutal and all but tilted the balance of power in the region to the moderate Arab states.

A renewed fervor for homeland security and interventionism also lead to the enactment of a new Patriot Act that gave unprecedented powers to the Executive Branch and federal agencies in a resurgent war on terrorism. Twice burned by a lack of vigilance, few Americans protested what they viewed as an infringement on their civil liberties, for those who did risked being labeled and dismissed as naïve and unpatriotic.

The new reality also called for an overhauling of the Hartman Energy Bill. With the approval of the Caine administration, plans to tax windfall profits were scrapped and incentives for alternative energy were reduced to pay for the production of several new nuclear power plants. In addition, offshore drilling over the Florida, California and Gulf coasts was reinstated by executive order – all in an alleged effort to end U.S. dependency on foreign oil. The measure passed both houses of Congress and was signed into law by the President just before Christmas.

There were also far-reaching economic consequences. On the day of the Kansas City tragedy, U.S. stocks plunged before trading was suspended for several sessions. The markets continued to decline for nearly a month, but then stabilized and eventually rallied strongly. Leading the way were energy and defense stocks, spurred by the spike in oil prices and a demand for new military hardware and technology. Production surged, employment rose, and corporate profits reached all-time highs.

On a wave of national sympathy and wartime fervor, Hamilton Caine ran for president the following election year and was easily elected – along with his running mate Harley Singleton – with a 61 percent plurality and nearly 400 electoral votes. Having succeeded James Hartman with 17 months left in his term, Caine qualified to run again four years later under the 21st Amendment. Thanks to a thriving economy, he scored another landslide with nearly 60 percent of the popular vote. Serving nine years and 5 months, his was the longest term of office of any president with the exception of Franklin Roosevelt.

As for his short-lived predecessor, there were numerous high schools, boulevards and turnpikes named in James J. Hartman's honor. Special editions of *Time* and *People* chronicling his life and legacy sold out on newsstands. Memorial coins, plates and other merchandise bearing his likeness were sold for a time online and in late night infomercials. A few biographies appeared on bookshelves and there was even an Emmy-nominated TV movie entitled "The Day That Changed America." There was also a Presidential Library and museum established by the surviving members of his family in their native Elmira, New York.

But aside from these compulsory tributes and exploitative marketing ploys, the ultimate consensus on Hartman among historians was simply that he had been a marginally successful president whose intentions may have been good, but whose ability to effect meaningful change proved limited.

One month to the day after the Kansas City tragedy, Wayne Kirkland resigned as Secretary of Homeland Security. Some saw it as an acceptance of responsibility for DHS' failure to interpret intelligence and protect the President and the United States itself from a domestic terror attack. It didn't help matters that DHS lowered the terror alert from orange to yellow following the release of the American hostages in Manila and the determination that Internet chatter leading up to the Kansas City tragedy was bogus. Others maintained that there was plenty of blame to go around, citing the FBI, Secret Service and the NSA for a lack of cooperation and due diligence. But that would have to be sorted out by yet another presidential commission.

For Kirkland, it was more than guilt that prompted him to leave – it was the realization that no matter what he had done or could have done, the outcome probably would have been the same. The world was a violent, unmanageable place where the worst would eventually happen simply because it could. That was confirmed for him in Beirut in 1982, though he chose not to believe it. It was reconfirmed on 9-11, but again he denied the truth. And now, Kansas City. Finally, he accepted the fact that one could stave off the horror for just so long, but not forever. And that made him irrelevant.

He and his wife retired to rural Pennsylvania, far enough from Washington, D.C., but close enough to his children and grandchildren in the Philadelphia area. There, he had plenty of time on his hands and he spent it catching up on his reading, riding roughshod on his beloved John Deere lawn mower over two and a half acres, and tinkering with his collection of model sailboats in bottles.

He would still frequently awake in the night to the horrific cries of limbless Marines buried in rumble. Other times he was imprisoned in dreams of ghostlike firemen and cops ominously emerging from the dense mist of fallen debris. And sometimes he was jolted from blissful darkness into waking consciousness by the jarring sound of a sudden blast and the ensuing screams of terror-stricken survivors. His fragile heart would be pounding like a bass drum, his throat drier than a patch of desert, a cold sweat sending his body into spastic shivers that chilled him to the core.

And on a bright Sunday afternoon the following spring, while riding his lawnmower across the lush green expanse of his own backyard, Wayne Kirkland was suddenly stricken with a hard and heavy pain in his chest. He tried to steer back toward his house, but the pain spread to his arms, rendering him virtually helpless. He took his foot off the accelerator and slowed to a stop beneath a huge elm tree. Doubled over the wheel, he gritted his teeth and endured the agony as long as he could. Eventually, though, he slipped into unconsciousness, surrendering to a void in which he would never return. At least, he thought in his final moments, the bad dreams were over.

While cruising the deserted streets of a St. Louis suburb at approximately 4:15 a.m., Officers Haley and Kravis pulled up alongside a black, late model Ford Explorer parked diagonally in the empty lot outside a local supermarket. At first, they assumed the vehicle had been abandoned. But upon closer inspection, they spotted the darkened profile of a driver behind the wheel.

"I'll go wake him up," sighed Kravis.

"Be gentle," his partner quipped, straight-faced.

Kravis lumbered out of the patrol car and slowly approached the vehicle on the driver's side. He pulled his flashlight out of his belt and shone it brightly through the window, illuminating the left side of the occupant's face – a middle-aged, white male with frosty gray hair and a double chin, his head slumped forward and his eyes sealed shut.

Kravis rapped gently on the glass. "Hey, buddy," he called. No response. He rapped harder. "Hey!" he called louder. "Wake up!"

It was then that Kravis noticed that the driver's right arm was slung to the side, resting on the front seat. He directed his light to the man's right hand. It loosely cradled what appeared to be a revolver. Gingerly, Kravis walked around to the other side of the vehicle and shone his light into the cab. Sure enough, the right side of the driver's face was soaked in blood from a gaping head wound. Next to the gun was what appeared to be a note.

"What's up?" Haley asked, rolling down his window.

"Looks like we got a suicide," Kravis replied calmly.

"Yeah, right," Haley scoffed. But when Kravis wandered toward the back of the vehicle, he realized he wasn't kidding, so he got out of the car to get a look for himself. "Shit …" he muttered, waving his own flashlight, impressed by the amount of brain matter splattered throughout the cab. "I guess we can forget about calling the paramedics."

"Don't touch anything," Kravis warned. "We've got to call this in. And run this license plate number – JTX 295, Missouri."

While Haley alerted the precinct, Kravis surveyed the entire perimeter of the vehicle, searching for any obvious clues. There were none -- not even a cigarette butt or wad of gum.

"Backup's on the way," Haley reported. "As for the plates – the vehicle's registered to a Peter Ames – 515 Palomino Drive, Richmond Heights."

"Uh-huh," Kravis grunted, reaching into his pants pocket and extracting a handkerchief.

"What're you doing?" asked Haley, watching his partner opening the passenger door of the SUV. "I thought you said not to touch anything."

"Just curious," Kravis muttered, reaching inside with the handkerchief to lift the note. Training his light on the piece of paper, he read aloud: "Forgive me, Doris. I just couldn't live with it."

"Huh," Haley grunted. "Couldn't live with *what*?"

Kravis glanced at his partner and, with typical cynicism, flippantly replied, "Probably Doris."

Just as he was dozing off, Gideon Burnett suddenly realized something and flinched into vivid wakefulness. The startled passenger next to him in coach, a middle-aged businessman with girlish bifocals and a laptop on his snack tray, eyed him with fearful suspicion. "Sorry," Burnett muttered, looking away through the aircraft window at a plush carpet of billowy clouds just below.

He had been recalling his last trip to Texas, of the dark room in the abandoned facility where he had been interrogated by Tattoo Guy and the Marlboro Man. He was remembering how clever he thought he had been in escaping when, in fact, he had merely been lucky that

Marlboro Man had left his lighter on the table where Burnett could reach it. Yeah, right … lucky. Like when they left the motor running in the van … and his wallet in the glove compartment. It was almost as if … they had wanted him to escape.

When the plane landed at Ronald Reagan Airport and Burnett disembarked, he shuffled through the terminal as if in a somnambulistic trance. Ever since the Kansas City catastrophe, he was haunted by his brief encounter with President Hartman. It was hard to believe that not long after that eventful meeting, the President was killed. And if it hadn't been for that meeting, Harley Singleton would be sitting in the Oval Office today. And if it hadn't been for that meeting, Pauline would still have a job and he would still have Pauline. What a world, what a world.

Weary from his flight but in no particular hurry, Burnett paused at an airport bistro and ordered himself a container of coffee. He plopped himself down in the nearest chair and poured a couple of packets of sugar into his brew. But before he could raise the cup to his lips, he glanced around the area and spotted a lone stranger sitting at another table. There was something familiar about the man's profile, and when he turned his head, his face became recognizable. Stunned, Burnett simply stared for a full minute. Eventually, however, he rose from his seat and approached the object of his astonishment. Just as the man looked up and their eyes met, Burnett murmured, "Kayton?"

"Excuse me?" the man responded.

"Ross Kayton. It's me – Gideon Burnett."

The man looked vaguely bewildered. "You must have me mistaken for someone else."

"No, actually, I don't," Burnett insisted. "You're Ross Kayton … from Beauville, Texas."

The man shrugged. "Afraid not."

"Oh, I see," Burnett nodded, glancing to his left and right. "You're on the run … using an alias."

"Huh?"

"I understand," Burnett played along. "I've been looking over my shoulder, too, ever since we met last May."

"Look, buddy," said the man, mildly irritated. "I don't know if you're pulling my leg or what, but I'm not whoever you think I am. Now, would you please leave me alone?"

Burnett gaped at him. "No," he calmly but firmly replied, "no, I won't. I've got questions and you've got the answers."

Sighing, the man took a final swig of his own cup of coffee, stood up and slung a piece of carry-on luggage over his shoulder. He started to walk away and Burnett grabbed his arm. "Hey!"

As the man roughly tugged his arm away, an airport security guard suddenly appeared. "What's going on here?" he asked.

"Officer, this man is harassing me," said the Kayton lookalike.

"Harassing you?" Burnett winced. "How the hell am I harassing you?"

"He insists that he knows me – which he doesn't – and he won't leave me alone."

"Is that right, sir?" the cop asked Burnett.

"I do know him. His name is Ross Kayton. He's from Beauville, Texas and we've had dealings in the recent past."

"My name is Jeff Abram, I'm from Winston-Salem, North Carolina, and I've never seen this man in my life. Here," said Abram, reaching into his back pocket for a wallet and handing it to the officer. "Check it out."

The cop examined the billfold's contents.

"That's my driver's license, bankcard, credit cards ..." Abram pointed out.

The officer glanced at Burnett. "Looks like you've got the wrong guy," he muttered.

"Let me see that," Burnett demanded, snatching the wallet out of the officer's hand. Sure enough, the I.D. contradicted Burnett's claim, but he wasn't buying it. "Either he's lying now or he lied to me when he said he was Ross Kayton," he maintained, tossing the wallet back to Abram.

"And who are you, sir?" the officer inquired pointedly.

"I'm Gideon Burnett. I'm with the *American Observor*."

"The *what*?"

"I'm a journalist," Burnett impatiently elaborated.

"Ah-huh," the cop grunted, clearly not impressed. "Is that alcohol I smell on your breath?" he asked.

Burnett stared at him. "What?"

"Have you been drinking, sir?"

"One Scotch and soda on the plane."

"One?"

"*One*. And what has that got to do with anything?"

"Sorry, Mr. Abram," said the security officer. "You're free to go."

"Wait a minute," Burnett loudly objected, "you ..."

"*Sir*," the officer sternly intoned, "you're causing a disturbance. I suggest you calm down and lower your voice."

"And I suggest you detain that man," Burnett replied as Kayton began to walk away.

"For what?"

Burnett huffed in frustration. "*He's not who he claims to be*. Look, can I go, too?"

"No. I want you to hang around a few minutes until Mr. Abrams is gone."

"So you're detaining me? Am I under arrest?"

"Not yet, but you will be if you keep this up," the officer warned.

"Okay, okay," Burnett cajoled unconvincingly. "I guess I made a mistake. Can I please go now?"

"Not yet, sir."

"*I'm not going to follow him*. I'm just want to go home."

"*Sir*," the officer cautioned, placing his hand on what Burnett recognized as a taser attached to his utility belt. "I'm not going to tell you again ..."

"All right," Burnett conceded, raising his hands in surrender, then lowering them to his sides. "All right," he sighed, watching Kayton fade into the distant crowd.

When he was finally allowed to leave, Burnett headed briskly for the nearest airport taxi stand. Along the way, he tried to call Paulsen on his cell phone, but only reached his voice mail. Rather than leave a hysterical message, Burnett decided to go directly to Paulsen's home in Georgetown. But when he got into the cab, he changed his mind and gave the driver his own apartment address. It was late – nearly midnight – and Burnett was exhausted. Besides, he needed to think this through first, fit the puzzle pieces together and build his case before sharing his suspicions with anyone. Otherwise, he'd come off like a raving lunatic.

Burnett's thoughts continued to swirl around his airport encounter as he placed his head on his pillow that night. It had to have been a set-up – Kayton luring him to Beauville, enticing him with incriminating evidence about Harley Singleton, his subsequent kidnapping and convenient escape – all calculated to create a false impression and a sense of urgency. The whole charade had compelled him to deliver the Uniplex files to the White House. But for what purpose? Simply to derail Singleton?

And then it hit him. If Kayton wasn't who he said he was, perhaps the objective wasn't what he claimed it was either. Maybe … just maybe it was to use Burnett to influence the President's choice for Vice President. Perhaps Singleton was just a stalking horse. Maybe the plan was to force Hartman to choose someone else, *someone with no apparent connection to Malcolm Everett Tate*. Perhaps the purpose of the incriminating Uniplex files was to sacrifice Singleton for the sake of installing Hamilton Caine – *just weeks before Hartman's assassination*. And what had precipitated this chain of events? The *accidental* crash of Air Force Two.

Though tired, Burnett didn't fall asleep until 3 a.m. Even his dreams were infested with images of the White House – the press room, the West Wing, the corridors and Oval Office – and faceless people in business attire moving from one office to another. He was traipsing the corridors in his night clothes, wearing only a pair of boxers, searching for someone. The President? But every door lead to another empty room in a maze of his own imagining.

And then suddenly, he paused, sensing a presence. Yet just as he turned around, he awoke with a start. "Huh?" he grunted, propping himself up on his elbows, bathed in sweat. Standing alongside his bed, barely recognizable in the dark were Tattoo Guy and the Marlboro Man. "Ha!" Burnett laughed, assuming he was still asleep and dreaming. Seconds later, however, detecting the subtle stench of the Marlboro Man's tobacco breath, he realized he was not.

Burnett tried to bolt from the bed, but the two men pounced and pinned him to the mattress. One of them – Tattoo Guy it appeared – drew a gun and pointed it at Burnett's face, instantly forcing him to stop struggling. Burnett looked down the barrel of what appeared to be a silencer. *I'm dead meat*, he thought. "How ..." he started to ask.

"Shhhhhh," Tattoo Guy hushed. "We wouldn't want to disturb the neighbors."

Burnett was too petrified to respond, breathing heavily and wondering why they hadn't already killed him.

After a long pause, Tattoo Guy said, "Open your mouth."

"Hm?" Burnett stared at him dumbfounded.

Tattoo Guy repeated, "Open ... your ... mouth."

Christ, thought Burnett, panicking. *He's going to blow my brains out. They want to make it look like a suicide.* He resisted, his lips and jaws tightly clenched and his nostrils flaring.

"If you don't open your mouth," Tattoo Guy said calmly, "I'm gonna' bust your teeth."

Reluctantly, Burnett let his jaw go slack, then gradually obeyed, parting his quivering lips. As he expected, Tattoo Guy shoved the barrel of the gun into his mouth. Gagging, Burnett struggled briefly, then settled down. Convinced he had moments to live, he gazed wildly into Tattoo Guy's shadowy eyes.

"Now that I have your attention," his assailant declared, "I want you to listen to me very carefully." He paused to take a deep breath, then continued. "Whatever you think you know, whatever ... crazy ideas you may have ... we want you to forget about them. Erase them from your mind. Okay? Move on. Go about your business as usual. Just ... let it go."

Burnett kept swallowing and gagging, repulsed by the taste of metal in his mouth, trying hard to focus on the menacing visage just inches away from his face.

"You see how easy it was for us to get to you?" Tattoo Guy asked rhetorically. "We can *always* get to you, Mr. Burnett. And if we can't get to you, we can always get to the people who matter to you. Your mother. Your brother. Your nieces and nephews. Your friends ... *Pauline*." Burnett abruptly stopped gagging.

"Ah, yes," Tattoo Guy acknowledged softly. "So many ways we can get to you, Mr. Burnett. However, the best outcome for us – and for you – is to put it all-l-l-l behind you."

Then Tattoo Guy abruptly removed the gun barrel from Burnett's mouth. And as he wiped it clean on the bed sheet, Marlboro Man gradually relinquished his grip on Burnett, who gasped for breath, but didn't move a muscle.

Tattoo Guy rose from the bed and holstered his weapon under the arm of his jacket. Marlboro Man retreated as well. "We'll be watching you, Mr. Burnett," he warned as they backed out of the room and faded into the darkness of the outer hallway. "Pleasant dreams."

Burnett held his breath until he heard the front door close. Then he let out a repressed whimper. He laid there for hours until the sun finally rose, staring at the ceiling all the while. He felt small and alone and filled with a sickening dread – almost wishing they *had* killed him.

Chapter 29

Several months after Hamilton Caine was sworn in as President of the United States, and a week after his resignation as White House Chief of Staff, Hunter Davidson decided that an unannounced visit to Provo was in order. He had told his wife he was flying to Utah to meet an editor who was interested in publishing his memoirs – a first-hand, behind-the-scenes account of the Hartman years. It wasn't the first lie he had told Melissa, nor would it be the last.

When he arrived in Salt Lake City, Davidson rented an economy car. It wasn't that he couldn't afford a more luxurious vehicle – he just wanted to be as inconspicuous as possible. Besides, he didn't really care what he drove. There were more pressing matters on his mind and lately, he was acting simply on impulse – like when he walked away from his prestigious and powerful job for "personal reasons." The media assumed he did it to explore new opportunities and/or because he didn't bond with the new president. Those closest to him assumed it was to escape the constant reminders of what was lost on August 25. But those were just convenient excuses; Davidson knew differently, and so did one other individual.

The drive up the mountain road to his intended destination was breathtakingly scenic, but Davidson might as well have been cruising along the Capital Beltway. He didn't give a fig about majestic, craggy peaks or sprawling vistas. He just wanted to get where he was going and say what he had to say and get the answers he needed to the questions that were devouring him from the inside out. He knew he had arrived when he spotted a sign that read: PRIVATE ROPERTY. VIDEO SURVEILLANCE. TRESPASSERS WILL BE SHOT. Undeterred, he drove on.

When he reached the guardhouse at the wrought iron gate of the estate, Davidson paused and lowered his window to address the expressionless sentinel who emerged from the booth, a towering and husky male with a shaved head and a thick, bushy moustache. "Hunter Davidson," he announced. "To see Mr. Tate."

The guard checked a clipboard in his beefy hand and replied, "You're not on the list."

"No," Davidson replied. "But he'll see me."

"I don't think so," the guard evenly responded. "You'll have to turn your car around and leave."

"Call him," Davidson persisted, immune to the guard's menacing glare. "Tell him who's here. He won't turn me away."

The guard stared icily for a few more seconds, then returned to his booth and picked up the phone. Davidson waited patiently until he saw him put down the phone and press a button. The gate opened. The guard glanced at him and motioned to proceed.

Davidson drove onto the long paved driveway leading up to the curb of the sprawling, multilayered, monolithic, concrete mansion. Its design reminded Davidson of one of Frank Lloyd Wright's creations – expansive and imposing like the man who owned it. He parked at the curbside, got out of his car and climbed a wide, steep slope of steps to the front porch.

A pair of security cameras perched high in the rafters announced his arrival and before Davidson could reach the threshold, the huge, brass front door was electronically opened. As he proceeded inside, into what looked like the main lobby of a hotel with its marble floors, high ceiling and crystal chandelier, Davidson was met by another guard, this one in a black suit and tie. He ushered Davidson through a metal detector, as if passing him through airport security.

Once he had cleared this checkpoint, Davidson was subjected to further search. "Arms out," the security guard muttered, brandishing a metal detector wand.

Bewildered, Davidson nonetheless complied, lifting and stretching his arms sideways as the guard ran the rod over his body. For good measure, the guard patted his chest and stomach over his clothing.

"I assure you, I am not carrying a weapon," Davidson smugly remarked.

The security guard regarded him with a mixture of amusement and suspicion. "It's not a weapon I'm checking for," he replied. Finally satisfied, the guard allowed Davidson to proceed. "Down the hall, last room on the left," he directed.

It was as if Tate had his own White House, thought Davidson as he strode through the impeccably decorated pathway. He had once seen pictures of the fortress in the pages of *Architectural Digest*. If he recalled, the interior spanned at least 20,000 square feet planted squarely on 50 acres of mountainside property with an extended balcony that was suspended over a cliff to provide a panoramic view of the Sierras.

When he reached the end of the corridor, Davidson made a sharp left into a large game room furnished with a billiard table, a huge circular card table and wall-encrusted bookshelves. He was startled to see numerous stuffed animal heads mounted on the walls – boars, mule deer, elk and a bobcat. Morbidly fascinated, he paused to review the gallery, turning slowly in place.

He was even more startled when he turned to see Malcolm Everett Tate standing before him, a tall if withering figure of a man dressed for the outdoors in boots, jeans, a red plaid shirt and a dark suede vest, a 12-gauge, Browning Citori Superlight Feather rifle nestled in the cradle of his right arm.

Davidson stared at the weapon nervously.

"Just back from hunting," Tate explained with a smile. "Quail." Sensing Davidson's anxiety, he set the rifle on a nearby armoire. "Follow me," he instructed.

Tate led Davidson to a nearby drawing room and shut the door behind them. "Have a seat," he said.

"I'd rather stand," Davidson replied.

"Suit yourself," Tate shrugged, settling into a comfortable leather arm chair. "Fix yourself a drink, if you like."

"I didn't come here to socialize."

"Oh? And exactly why *did* you come?" asked Tate, opening a cedar box humidor on an end table beside his chair and withdrawing an elongated Churchill. "I thought we had agreed not to meet face to face," he said, clipping the nub of his cigar. "Especially in my home."

"We agreed on a lot of things," Davidson said with a hint of bitterness.

Mildly amused, Tate leisurely placed the cigar in his mouth, crossed his legs and struck a wooden match against the sole of his boot. He took his time lighting the cigar, puffing briskly until dense clouds of white smoke drifted to the ceiling. Then he shook his hand to extinguish the flame and discarded the charred match into a nearby ashtray. Finally, with a smoky sigh, he inquired, "Well, what's on your mind, my friend?"

Davidson recoiled at the insinuation. "First of all, I'm not your friend."

"Figure of speech," Tate shrugged. "Would 'accomplice' be a more suitable term?"

"You lied to me," Davidson angrily accused.

"How so?" Tate calmly wondered.

"The plan was to bring balance to the administration, to install a vice president sympathetic to your business interests, not – not ..."

"Plan?" Tate replied with mock bewilderment. "What plan? I don't know anything about a plan. I haven't the slightest idea what you're talking about."

"You treasonous bastard," Davidson muttered with utter contempt.

"You know damn well what I'm talking about. You were responsible for what happened to the President in Kansas City."

"Whew," Tate whistled, rolling his cigar between his fingers. "That's quite an outrageous accusation. But I'm afraid you're mistaken. James Hartman was assassinated by foreign terrorists. Don't you read the papers? Don't you watch TV? They've been acting up for months – chattering away on the Internet … kidnapping Americans overseas. Homeland Security should have seen it coming."

"I'm not stupid, Malcolm," Davidson bristled. "I know *exactly* what happened. This was a coup d'état and you were behind it."

"On the contrary, you *are* stupid," Tate viciously replied. "Stupid *and* naïve."

"For trusting you? Absolutely. I didn't realize it when Clayton Talbot died. I thought that was just a convenient accident."

"*Mechanical failure*," Tate corrected. "That was the official conclusion."

"All I know," said Davidson, "is that it made things easier. Instead of having to convince the President to drop Clayton from the ticket in the next election, I just had to steer him toward the right replacement. But after Kansas City and now the subsequent military action in the Middle East, it's all become clear. I know you were behind the crash of Air Force Two. And I know you staged the attack that killed Hartman and 600 other innocent Americans."

Tate glared at Davidson, then abruptly burst into laughter. "Well," he chuckled, taking a few puffs on his cigar, "you're just full of allegations, Hunter. Which is quite surprising … coming from someone who was so intimately involved in the alleged plot."

"I had no idea you would go to such lengths," Davidson insisted.

"I would go to such lengths? You're in denial, dear boy. Your hands are no cleaner than anyone else's."

"All I did was influence the President's decision."

"Oh, and how well you did your job," Tate chuckled. "Presenting the President with a short list ripe with flawed candidates. Guiding him toward eliminating the weakest of the lot. Steering him away from Gardner with nothing more than unsavory innuendoes. Then advocating on behalf of Singleton, while positioning Caine as the fallback candidate. A masterful bit of misdirection on your part. The old bait and switch. You played it to perfection, Hunter, to perfection. Just like a chess master ..."

"That was the extent of my involvement," Davidson insisted, "delivering Caine. I had no idea there was more to the plan than installing a vice president covertly aligned with your business interests."

"Don't be ridiculous," Tate scoffed. "You're in no position to plead ignorance ... or innocence. You have a numbered Swiss bank account, not to mention incriminating meetings with *certain* people – all videotaped, by the way."

"You had me *under surveillance?*"

"Well, of course, you dolt."

"Why?"

"Why? Insurance. Leverage." Tate paused to take a drag and blow a perfect smoke ring into the air. "You see, I'm a chess master, too."

"Do you think you can blackmail me into silence?" Davidson challenged.

"I don't need to," Tate confidently replied. "There's no linkage between you and me. Or between me or any of this nasty business. Our extensive chain of messengers saw to that. I've got multiple layers of plausible deniability. Unfortunately, you do not. Your fingerprints are all over the place. Hell, you even shredded evidence. You see, you're really in no position to make waves."

"I don't care," Davidson boldly claimed.

"Of course you do," smiled Tate knowingly. "Even the hint that you betrayed your president ... your *friend* ... would damn you for generations to come. You wouldn't want that – believe me. There's also the matter of your legal culpability. There's no country club prison for treasonous traitors. And if I thought for one moment that you could possibly implicate me," he added ominously, "well, I'd have to deal with that. Wouldn't I?"

Davidson was tempted to retrieve the rifle from the other room. For a fleeting moment, he even imagined blowing Tate's head off. But with his luck, it probably wasn't loaded. Of course, he did nothing but scowl at the old bastard's snickering face.

"However," Tate continued, smugly puffing away on his cigar, "we both know you don't have the nerve to come clean. Plus, you have others to think about besides yourself. Your wife, your children ..."

"Are you threatening me?" Davidson glowered.

Tate lowered the cigar and leaned forward in his chair. "You're damn right, I am," he assured. "It's much too late to develop a conscience, Hunter. If you so much as raise an eyebrow, you'll lose everything you treasure. So get off your high horse and count your blessings. That little nest egg of yours in Zurich can buy an awful lot of rationalization. It'll pay for your children's education and your wife's eventual facelift ... not to mention a lot of hot, young *cooch*."

"You're vile," Davidson sneered.

"I'm a lot of things," Tate acknowledged, tapping ashes into a tray built into the arm of his chair. "But one thing I'm not is a fool. No, that's your department. Oh, how easy it was to use you. To *buy you*. And how eagerly you played your part. And now you have the audacity to come here and play the victim. Have you any idea how pathetic you are?"

Ashamed, Davidson lowered his head and swallowed hard. "Tell me it wasn't all about money," he entreated, "triggering a war for profit, ensuring years of lucrative government contracts and higher energy prices just to line your pockets and those of your ... business partners."

"It's never that simple," Tate replied philosophically, staring up at the rising, writhing mist of his cigar smoke. "It's about maintaining the natural order of things, the balance of power. That's what it has always been about – and always will be about. This country … hell, *this planet* must function in a certain way to stave off chaos and upheaval. Haven't you learned that yet?"

Davidson had no ready reply.

"Apparently not," Tate derisively surmised. "To boot, you're obviously a glass half-empty kind of guy. A lot of good will comes from our new world order. For one thing, we'll get a decisive upper hand on global terrorism. We'll enhance American military capability and strengthen our defenses, as well. We'll end our dependency on foreign oil, bolster our economy and strengthen the dollar …"

"At what price?" Davidson demanded.

Realizing his argument was falling on deaf ears, Tate simply took another puff of his cigar and casually replied, "The mere sacrifice of one inconsequential politician."

"What about the others?"

Tate looked puzzled. "The others?"

"*The 647 innocent people who perished in Kansas City*," Davidson bitterly reminded him. "Were they also *inconsequential*?"

"No," said Tate, stamping out his cigar in the ashtray. "They were unfortunate."

"Maybe you can live with the guilt," Davidson maintained, looking down with an expression that approximated anguish. "But I can't."

"Oh, give it time," Tate advised, rising from his chair. "Eventually, you can live with anything. Besides, your role wasn't as crucial as you might think."

"What do you mean?" asked Davidson.

Tate regarded him with perverse amusement. "Do you honestly think you were my only mole in the White House?"

Davidson's heart skipped a beat.

"Because if you do," said Tate, "you're an even bigger fool than I thought you were."

Disheartened beyond words, Davidson stood in stunned silence, studying every crag in Tate's face until the blasé billionaire muttered,

"Now if you'll excuse me, I'd like to have some lunch. I am quite famished." He ambled toward the door, paused and added, "I believe you know the way out," then left the room.

Alone, Davidson contemplated his immediate future, oddly unable to see beyond the next few days. He'd return home, of course. Tend to his affairs, play with his children, and make love to his wife. Eat, drink and sleep. He would go through the motions, do what was required, and exist from moment to moment. But for all intents and purposes, the remainder of his life would be an empty void.

Such was the burden of an unspeakable secret – and an unforgiving conscience.

Chapter 30

Despite the morbid curiosity of the media-saturated society in which she lived, Irene Hartman's widowhood was as low-profile and reclusive as possible. She neither courted sympathy, nor did she receive unnecessary pity. She did not haunt the social or political landscape like the tragic ghost of a bygone era. She did not impose her will or offer unsolicited advice of any kind to anyone. And she certainly did not depend on the kindness of strangers.

For their part, most people – even the more aggressive members of the world press and paparazzi – made every effort to respect her privacy. After all, she was no Jackie O and she rarely provoked attention by socializing in public except, perhaps, to attend an event commemorating her husband's life and short-lived legacy. Even on those rare occasions she would often appear on videotape, her remarks reverent and thankful but usually brief. The sometimes dazed and vacant look in her eyes, the tentativeness of her speech, and the reticence of her demeanor suggested a woman who just wanted to be left alone. And who could blame her?

Occasionally, candid shots of her strolling along a city street incognito or sunning herself on an oceanfront balcony in a modest one-piece bathing suit surfaced in one of the tabloids. But for the most part, she was out of sight, though never completely out of mind. In fact, for the rest of her life, she would consistently place at or near the top of the list of the most admired women in the world. Some cited her as the perfect example of how a former First Lady should act – a dignified part of the public consciousness, but as unassuming as a shadow.

Unbeknownst to all but her closest advisors, her private investments had prospered in the first few years after she left the White House, affording her a life of comfort and security. She served on the board of several charitable foundations and universities, and she split her time between living in a finely-furnished Victorian duplex in Boston and a luxury condominium in Boca Raton, Florida. She turned down a lucrative offer to pen a memoir and declined interviews for an unauthorized biography. Not even close friends such as Barbara Walters, Oprah Winfrey and Diane Sawyer could convince her to do a sit-down interview. She lived her life on her own terms and, obligingly, that was how everyone preferred it.

The summer following the horrific events of August 25, Irene Hartman decided to take a long vacation, cruising the Mediterranean on *La Grande Madame*, the 150-foot yacht of her old friend and college roommate Mitzie Callahan Dauphin and her husband Charles, a charming French financier and graduate of the Wharton School of Business. Setting sail from Monte Carlo, they leisurely charted a course along the western Italian coastline, around the boot and up the Adriatic, then down to the Ionian and around to the Aegean with sightseeing stopovers in Corsica, Sicily, Venice, Dubrovnik, Kythira and Skyros.

Along the way, they would swim and snorkel and fish and feast on local delicacies, enjoying virtually perfect weather and calm seas, attended by an able crew and protected by a special detail of U.S. secret service agents. The month-long trip allowed Irene to rest and relax, to catch up on old times with Mitzie and get to know Charles, and otherwise put a great deal of baggage behind her.

One day, while lounging on the main deck in a flattering yet tasteful pair of white shorts and a red-striped blouse knotted at the waist, sipping a Mimosa and reading a book on medieval culture, Irene finally reached an elusive level of serenity. She momentarily rested the book on her lap and gazed out over the bow at the clear blue Aegean waters glittering in the sunshine.

Anchored in a secluded cove, the yacht gently rocked like a cradle on the lapping tide, the only sound an occasional gust of wind that whistled softly in her ears and swept through her flowing hair like an unexpected caress. It momentarily reminded her of a day long ago when a certain young man ran his fingers through her tossed and tussled mane as a prelude to a deep and lingering kiss.

For once in a long, long while she was at peace, her thoughts transcending any lingering bitterness, regret or recrimination she had felt in the past. What was done was done, and there was no use looking back with anger or disdain. The rest of her life lay before her like a banquet. She was whole. She was alive. And she was free.

And then suddenly, the spell was broken by the mellifluous chimes of a classical music ring tone. She lazily reached for her cell phone, which rested on the arm of her chaise, next to her cold drink. Shielding her eyes from the brilliant sun, she squinted to read the phone's display. Recognizing the nickname and number, she smiled and took the call.

It was mid-afternoon where she was, dawn at the source of the call. So with all the pleasantness of a dear and faithful friend, she sweetly greeted, "Good morning, Malcolm."

Also by Robert Stricklin

A Necessary Evil